A GENTLEMAN IN SEARCH OF A WIFE

THE LORD JULIAN MYSTERIES

BOOK FIVE

GRACE BURROWES

GRACE BURROWES PUBLISHING

A Gentleman in Search of a Wife

Copyright © 2024 by Grace Burrowes

All rights reserved.

Cover photo by Cracked Light Studios LLC

Cover design by Wax Creative, Inc.

No part of this book may be reproduced in any form or by any electronic or mechanical means, including information storage and retrieval systems, without written permission from the author, except for the use of brief quotations in a book review.

If you uploaded this book to, or downloaded it from, and free filing sharing, internet "archive" library, or other piracy site, you did so in violation of the law and against the author's wishes. This book may not be used for artificial intelligence program development or training purposes *whatsoever*.

Please don't be a pirate.

DEDICATION

**To those who have bungled
and don't know how to make it right**

CHAPTER ONE

"You have to help him, Julian." Hyperia West put her plea to me quietly. "John Tait is one of my oldest friends, and he can't ask anybody else for this sort of assistance."

We strolled along Caldicott Hall's lime alley, the ground beneath our boots dotted with golden leaves. The time of year was sweet, also sad—my only surviving brother was soon to take ship for an extended tour of the Continent. The closer the date of Arthur's departure came, the more melancholy my mood grew.

"The estimable Mr. Tait is not, in fact, asking me to aid him," I replied. "*You* are putting his case to me in his stead."

At first glance, Hyperia West was an unremarkable specimen. A trifle too abundantly curved for current fashion, shortish stature, medium brown hair, and a bit long in the tooth by Mayfair's matchmaking standards.

I nonetheless loved her dearly, and if I did take an interest in John Tait's situation, I'd do so because Hyperia expected it of me, rather than out of noble generosity on my part.

"John has his pride," she said. "I assured him he could trust your discretion."

If so, he'd be trusting the discretion of a former officer whom most of Society regarded as a traitor. "What is the urgency, Hyperia? You tell me Tait's wife has been missing for some time. Why does her husband wait until now to investigate her fate?"

We walked along in the afternoon sunshine, leaves crunching underfoot, a gentle breeze riffling the lush autumn grass.

"I suspect John is finally ready to move forward," Hyperia said. "Some of his habitual sorrow has left him. He blames himself for Evelyn's departure, and the guilt has been a heavy burden. I sense he's focused more on the future lately and less on the past."

As was I, oddly enough. "How long have you known him?"

"Since childhood. Our mamas were old friends. His mama is my godmother. You know how that works."

My own godmother, Lady Ophelia Oliphant, was a frequent guest at Caldicott Hall. Godmama was a terror when it came to Society's secrets and foibles, and she could be blunt to a fault when dispensing her opinions. She also served as Hyperia's nominal chaperone, and thus I rubbed along with Godmama as best I could.

I dreaded the day when I had Caldicott Hall to myself, if such a thing could be said about an edifice with sixty rooms abovestairs and staff sufficient to keep them all dusted.

"I will discuss the matter with Tait," I said. "I'm not promising I can find his errant wife, but I'll hear what he has to say. I assume he's petitioning the courts to have his wife declared dead?"

"I don't know as she's been gone long enough, Jules. That aside, litigation is expensive, and the courts drag their feet for years. John is almost certain that Evelyn met an untimely death. He believes she would have written, if not come home, if she'd been able to. They were very much in love, but two strong personalities can clash, especially two strong, proud personalities."

Despite my low spirits, questions began to swirl in my mind: Had Evelyn left a note? What had she and her spouse quarreled about if a spat had precipitated her flight? Where had John Tait searched for her? Where else might she have found a safe refuge?

Did she speak any foreign languages? How much coin had she taken with her?

Had Tait murdered his wife, and was he only now going through the farce of investigating her disappearance because incriminating evidence was no longer a worry?

As a former reconnaissance officer, I had a penchant for assembling observable facts into theories. Why was the priest the only stout person in a poor Spanish village? Was he perhaps augmenting his meager income by informing against his parishioners? Why did a woman who claimed to be illiterate have pencil, paper, and a radical pamphlet in her reticule?

Those sorts of observations.

Since coming home after the Battle of Waterloo the previous year, I'd turned my investigative abilities to discreetly solving the problems that vexed polite society. A missing heir, a missing prize hound, the provenance of a small boy—my own nephew, as it happened—left to fend for himself in a disobliging world...

I wasn't defeating the French Army single-handedly, but I was fighting a war of my own against gossip and slander. Contrary to the gossip, I had not betrayed my country, my command, *or my late brother, Harry*. I refused to oblige malicious whisperers by fading from Society when there were puzzles to be solved.

Then too, I enjoyed the challenge of ferreting out truths that malefactors preferred to keep hidden.

"So I'm to find proof that Evelyn Tait has been gathered to her reward, preferably by natural causes?" I asked.

"Or find Evelyn Tait."

I paused to regard Caldicott Hall, sitting on its slight rise on the opposite bank of the creek. My boyhood home was aging well, and yet, its simple, Palladian dignity looked lonely in the mellow afternoon light.

Which was utter rot, of course. "How long has Evelyn been gone?"

"Five years."

I was a competent tracker. Had the lady been gone five days, I'd have had some cause for optimism. "Five *years*, Perry? I will hear what Tait has to say, but I make no promises."

"Thank you, Jules." Hyperia bussed my cheek and set off in the direction of the Hall.

I followed, though I wanted to tell her not to kiss me like that—no warning, no time to savor the pleasure—but then she might decide not to kiss me at all, so I kept my remonstrations to myself.

"Why the forced march back to camp?" I asked, catching up with her easily. "You haven't given me the Town gossip, and I haven't told you all about Arthur's latest plans."

"Arthur changes his itinerary as often as I change my gloves. I vow I will be relieved when he and Banter take ship. Lady Ophelia says the same."

I would not be relieved. Not at all. I had some good memories of my time in uniform. My older brother Harry and I had frequently crossed paths, and because we'd both been reconnaissance officers, we'd had plenty in common besides the usual sibling connections. On the whole, though, my time on the Continent had been grueling and lonely, even before I'd fallen into French hands.

"Lady Ophelia will follow Arthur and Banter to Paris in a few weeks," I said. "Or, that's the plan. They will send George home with her." George being Banter's young godson. "Will you travel with her?"

"I might. Probably not. You?"

"If I never set foot in France again, it will be too soon."

Her steps slowed. "You are doing better, Jules. You seem to gain ground with every investigation you take on."

She was right—I was improving—but I still needed my blue-tinted spectacles in strong sunlight, I still had nightmares, I still lacked the stamina I'd had in uniform, and I was still prone to low moods and fretfulness.

"I doubt I can do much for your friend Mr. Tait," I said as we crossed the arched stone bridge that was rumored to date from Roman days.

"People don't just disappear, Jules. If Evelyn is alive, I know you'll find her."

People *did* disappear. They sailed to the Antipodes. They expired in obscure locations. They changed their names and nationalities in an afternoon and were never heard from again. I'd done plenty of disappearing on reconnaissance in Spain and France, though those experiences ought to aid me in locating Mrs. Tait.

I stopped halfway across the bridge. "Whose coach and four is that?"

"John's. I told him to pay a friendly call. Arthur is the ranking title in the neighborhood, and His Grace is preparing to go on extended travel."

Arthur, also styled His Grace of Waltham, was one of the leading titles in all of Britain. "Perry... if I'd declined to involve myself in what is very likely a hopeless case, the situation would have been awkward."

"But you didn't decline, did you?"

"I still might."

Except that I wouldn't. Not as long as Hyperia West had put the request to me.

Mr. John Tait had climbed down from his coach. He stood at the foot of the terrace steps, his attire that of the country gentleman whose Bond Street accounts were quite current.

He was tall, broad-shouldered, and possessed of wavy dark hair and a pair of limpid blue eyes.

"My darling Hyperia." He took both of her hands and bowed, which should have looked ridiculous, but on him it appeared charming. "You truly do grow more lovely every time I see you. John Tait, my lord, at your service."

Forward of him, to introduce himself when Hyperia was on hand to see to the courtesies.

I bowed. "Lord Julian Caldicott. A pleasure to make your acquaintance."

I was lying. John Tait was so robust and hearty, so genial and composed, that I resented him on sight. He was what I had once been—an exuberantly masculine blend of innocence and arrogance. I would find his missing wife if she yet drew breath, because Hyperia had asked it of me. Also because this handsome bounder had no business putting on bachelor airs when he was, in fact, no sort of bachelor at all.

Assuming, of course, the lady wanted to be found.

∽

"I loved Evelyn," Tait said, his soulful gaze roaming between me and Hyperia. "I still love her, but she's become a shade, and life is for the living. As I've grown older, I've felt a greater need to know the truth. I hoped she'd return—for years, I've hoped—and now... How can a mere mortal man subsist on hope alone, my lord?"

Tait was subsisting on excellent tucker, fine tailoring, and at least five thousand pounds a year, based on available evidence. The signet ring on his smallest finger was gold and matched his ornately figured cravat pin. He had good taste—to concede the obvious—but his version of subsisting would be the envy of most.

"Nobody judges you, John," Hyperia said. "Julian might well find that Evelyn is happily dwelling in a bigamous relationship with a Dover sea captain. For you to face that prospect takes significant courage."

Tait gazed manfully into his tea cup. "As long as she's happy, I could bear that. I'd even pursue an annulment, if she asked me to. Evvie is still a young woman, if she's extant. I'm not exactly doddering myself." He aimed a beamish smile at Hyperia, which she graciously returned.

I swirled my tea and considered accidentally spilling it on Tait's skintight chamois breeches.

"Oh, there you are!" Lady Ophelia, occasionally doting and more often vexatious godmother-at-large, paused in the parlor doorway. She had a gift for making entrances, and one ignored her at one's peril. "You young people have no sense. On a day this glorious, you should be taking tea on the terrace. John Tait, the last time I saw you, you were just down from university. You may make your bow and then tell me all the best gossip."

She swanned over to our guest, who—like me—had risen at her arrival, and proffered her hand. Tait did the pretty damnably well, and then her ladyship was accepting a cup of tea from Hyperia and directing the gents to resume their seats.

She inquired after Tait's sisters and declared him to be a naughty fellow for playing least in sight for so long. Town was always in want of handsome swains who could stay sober long enough to dance an entire quadrille. And really, if everybody took to hibernation as dear Julian had, London would be a dull place indeed.

"I have come out of hibernation," I said. "Be fair."

Lady Ophelia twinkled at me. She was a willowy blonde, aging splendidly despite being twice widowed. To the casual observer, she was just another chattering specimen of a beautiful, vain, and largely pointless Society.

On closer inspection, she had a nigh infallible memory, grasped human nature with a connoisseur's expertise, and knew the origins and denouement of every scandal in the last half century.

Some of which, she'd instigated. The Regent took care to remain in her ladyship's good books, and on my better days, I did too.

"My darling boy," she began, "venturing down the carriageway with Hyperia in broad daylight is hardly resuming the social whirl, though it's true you no longer strictly qualify as a recluse. When His Grace is absent, you will be expected to entertain in his stead. I've been meaning to discuss this with you, but how much more pleasant to catch up with old friends." She sparkled in Tait's direction, then swiveled her gaze to Hyperia.

"My dear, I simply must steal you for a moment or two. We're hosting company for Sunday supper, and the menu... Mrs. Gwinnett tries, I know, but you have such a way with a delicate conversation, and I'm afraid His Grace will take ship early if we inflict eight full courses on Vicar in the middle of the day." She rose and left Hyperia no choice but to attempt to speak peace unto the kitchen.

The ladies departed, and Tait held out the plate of tea cakes to me. "Hyperia is such a treasure. She insisted I speak with you about Evelyn's situation, or my situation. Our situation."

I shook my head, and Tait helped himself to three cakes.

"While we have some privacy," I said, "I should arrange for a lengthy conversation with you where we will not have an audience."

"Hyperia and I have no secrets." He popped an iced cake into his mouth. "We're old friends. Our mothers are old friends. Our grandmothers were old friends on back to the Flood. You know how it is among gentry who prefer to ruralize."

"Nonetheless, I will call upon you tomorrow for a private interview. Between then and now, please consider that ignorance of your wife's situation might well be preferable to the truth."

"The dashing-sea-captain sort of truth?"

I had been to war. Tait had not. I had been taken prisoner by the French and subjected to horrors that had for a time parted me from my reason. My capacity for imaginatively peering into abysses of human depravity doubtless exceeded Tait's on his gloomiest day.

"What if she caught a packet for the Low Countries, Tait, and was sold into bondage fifteen minutes after reaching her destination? What if she's dying of consumption in a London brothel? What if she's borne three children to another man and will swear that you tried repeatedly to kill her if you ask her to leave that man? What if she has lost her reason?"

Tait considered his second tea cake. "One hears you did not fare well in uniform, my lord. I understand that you mean me no insult. You are parsing hypothetical conjectures, each one more alarming than the last. I have considered them all and well know that Evelyn remains my legal responsibility, regardless of her situation. I married her because I esteemed her deeply and held her in great affection. I will soon reach the thirtieth year of my age. The time has come to face the truth, whatever that truth may be."

Birthdays could provoke introspection, and yet, I suspected Tait had some other reason for this sudden bout of connubial courage. An inheritance, perhaps, that could not come to him until his wife was declared dead. I would investigate that theory, but not when the ladies were due to return any minute, possibly with Arthur in tow.

"Very well, the truth wherever it may lead," I said, "and you should know that when I investigate a situation, I do so discreetly. I will not confer with Hyperia or His Grace or Vicar, for that matter, unless I believe they have relevant evidence to share."

"My secrets are safe with you?"

If I didn't plant this poseur a facer before I found his wife, I would deserve at least a long afternoon shopping at Hatchards.

"Secrets are a burden on the soul, Tait. To know somebody else's intimate business is far from enjoyable." I was privy to secrets—Arthur's, some of our late brother Harry's, and a few picked up along the way when snooping on behalf of His Majesty's loyal forces. Secrets and confidences weighed on the soul, and before Evelyn Tait's whereabouts were known, her husband might learn that lesson too.

"You are reluctant to pry," Tait said, "and you don't tell tales. I understand such delicacy and appreciate it, particularly when Hyperia West's opinion of me matters. If the issue you're dancing around is compensation, my lord, then let's not mince words. I am prepared to pay handsomely to learn of my wife's fate."

Oh, for pity's sake. "We will not discuss money, Tait. We will discuss much else, but not that."

He sighed and munched the second tea cake into oblivion. "If you want to know my every fling and flirtation, I can list them, but I hardly see what that ancient history has to do with Evelyn storming off in high dudgeon."

For the first time in days, I felt a hint of pleasure. "Every unmarried woman with whom you exuberantly *flung* or *flirted* had a motive to do away with your wife, particularly if you got the unfortunate lady with child."

Before Tait could remonstrate with me over that logic—and I was applying nothing save pure reason—the ladies rejoined us. Lady Ophelia invited Tait to join us for Sunday supper, a bit of meddling I could have done without.

When our guest finally rose to take his leave—such a pity, the duke was still out—I noticed that Tait departed without eating the third tea cake.

Good, if that meant I'd given him something more serious to chew on.

"Julian," Lady Ophelia said as we watched Tait's chestnuts with matching white socks trotting down the drive. "I do not care for that man. I have my suspicions where he and Hyperia are concerned. Ancient history, but he bears watching."

My mood took another turn for the worse. "He trifled with Perry?" My darling Perry, who'd left us in the foyer after offering Tait a farewell kiss on the cheek? *That* Perry?

"They might have trifled with each other. Hyperia is the soul of discretion. This would have been years ago, after Evelyn's departure and while you were... away."

At war, losing my mind and my reputation. *Splendid.* "Might you do me a favor, my lady?"

Lady Ophelia took my arm and steered me back into the house. "If this favor involves seducing Tait, no. My seducing days are behind me, and he presents no challenge in any case. One must have standards even in one's trivial amusements."

"All of St. James's will mourn your retirement into propriety. I want to know with whom Tait flirted and cavorted when Evelyn was on hand. I'd ask Hyperia, but your knowledge will be more comprehensive."

She stopped at the foot of the grand staircase. "I won't protect him, you mean?"

"That too." I was enlisting Lady Ophelia's assistance at the first opportunity, which slightly contravened my assurances of discretion. Slightly. Somewhat. But she wasn't Arthur, Hyperia, or Vicar.

"Has it occurred to you, my boy, that Tait might well have done his wife an injury, and when the wound proved fatal, he buried her beneath the roses by dark of night? These things happen, you know."

"My lady has been reading lurid novels again."

She patted my arm. "I read the Society pages and the financial pages, which are lurid enough. You will be careful, Julian?"

In my foul mood, I should have resented her question, but she apparently grasped what Hyperia did not. The investigation could grow dangerous—for me, for Tait, or for Evelyn, if she yet lived.

"I will be exceedingly cautious. I'd leave Tait to his uncertain fate, but Hyperia asked me to take a hand in matters."

"She might regret that request ere long, Julian."

As it happened, we both did. Bitterly.

CHAPTER TWO

"My lord, do come in!" Tait greeted me as if we'd matriculated in the same public school form and shared memories of the same boyish pranks. "I've been anticipating your call."

We shook hands—a presumption on Tait's part, a ploy on mine. If I was to find answers for Tait, I needed to earn his trust, lest my time be wasted.

"Shall we do the tea tray, indulge in a tot, or get down to business?" Tait asked, ushering me into a dim foyer notable for its wooden herringbone parquet floor. Old-fashioned and durable, but in need of some polish.

"Lemonade or cider wouldn't go amiss, once I've had the use of a washstand," I said. "If you'd rather speak out of doors, I'd enjoy a ramble in the garden." That ramble would take us a sufficient distance to ensure privacy.

Tait bellowed for a footman, ordered a tray of lemonade and biscuits by the sundial, and escorted me through a country manor midway between prosperity and poverty. I washed my hands in a breakfast parlor that boasted a table too large for a household of one, though the windows were sparkling and the sideboard recently polished. The house was generally free of cobwebs, stains, and dust, but the hall runners were thin, only half the sconces had lamps, and the art on the walls was a collection of bucolic mediocrities.

"I haven't done much with the garden since Evvie left," Tait said, leading me onto a wide flagstone terrace at the back of the house. "I still don't know how to talk about her departure. Did she leave? Was she kidnapped? Did she come to grief at the hands of highwaymen? Did she succumb to food poisoning at some coaching inn between here and London, her valuables ransacked by the innkeeper? England is not what it once was, with tens of thousands of soldiers home, all looking for work or looking for trouble."

His point, while mildly insulting, was valid, more so because all of those former farm boys, apprentices, and drovers had grown comfortable with firearms, inebriation, and violence while taking the king's shilling. Wellington had referred to his army as infamous for good reasons.

We jaunted down the steps into a garden fading toward autumn. "We can take comfort," I said, "from the fact that those soldiers were still on the Continent at the time of your wife's disappearance, and highwaymen have become rare."

"True enough, but I don't know what became of Evelyn, my lord. The not knowing eats at me like a malaise of the soul. Did I inspire my spouse to take her own life? Is she kicking her heels as some alderman's ostensible wife, heedless of my torment or even gratified by the thought of it? Sometimes I think I'll go mad with wondering. Other times, I can pretend the whole business is behind me."

Tait's lament struck a reluctant chord with me. I was not entirely certain what had led to my brother Harry's death and less certain still what role I had played—if any—in his demise. I had followed him from camp one night, thinking to safeguard him on whatever mischief he was about. To my shock, he'd been waylaid by a party of French officers, and he'd surrendered without a fight, perhaps because he'd sensed my presence and thought to protect me. I'd presented myself to his captors as well, thinking that Harry and I stood a better chance of escaping together than Harry did alone.

I'd had no opportunity to ask Harry why he'd left camp against standing orders, though he most assuredly had. Harry was dead, I had endured torments in captivity that haunted me still, and this enigma in my recent past no doubt fueled my interest in solving other people's mysteries.

"You manage," I said to my host. "Good days and bad days, sometimes terrible days and worse nights. Life goes on, and marriage, while important, does not encompass all that gives life meaning."

"You describe me as a cross between a career infantryman and a youngish spinster."

Touché, did he but know it. "We are all soldiering on as best we can, Tait."

A housekeeper in a mobcap and half apron descended into the garden, laid a tray on a small weathered table near the sundial, curtseyed, and withdrew. She was doubtless doing the footman's job, the better to get a gawk at the titled caller. She was younger than most housekeepers and pretty in a sturdy, freckled way. Something about the lone glance she'd sent Tait stirred questions in my mind.

Because the garden was sunny, I donned a pair of my blue-tinted eyeglasses.

"Hyperia likes your spectacles," Tait said, settling on a wooden bench beside the table. "She says they give you a scholarly air."

"They protect my eyesight." I sat about two feet from my host, the bench warm at my back. "Tell me about the last time you saw your wife."

Tait handed me over a glass of lemonade and took one for himself. "The fourth of October, five years past. The anniversary is at hand, and that always makes me melancholy."

The melancholy might fade to introspection in time. "Did you part in anger?"

He sipped his drink and looked all brooding and handsome even while engaged in that mundane undertaking. "Has Hyperia been telling tales out of school?"

"She respects your confidences. My questions are my own. If Evelyn is alive and well, then she is apparently *choosing* not to communicate with you, *choosing* to remain at a distance while she holds your future hostage. Those are not the behaviors of a happy wife."

"Your thoughts echo my own, closely followed by, 'And is she justified in her anger?' Was I that bad of a husband? I loved her, I never laid a hand on her, I thought she loved me…"

I waited. Tait had philosophized and regretted and speculated, but he was taking his jolly time getting down to a recitation of relevant facts.

"We quarreled," he said. "All couples do, though some manage their skirmishes mostly in private and in civil tones. Evvie and I were loud. We were young, and the lack of children became a sore point after a couple of years. We both wanted children, and providence thwarted our wishes. This has an insalubrious effect on marital relations."

I let that understatement pass unremarked. My manly humors had suffered some sort of casualty during my time in uniform and had yet—thus far—to reassert themselves.

"Was the last quarrel the worst?"

Tait smiled ruefully at his drink. "It is now, of course. At the time, it was just another row. I'd tracked mud onto the carpets in the formal parlor. This misdemeanor is committed by every rural husband whose abode boasts such a parlor, but I'd given offense once too often. I was a disrespectful lout. She rued the day she'd accepted my suit."

I sipped my lemonade, which was good. Cool, neither too tart nor too sweet. "And you returned fire?"

"Don't we always when the ladies take us to task? She was a nag who cared more for a spot on the carpet than she did for her own husband, and the only people to see our formal parlor were her gossiping friends and the vicar's sermonizing wife. Their opinions of my manners meant less than nothing to me, et cetera and so forth. I rued the day I'd offered for her hand, and that was her opening to storm off, stage left. Cue ominous violin tremolo. Within the hour, she'd summoned the coach to take her the five miles to Bamford. Several coaching routes converge there, and I haven't been able to trace her movements from that point forward."

His circumstances resonated too well with my own. I'd trailed Harry into the night half on a lark, thinking to catch him out in a tryst or hoping to eavesdrop on a meeting with one of his myriad informants. Nothing about the night marked it as the start of a tragedy, much less a harbinger of ignominious death.

"Your wife did not leave you over one spot of mud on the carpet, Tait."

And I had not trailed Harry strictly on a lark. My motivations had included overweening curiosity, boredom, genuine fraternal concern—and sibling rivalry.

"Oh, we had our differences, my lord. I was not strictly faithful. She flirted to annoy me. I suspect the final blow was that October the fourth was our wedding anniversary, and I had forgotten the significance of the date. Evvie set great store by such dates. She always made a fuss over holidays, birthdays, that sort of thing."

And now every holiday and birthday was a reminder of Evvie's departure. "You sent inquiries when she didn't come home?"

"A few, but ours was the typical polite-society courtship. I went up to London in search of a wife. I'd done my bit at university, the land was prospering at the time, and my mother was appealing to my conscience. She longed for grandchildren. According to her, had my father been alive, he'd have counseled me to take a bride. I had means, land, looks—according to my mother. I was remiss for remaining a bachelor. You know how the ladies go on."

I didn't, quite. As the second spare in a ducal family, I'd not faced the pressure to marry that my older brothers had, though I faced it now. The Waltham ducal succession rested on my tired shoulders, and I keenly felt the burden.

"You and Evelyn met in Town?"

"In spring, when all is gaiety and fashion. The Season is a handful of weeks, really, and at first you are agog at the splendor. Up every morning to see and be seen on the bridle paths, socializing by the hour at the tailor's, the bootmaker's, the clubs. Dancing until the small hours, then pretending to cut a dash at the gaming hells. I had never been so exhausted in all my born days, and I am a countryman in my prime, my lord."

My older brothers had made sure that I knew my way about the clubs and hells. My social standing alone had guaranteed me entrée into the ballrooms. For a gentry bachelor in search of a bride, Town had likely been a more daunting proposition.

"You hadn't spent much time in London previously?"

Tait set aside his glass and stretched out his legs to cross them at the ankle. "Papa took me up to London a few times, but tagging after him at Tatts or going for an ice at Gunter's doesn't really show a boy much of Town life. Then Papa fell ill, and off to university I did go."

For three years of scholarship, inebriation, and—for the most part—sexual frustration. "Was Eveyln in her first Season when you met?" I finished my drink and poured myself another, because Tait's recitation was only getting started, and the sun was gaining strength.

"She was in her *only* Season. Evvie is one of four daughters. The family had the means to give each young lady one Season, or so the parents decided. Evvie was well dowered, and I suspect the single Season edict was to inspire seriousness of purpose, lest a younger sister's prospects wane while an elder sibling enjoyed a third or fourth turn around the ballrooms. Evvie was the second oldest and intent on seizing the day."

Among the aristocracy, the rules about sisters marrying in birth order tended to be honored in the breach, while gentry and cits intent on ascending were less flexible.

"Evvie seized you?"

Tait uncrossed his ankles and crossed his arms. "April turns into May, and the matchmaking becomes desperate. You realize you have a fortnight, a month, six weeks at the most to find gold, or you'll return to the shires without a wife. Evvie was so frank and good-natured about it all, and to be honest, she flattered me. She struck me as a woman of substance who knew what she wanted. She wore too much jewelry for such a young lady, though the pieces were always good quality and would have raised no comment on a married woman.

"Evelyn wore heeled slippers," he went on more softly, "despite being quite tall, and she wore bold fragrances—muguet or Parisian blends rather than the usual orange blossoms or attar of roses. I was a veritable bumpkin with the usual struggling acres, by London standards, and yet, Evelyn always saved a dance for me. I screwed up my courage, had the requisite discussion with her mama, and the rest was pretty much a blur of longing gazes, furtive caresses, and stolen kisses."

Evvie, in other words, hadn't been foolish or besotted enough to allow Tait any anticipation of the vows.

"You tell me this," I said, "to explain why you were at a loss when it came time to search for your wife?"

"I was at a loss and equal parts furious and humiliated. I had no idea to whom she might have gone, other than to her sisters, and they claimed ignorance. I tried the only governess I'd heard her mention—but that was a finishing governess rather than a family retainer. Evvie had the two years at finishing academy required by holy writ, but I could not bring myself to write to the headmistress."

In Tait's shoes, I might have been similarly reticent. I'd tell myself each day that Evvie could already be on her way home, and each night, I'd promise myself that tomorrow, I'd send a note to the headmistress…

While the trail grew colder and more overgrown.

"Write to the headmistress now," I said. "That your wife left you has long since made the rounds of the gossips. Some might conclude you and she have simply decided to live apart, and thus they don't think it odd that they spotted Evelyn taking the waters, or coming out of a Paris hat shop. Can you ask the sisters for the names of former housekeepers, governesses, and close friends?"

Tait sat up, no longer the young gentleman at his leisure. "I was hoping you'd check those traplines."

"Those ladies are your family."

Tait poured himself a half glass of lemonade. "They have more or less closed ranks against me. They claim I was a bit too flirtatious with the youngest sister—she's since married, of course—and the eldest sister held the misunderstanding against me, and then Evvie ran off. The sisters and I can be civil, but I am no longer part of their circle."

"Tait, please tell me you did not compromise the youngest daughter."

He shook his head. "Hanged for a sheep, and all that. Ardath was something of a featherbrain. Most of the time she was jolly, as Evvie had once been jolly, but I never crossed the most important lines."

I wanted to smack him on the back of the head. He'd apparently crossed *other* lines, lines that could just as easily have seen Miss Ardath cast from Society's favor. A brotherly kiss that did not land on her forehead, an embrace that lasted longer than a friendly squeeze.

"You were trying to make Evvie jealous?" I could come up with no other halfway credible excuse.

"Tit for tat. Evvie was a flirt, I became a flirt, and sometimes more than a flirt, and by the time she left, we were both convinced that we'd been victimized by a cruel and unfeeling spouse who did not deserve our loyalty. Children would have helped, even one child, but that consolation was denied us."

I sipped my second drink, repositioning my mental artillery and arranging infantry and cavalry in light of the discussion. My job was not to judge two young people who'd made a hash of their marriage—what did I know of those challenges?—but rather to find the missing party.

"I need a list, Tait, of your flirts and especially your more-than-flirts. Leave nobody off. Not the scullery maid at the posting inn, not the second parlor maid you had to pay off after only a summer." Nor the pretty, youngish housekeeper with the longing glances.

"Those people won't know where Evelyn is, assuming my wife is yet alive."

"They might well have facilitated her exit, heard her plans, or arranged to have her done away with. I will call upon her sisters to learn what I can of Evelyn's side of the equation."

Tait's handsome countenance took on a sullen cast. "I hate that you must pry into my affairs, and yet, that's what I've asked you to do."

I wasn't much looking forward to the exercise myself. "Then dismiss me from the ranks, Tait. I follow your orders in this undertaking. If you want your lady wife found, I will march out smartly. If you want to continue on in the same ignorance you have enjoyed for five years, then say so now. Harvest is upon us, and I can make myself useful elsewhere."

More accurately, I could lounge about at the Hall, counting the days until Arthur's departure and playing Vikings with little Leander in the nursery. Harry had always preferred Vikings to Highlanders or explorers. I had recently taken on managing the household correspondence, as much for something to do as to prepare for Arthur's absence.

"Commence searching," Tait said. "I will send a note to the oldest sister, Mrs. Margery Semple. She bides about ten miles to the west, not that far from Caldicott Hall."

The name was unfamiliar to me, but then, I hadn't been home much in recent years. "Tell her to expect me tomorrow at midmorning. I can see myself out." I finished my drink and rose. "Is there anything else you think I should know?"

Tait stood as well. He lacked about an inch of my six-foot-two-inch height, but he was a fine specimen. His flirtatious overtures had likely been well received in many quarters and bitterly resented in others.

"I'm sure I'll think of something—a thousand things—just as soon as you trot down the drive, my lord, but at present, no. I've revealed the unhappy nature of my union, my part in creating the misery, and my desire to see Evelyn found or properly laid to rest. I'm not sure what else there is to tell."

He could tell me which shops she'd patronized in Town, with whom she'd corresponded, whether the same housekeeper still served the Tait domicile... I had much ground to cover, but I sensed that I'd reached the limit of Tait's willingness to talk, for now.

"You have lied by omission," I said, surveying the tired garden. "I understand that, because your pride is involved. You well know which fellows you suspect of making a cuckold of you, which fellows listened too sympathetically to Evelyn's woes in the very churchyard.

"I will be back," I went on, "and I will compare what you tell me about those fellows with what the sisters have to say. I will traverse the terrain of your marriage over and over, focusing first on this bit of gossip, then on that odd silence, until I know your past better than you do. Understand that now, Tait, and either support my endeavors or end the search before it begins."

He studied the sundial, a venerable relic defaced by the passing of some disrespectful bird. A wife would have seen the sundial regularly scrubbed, the herbaceous borders trimmed, the gravel walks raked. A wife would have done a tidier job of mending the seam of Tait's morning coat, and a wife would have ensured that the kitchen had put at least a pot of violets on the drinks tray.

Tait seemed to mentally inventory all those touches missing from his life before making his decision.

"Do your worst, my lord, or your best. If you cannot find Evelyn, then I must wait years for the courts to free me from her ghost, and I will bankrupt myself in the process. Hyperia is right that you are my best option, though admittedly, one I embrace with reluctance."

As noble speeches went, that one was at least brief. "I will return tomorrow afternoon, after having called on Mrs. Semple."

I bowed my farewell and left him in a brown study by the sundial. My ride home was taken up with the question of timing. Why start the search for Evelyn now? Tait's feelings for his wife were clearly mixed, while she might despise the ground he strutted upon—assuming she was alive.

And I had not been strictly forthcoming with Tait either.

He'd said he'd never raised a hand to his wife. Many husbands bragged of the same accomplishment, as if having the self-restraint of a seven-year-old at choir practice was somehow indicative of great forbearance. Tait might well have taken a riding crop to his wife, or otherwise given her reason to fear him.

If Evelyn had been unsafe in her marriage, then, should I find her, I would keep her whereabouts from Tait, no matter how many speeches he made or husbandly regrets he expressed.

CHAPTER THREE

Mrs. Margery Semple was a pillar of the parish in both moral and physical senses. I put her at about five foot ten barefoot and thirteen stone standing in her shift—a daunting prospect even in my imagination. She had begun a stately progress toward middle age, one embroidered sampler, chubby child, and pressed flower arrangement at a time.

"I have no idea where Evvie got off to, my lord," she said when we'd dispensed with two cups of tea as well as the requisite rounds of *have you met...?* and *I believe you might know...* By diligent pursuit of my particulars, Mrs. Semple had established that she was indirectly acquainted with Lady Ophelia and had been introduced to His Grace at the last village fete.

We were practically cousins, all unbeknownst to me.

"You and Evelyn were not close?" I asked as a pug waddled into the parlor and gave me a panting perusal.

"I am several years Evvie's senior, and thus we moved in different circles. By the time she made her come out, I had already married Mr. Semple and set up my nursery. I tried to warn Evvie about what Town would be like, but warning Evvie at that age was like explaining a republic to Napoleon. You can shout *liberté, égalité, fraternité* all you please, and he will even wave encouragingly, but then he insists on crowning himself emperor."

Recent French history in a nutshell. "Were Evvie and John a love match?"

Mrs. Semple patted her knee, and the dog crossed the room to turn adoring eyes on his mistress.

"At that age, my lord, who is capable of love? We mistake infatuation and animal spirits for grand sentiment. I'm sure Evvie and John fell prey to nature's lures, but love? I don't believe Tait is capable of truly loving another. His mother spoiled her only son shamelessly, and we gentry do pride ourselves on our acres. He inherited a very pretty property and isn't bad-looking himself. Evvie supposed herself lucky to win an offer from him."

Tait was handsome, dashing even, and charming. "You don't care for him?"

She picked up the dog, who sighed gustily and made himself at home on her lap. "I wanted to like John Tait. At first, we did like him. He was witty, doting, and friendly. Let it be said that dear Evvie had no other offers, so we looked upon John as the answer to a prayer. After the marriage, it became apparent he was too friendly with the wrong parties for Evvie's peace of mind. By the first anniversary, we were all regretting Evvie's choice, perhaps Evvie most of all."

"Might Evvie have found somebody with whom she was more compatible?" The simplest explanation for her absence was that she'd eloped with a lover.

Mrs. Semple stroked the pug's ears, and the dog closed his eyes on a rapturous grunt. "Evvie was no longer a young heiress new to Town, my lord. She'd put on some weight during her years of marriage—we Hasborough girls are not dainty to begin with—though she nonetheless exerted herself to be charming to certain young men. I doubt there was anything to it, but I am kept busy raising my own brood, and Mr. Semple advised a prudent distance from Evvie and John's drama."

"Tait apparently became overly friendly with your youngest sister, Ardath. Where might I find her?"

Mrs. Semple ceased fondling her dog. "In Town. Ardath is now Mrs. Humphrey Deloitte. He deals in fine cloth, wallpaper, and drapery. They bide on Hammersleigh Court. Ardie was always closer to Evelyn than I was. Ardie can tell you much more about Evelyn's married years than I ever could. Do have some more tea, my lord. I rarely have a chance to get off my feet in the middle of the morning, much less to further my acquaintance with a distinguished neighbor."

Mrs. Semple had not corrected my characterization of Tait's behavior with Ardath, for which I applauded her. A pragmatic sort of woman. Tait's term—a woman of substance—fit her in a mostly complimentary sense.

"Was Tait abusive? I ask because, if so, I will purposely fail in my quest as far as he's concerned, even if I locate his wife. The lady left him for reasons, and he's waited five years to take her departure seriously. That raises questions in my mind."

Mrs. Semple poured us both more tea. "Tait was a scoundrel, cavorting shamelessly right under Evvie's nose. I understand that men grow bored with their wives, and temptation is everywhere for those with weak characters, but Tait was unkind. I fault him in passing for straying, and straying so early in the marriage, but I hold a serious grievance with him for being cruel about it."

The tea was hot and strong. I ventured a question I would not have put to just anybody. "Was Tait trying to compensate for an empty nursery?"

My hostess stirred honey into her cup. "Oh, very likely, and was Evvie engaged in the same foolishness? All three of her sisters have children—note the plural. I doubt the fault lay with her, if an empty nursery is a fault. England is awash in children without bread to eat or shoes to wear. More little dears are arriving by the hour. That 'be fruitful and multiply' business is fine for when you have a single breeding pair and all of Eden to populate, but here in the land of Nod, those conditions hardly apply, do they, my lord?"

I had seen too many orphans in Spain and London, all with the same weary despair in their eyes, the same wretched rags for clothes...

"I take your point, Mrs. Semple. Tait has said he would entertain an annulment, and childlessness will aid that cause if and when a petition is brought. If Evelyn wants to be free of Tait, I need to find her and tell her that, but I have no idea where to look." Not quite true. I had a few hunches and suspicions.

Mrs. Semple sipped her tea, and such was her self-possession that I could not tell if she was inventorying memories or deciding just how honestly to respond.

"Evvie attended the Ellington Academy, my lord. We all did, in our turns. Schoolgirls can become friends for life, and Evvie was particularly close with the Wilner girl. Evangeline Wilner—Evvie and Evie, they styled themselves. They both accepted offers in their first Season, but I am dashed if I know the name of Evangeline's husband. Ardie might know."

Lady Ophelia would of a certainty. "One more question before I take my leave: With whom did Tait disport most notoriously?"

"With whom didn't he? Several maids came and went from the household in close succession, all young and gullible. The vicar's cousin visiting for the summer from Yorkshire—a *vicar's cousin*, and Tait had to slobber over her hand and recite poetry to her at the assembly. A Mrs. Probinger from the village on your brother's estate caught his eye... Lovely widow, though I suspect she hadn't much time for him. His tastes were eclectic and shamefully unrestrained. Mr. Semple offered to have a word with Tait, but Evvie wouldn't hear of anybody criticizing John's flirtations. We settled for limiting our association with him after Evvie left."

Why would a new husband stray that often and exuberantly? Why would any husband? "Might I call again if I have more questions?" I asked, getting to my feet.

She set the dog on the floor, and the creature affected a gaze of crushing heartbreak. "My lord, you must call even if you don't have questions." Her smile was so gracious that I did feel a sense of welcome, a sense of having formed an ally in an unlikely place.

Exactly the impression a skilled liar would want me to form, alas.

"Lady Ophelia Oliphant and Miss Hyperia West are biding at the Hall," I said. "You might consider calling upon them if you have the time to spare." I did not suggest she call upon the duke, of course. Arthur would fillet me for that much presumption.

"Thank you," she said, rising without assistance and escorting me from the room. "I shall do that, and I might even inveigle Mr. Semple into coming with me. That will cause talk, my lord, depend upon it."

She sailed to the front door and passed over my hat and spurs. "I hope you do find Evvie. She was always restless, and I have worried about her, but the one characteristic Evvie has to a fault is determination. If I were a betting woman, I'd wager she's landed on her feet."

"Let's hope so, for the sake of all concerned. Tait acknowledges that he was a poor husband, and I believe he seeks to atone for his shortcomings, one way or another."

"Is that what he told you?"

"Yes, more or less."

She opened the door and accompanied me onto the porch. A boy rose from the mounting block at the foot of the steps and trotted off in the direction of the stable.

"Do you believe John Tait has recently acquired a conscience, my lord? That he suddenly seeks to put right harm he inflicted years ago?"

The day was sunny, so I put on my blue eyeglasses. "I believe he might have slowly acquired a sense of shame for how he behaved. He's apparently much more circumspect now and reasonably well thought-of." By Hyperia, though not by Lady Ophelia, interestingly. "Then too, he describes a situation where both parties have a basis for regrets."

Mrs. Semple shaded her eyes as the boy returned with my horse, Atlas, in tow. "That's possible, of course. Young people can be hotheaded and sharp-tongued. You ride a fine animal, my lord."

"I brought Atlas home with me from the Continent. His good sense is equaled only by his bottom."

"Perhaps one might say the same of his owner. Good day, my lord." She curtseyed, came about, and tacked into the house before I could decide whether I'd been complimented, teased, disrespected, or all three.

I swung into the saddle, intent on joining the ladies at the Hall for my midday meal. As Atlas trotted along, I reviewed my discussion with Mrs. Semple, plagued by a feeling of dissatisfaction.

I hadn't learned much at all. Was that because Mrs. Semple was truly ignorant of her younger sister's situation, or because ignorance was the impression with which my formidable hostess had decided to leave me?

"Lina Wilner married..." Lady Ophelia gazed off toward the home wood as the midday breeze pushed a few dry leaves across the Hall's back terrace. "She married George Hanscomb, though everybody called him Handsome, and that was cruel because the poor fellow was as plain as the back end of a donkey."

"I remember that," Hyperia said. "His family was quite well fixed. They import hardwoods from the tropics, and I forget what else. He's an excellent dancer, doesn't put on airs. Jules, please pass the olives."

I complied, letting the ladies reminisce and chat in response to my questions. Arthur had deserted the ranks to meet with the head steward, which was pure tripe. If His Grace had truly been meeting with the steward, he would have dragooned me into accompanying him. I was to hold the reins at the Hall in His Grace's extended absence, after all, a prospect I dreaded only slightly less than I dreaded the thought of a return to France.

"The Hanscombs had two children at last count," Lady Ophelia said, swiping an olive from the dish when I'd set it by Hyperia's elbow. "A boy and a girl, but I cannot recall which is the elder."

"And what do you know of Ardath and Humphrey Deloitte of Hammersleigh Court?" I asked.

Lady Ophelia snitched another olive. "Silk and velvet are his primary lines, I believe. Owns a warehouse rather than a retail establishment, if you take my meaning. Doing quite well now that the war is over and people can go shopping again."

Some people could, the people who draped themselves in elegance. Other people—the vast lot in London's slums—were hard put to afford bread.

"Jules, you're scowling," Hyperia said. "Did the meal sit poorly with you?"

"The food was lovely, but I have promised Tait another call this afternoon. The two of you can anticipate a visit in the near future from a Mrs. Margery Semple, who has already been introduced to His Grace and whose acquaintance I made earlier today."

Hyperia took her time choosing her next olive. "She's Evvie Tait's older sister. You called upon her in an investigative capacity."

"And learned nothing." So far. Further reflection might reveal information in our exchange I had initially overlooked. "I put questions to Tait yesterday and gave him the night to ponder his answers."

Hyperia considered her olive. "Shall I come with you?"

"Thank you, no. Tait might well apprise me of behavior he's ashamed of, and in that case, a smaller audience is more likely to result in accurate disclosures."

Lady Ophelia looked from Hyperia to me. "The gentlemen will discuss *indiscretions*, Hyperia. Oh, the scandal! But, Julian, you must know that ladies discuss and even *participate in* indiscretions too. I have committed a few myself, shockingly delightful frolics, though you will find that hard to believe. You need not be delicate for our sakes."

"I must be discreet for Tait's sake. I promised him I'd keep the business to myself to the greatest extent possible, and I will hold myself to that promise."

Hyperia set the thoroughly examined olive on her plate. "I could be useful, Jules. John has no secrets from me. We are old friends. I can prod his memory and correct his erring recollections."

What to say to that? Would *John* admit to me that Perry had been among his conquests if she was sitting next to him? Would *John* be too busy flirting with her to give me honest answers?

"*We* can be of use," Lady Ophelia said. "I shall consult my journals and so forth and look for any mention of Tait and his wife. Five years ago, they were newlyweds, and the Peninsular hostilities were just heating up. Hyperia, you had been out for a year or two and were doubtless becoming an astute observer of the passing scene. We will put our heads together and be helpful within the bounds of Julian's vast and dunderheaded discretion."

I could not stop them from conferring, and Godmama was right: They might recall some on-dit or innuendo that shed light on Tait's circumstances.

"Consider any young ladies Tait might have led to believe he was courting that same Season," I said. "Young ladies who'd resent Evelyn's success on the marriage mart."

Hyperia set her table napkin beside her plate, and something in her manner suggested frustration—with me. "The list will be long, Jules. *Any* young lady who completes her first Season with an offer in hand is resented by *all* of the young ladies who did not."

Delightful. Hyperia when peevish could rival the Regent in a taking. The difficulty was, her injured pride was understandable.

"I'm interested only in young ladies who were smitten with Tait." I was *not* interested in learning whether that list had included Hyperia. "If you will excuse me, I will set off on my afternoon errand."

"I'll walk you to the stable." Hyperia rose, and short of rudeness, I could not decline her company.

I made my bow to Godmama and offered Hyperia my arm.

"My regards to young Tait," her ladyship called, waggling her fingers at us in farewell. "Don't be too hard on him, Jules, unless of course he murdered his wife and is using your good offices to muddy the waters. Then you must be the sledgehammer of justice. I'll spend the afternoon in the company of my diaries. Always a pleasant and entertaining prospect."

She blew us a kiss and wafted into the house on a breeze of gardenia and mischief.

"I want to grow up to be just like her," Hyperia said. "Except that Lady Ophelia is a true original, and thus one cannot emulate her exactly. One never sees her at a loss."

I thought back over the years of my interactions with her ladyship. "She was distraught at Papa's funeral service. Utterly silent. I accompanied the other men to the graveside, and I recall her standing in the churchyard, looking..." *Bereft. Shattered.*

Everlasting providence. Had she counted Papa among her indiscretions?

"Don't think about it, Jules," Hyperia said, leading me toward the terrace steps. "Their generation did things differently, and it was all a long time ago, and consenting adults and eight other platitudes. John did not kill Evvie."

I didn't think he had. "The only person who could know that for a fact, Perry—besides John Tait—is the person who did kill Evelyn."

"I hate that you can think like that, but that is precisely why you are the ideal resource to aid John now."

John. If ever the Almighty blessed me with male offspring, not a one of them would be named John. Not for a middle name or a nickname. Not John, Jean, Ian, Ivan, Jan, Johann, Giovanni, Jonas, Seán, or Vanya... The boar hog at the home farm was welcome to call himself John.

"I doubt the situation involves murder," I said as we took the path that led to the stable. "Rather, I doubt Tait had any hand in murder."

"You may be assured he is no murderer."

English choirboys were capable of enthusiastic murder when the French cavalry charged them. "I, too, acquit Tait of murder, Perry—

provisionally—because if Tait had killed his wife, his best course would be to let another few years go by, then petition the courts to have her declared dead. The longer he waits to bring a lawsuit, the more any evidence of bickering and infidelity fades from memory and the longer Tait has to cultivate a reputation for probity." Then too, the statutory seven years would have elapsed, making the timing less suspect.

"You truly don't care for him, do you?" Hyperia asked.

"I barely know the man, and I have more sympathy for his circumstances than you might think. We have no idea where Harry is buried, whether he took his own life to thwart his captors, died under torture, succumbed to jail fever... No idea why he left camp, whether he thought he was following orders or possibly *was* following orders. Tait is right—the not knowing is a malaise, and the only cure is the truth."

Hyperia stopped and gathered me in a hug. "I'm sorry, Jules. Of course you understand John's situation." She let me go as swiftly as she'd embraced me. "I almost hope Evelyn is dead, though you mustn't tell anybody I said that. A painless, swift, and noble death, too, of course."

"Perry, she was not yet thirty and was as deserving of a long and happy life as the next soul. Why would you say such a thing?" Had Tait said such a thing to Hyperia?

"Because then John could at least put her money to use, Jules. Show me a farmer who doesn't need an infusion of cash, and I will show you a liar. She was well dowered—all four Hasborough girls were—and she died without issue. Somewhere, a pot of money is sitting idle, or gaining interest at a very slow rate."

Dear Perry might well have solved the riddle of Tait's timing. Perhaps he could not *afford* to wait for the courts, and if Evelyn had been laid to rest in some rural churchyard two years ago, why should he?

"How destitute is he?" I asked as the stable came into view.

"I never said John was destitute, but he doesn't entertain, he seldom goes up to Town, and he's awash in acreage."

Land-poor. The all-too-common story. Wealthy in real property, but in want of cash. Or was Tait simply a squire without a hostess to put fresh bouquets on his sideboards and choose menus worthy of guests?

"I will ask about Evelyn's settlements," I said. "Your mention of that line of inquiry is very useful, Perry, and I thank you for it."

She parted from me on that note, and I wanted to call her back—to apologize, to interrogate, to simply hold her. This business with Tait sat increasingly ill with me. I was comforted not at all to conclude it sat increasingly ill with Hyperia too.

～

"You got your card in your pocket, guv?" Atticus posed his question from atop a bay equine whose antecedents might have numbered among the native specimens of North Devon. The beast, Ladon by name, was technically a large pony, though for the sake of Atticus's pride, I referred to his mount as a small horse. Height aside, Ladon—named for the mythical dragon who guarded Hera's golden apples—was coming off summer much in need of exercise.

Atticus, my tiger, was much in need of time in the saddle, and for my part, I needed a reliable report on the situation belowstairs at Tait's domicile.

"Eyes up, Atticus. Staring at the horse's mane won't help when he shies at a rabbit. My card is always in my pocket." I referred not to a calling card, but to a few lines written in my own hand, explaining—*to me*—that I was prone to short, complete lapses of memory, and I could return to the Duke of Waltham for safekeeping until the bout passed. The card had been Hyperia's idea, and writing it in my own hand provided a means for me to authenticate its authorship even when a lapse was upon me.

"A lad don't have to worry about rabbits scarin' 'is 'orse in London," Atticus replied, dutifully lifting his gaze to the road ahead.

"No pickpockets, confidence tricksters, sponging houses, or blacklegs in the countryside. Ready to try some trotting?"

"I hate trotting."

"Because you don't post. Watch me, watch how I rise with each step and descend to the saddle with the next. Once you get the knack, you never forget it. Posting is much easier on the horse's back and on your rosy fundament too. I'll go first."

My trusty Atlas, having learned the drill a fortnight past, adopted the slowest trot he was capable of, a sort of lazy horse's passage. Atticus gamely thumped his mount's side with booted heels. Ladon lifted into the trot, and Atticus bounced upon his back like a busker's puppet jigging on a barrelhead.

"Up, down, up, down," I sang out in rhythm to the smaller equine's gait. "One, two, up, down, one, two, up, down…"

Atticus's backside and the horse's spine were both taking a pounding. I gave up after another few hundred yards, because the boy was simply not catching on. Children were supposed to be natural riders, but in some regards, Atticus, for all his youth, hadn't much childhood left in him.

"Enough," I said as Atlas dropped back to the walk. "Let him blow for a bit."

"Ladon isn't tired," Atticus retorted as the pony returned to the walk. "I'm just no good at riding."

"Every skill takes time to acquire, my boy. Miss West tells me you are becoming a prodigious reader. A few months ago, you could barely spell your name."

"Miss West makes reading easy, and the newspapers never use big words. So what am I supposed to listen for when I'm having my kitchen beer?"

A good question, though I wished Atticus were more curious about equitation. The ability to handle a horse was a salable skill and a gentleman's art. The boy would do well to master it.

"Tait's wife ran off five years ago," I replied, "or so he would have me believe. He says they were devoted, but they bickered constantly. I'm to locate the lady or discern her fate, no matter how unfortunate."

"Bickering can be fun, to hear some tell it," Atticus replied, patting his pony. "Bickerin' and kissin' and kissin' and bickerin'. When I worked at Makepeace, the maids and footmen were always up to one or t' other."

At Makepeace, the manor house where Atticus had previously been employed, he'd been the boot-boy, general dogsbody, and drudge-at-large, despite his tender years. Nobody had been educating the lad. Nobody had been preparing him for a trade, much less contemplating articles of apprenticeship for him. The situation had offended my sensibilities, particularly when Atticus had shown himself to be resourceful, and—in his own dear, foul-mouthed, pigheaded way—honorable.

"You listen," I said, "for any sense of how long the staff has been in service to Tait. You gently inquire as to where the missus is, because nobody tells you anything, and you haven't been with me very long to know what I'm about. You compliment the cook on her ale and make a discreet inspection of the lower reaches."

"Nose about? I'm good at that."

He was, the little blighter. "And so modest too. I want a sense of Tait's finances. I can understand why a man would look for a missing wife, but Tait has waited five years to get serious about searching. Why that long, when in another two years he'll have recourse to the courts?"

"You mean he needs to marry for blunt? I thought only you nobs did that."

"We might have invented the game, but anybody can play it, especially gentry." Could and did play. "Keep an eye out for excessive economies, debts overdue, wages going unpaid, scanty stores in the larders, that sort of thing. Chat up the outside help, too, if you can manage it."

Atticus gave his pony a slack rein, stood in the stirrups, and settled back into the saddle. "Doesn't seem right, though, does it? Tait asked you to find his missus, and you start off by snooping about in Tait's own castle. So what if he's in dun territory? Most folk are. Most nobs are. How does that tell you where his missus got off to?"

Who needed a conscience when Atticus was on the job? "The state of matters belowstairs won't tell me where Mrs. Tait has got off to, though Tait might well have lied about his finances and made promises in the settlements that he could not keep. We need to know if dishonesty on his part or looming penury drove Mrs. Tait to seek greener pastures."

I was improvising, trying to excuse my own curiosity. My own nosiness.

"You think he's sweet on Miss West, and you hope he's a pauper."

No... and yes. "Don't be impertinent." I brandished my riding crop with mock sternness in Atticus's general direction. Not for anything would I have truly threatened the boy with it. Atticus had known enough of corporal punishment, often for de minimis transgressions.

Ladon, though, well knew what the intended purpose of a riding crop was and took off smartly not at the trot, but at the canter. Atticus hadn't cantered to speak of, that gait being appreciably faster than the trot.

The boy nonetheless stood in the stirrups when he ought to have pulled on the reins, yodeled like a dragoon on the tail of a retreating French column, and waved a fist in the air.

"Catch him," I muttered, nudging Atlas into pursuit.

We hung back until the pony began to tire, and the whole time, Atticus hovered over his mount's withers, happy as a Cossack and completely at ease with the horse's rhythm. When Ladon finally broke to the trot, Atticus posted along with the natural grace of a lad born to the saddle, until he brought his mighty steed to the walk.

"That were glorious wonderful," Atticus announced, thumping Ladon's hairy shoulder. "The best. Ladon is fast, isn't he?"

Ladon was a sloth with four hooves. "He was nigh galloping, my boy. He'd be halfway to the sea if you hadn't pulled him up."

"Let's do it again."

"Ladon needs to blow, Atticus. He's not used to a rider who likes to go fast. He's been indentured to the pony cart for too long."

"That's rubbish," Atticus retorted. "A fellow needs to stretch his legs from time to time, and Ladon deserves some fun."

Don't we all? Ladon's idea of fun was a half-dozen apples and an afternoon spent napping and grazing. "We'll get him legged up, but you must be patient with him. He's a man of mature years, and his greatest strength is surviving on short rations."

"More bleedin' rubbish. I hate short rations. Race you to the next gateposts!"

I did not let Atticus win the race, though when Atlas and I pounded along on Ladon's heels, the pony gamely approximated a true gallop for a few strides before we overtook him. By the time we turned through Tait's gateposts, Atticus was threatening to become a jockey.

I let him blow, so to speak. Tomorrow, he'd be hard put to get out of bed, given today's exertions. Fun was all well and good—even Wellington had understood the need to occasionally entertain the troops—but frolic always came at a price.

I handed Atlas off to a groom, removed my spurs, and prepared to interrogate Tait on the subject of his frolics and the price he might still be paying for them five years on.

CHAPTER FOUR

"That's the list," Tait said, passing over a piece of foolscap with a half-dozen names on it. "As best I recall. I was raised in a household of mostly women—two sisters, an auntie, my mama. Papa and I were allies while he was extant, but I learned to be agreeable to the fairer sex from a young age."

So had I, but if I'd had to list the ladies who could claim I'd toyed with their affections... Hyperia alone might qualify, and she had forgiven me my presumptions.

"A few details, please," I said, moving two feet to the right to take advantage of the shade available in Tait's gazebo. We were in that time of year when mornings and evenings could be nippy, but midafternoon still carried some warmth. I needed my spectacles because even winter sunshine could be too bright for my eyes, and the worst torment of all was sunshine on fresh snow.

"The vicar's cousin," Tait began, "Miss Sally Brown, is the first on the list." He rose and leaned against one of the gazebo's support posts, making himself a portrait of handsome melancholy. He'd asked that this interview be out of doors for privacy, and the octagonal fancy on the rise behind the garden had seemed an ideal location.

"Sally was far from home," he went on, "and sent south in something like disgrace. We were comrades in naughtiness and resentment, nothing more. Between the vicar's vigilance and summer being a busy time generally, I never managed any serious sinning with her. She went back north with a fond wave and a smile."

Plausible. "Amanda Goodenough?"

"A spinster who dwelled in our village at the time. She has since married some squire or other over in Kent. Pretty, sweet, in need of some flirtation. We took long walks by the river, and she listened to me whine about Evvie's many shortcomings. We kissed a few times, and I was willing, but she... deserved better and knew it."

Every woman deserved better than to be a spoiled young husband's crying towel. "Davida Hearst?"

"Lively." Tait gave a mock shudder. "We crossed paths at a house party near Portsmouth, and she turned up at several other gatherings thereafter, by design I suspect. I literally found her in my bed, and... I did not acquit myself as a gentleman, my lord. She did not acquit herself as a lady either. Evvie got wind of it. She went quiet on me for three months, and they were the longest three months of my life."

"And what became of Miss Hearst?"

"*Mrs.* Hearst. She was a widow. She took up with some French comte and was living on the Continent, last I heard. She's a comtesse now. She'd fit in well there. The French are more blasé about extramarital adventures."

The French might be surprised to learn that. "Mrs. Emelia Probinger?" I'd met the lady. She was a military widow, self-possessed, nobody's fool, and inclined to enjoy a widow's privileges, though never with me.

"Emmy... She led me a dance, my lord. Sampled my charms a few times and found me wanting, as was her right. We are cordial if we end up at the same quarterly assembly. She refused to hear a word against Evvie, and I think it was Evvie's unhappiness that eventually cost me the association."

The back of Tait's neck grew pinkish.

His recitation was consistent with what I knew of Mrs. Probinger. She was no prude, but neither was she a predator. One frolicked, one did not poach. A husband might be unfaithful to his wife, but never disloyal. If Tait had mentioned a single disparaging word about Evelyn, Mrs. P—whose own marriage had weathered a few storms—would have dropped him flat.

"Pamela Walters?"

Tait resumed the bench across from mine. "Five Seasons, no offers. She was past all discretion as five-and-twenty breathed down her neck. I think she was angling to get sent to her auntie in Paris, and she eventually succeeded with my assistance. We were seen canoodling among the biographies at the lending library. I have not set foot in that establishment since."

Of all places to risk being interrupted... Apparently, both parties had been past all discretion. "And finally, Dorothea Smith."

"She was bored while her husband was frolicking up in Town. They were leasing the Claridge estate for three years, and I gather Mr. Smith used the place mostly to stash his wife when he sought surcease from her company. She used me to while away the occasional afternoon, nothing more."

The list was unremarkable in one sense. Petty affairs born out of fleeting attraction, opportunity, and venal self-interest, but the list was also... pathetic. None of these women had been smitten with Tait. None of them had found much about him worth lasting attachment.

"Two of the ladies went on to marry happily," I noted, "one returned north without violating any commandments with you, one sent you packing, and another left the area for livelier surrounds. Were any of these women on hand when Evvie went missing?"

"Amanda had left about two months previous. Mrs. Probinger, yes, and though she was gone for a time, she's back among us. The rest, no."

I considered the list. I would waste a lot of time verifying Tait's comments, or I could call his bet and save myself a lot of effort.

"Either you are trying to distract me with irrelevant information, or you are growing forgetful in your dotage, Tait. Tell me about the domestics."

The gallant squire sent me a petulant scowl. "I don't force myself on anybody."

I was in the presence of rank stupidity, and yet, Hyperia called this man her friend. Her dear friend. "You gave the ladies you employed to understand that you would be receptive to their offers. No woman in service courts the loss of her post and her reputation without some encouragement, Tait. Without a lot of encouragement."

"My great lapses with the staff amounted to dallying with a pair of undermaids. One after the other, not at the same time. Evvie was being particularly... stubborn, and I was feeling neglected. I was an idiot. We need not debate the point. The first woman knew what she was about and agreed to leave without a fuss when Evvie confronted her. Demanded a good character and severance and told Evvie I wasn't worth putting any woman's nose out of joint. The second was simply stubbornness on my part. I wanted to prove to Evvie that I could tempt younger, prettier women."

Tait stared past me at the edifice he called home. "I look back on myself then," he went on, "and I want to puke. I don't blame Evvie for leaving. We were so young and so... overwrought about nothing. I was unworthy of her affection, and she was unforgiving of the smallest slight. If one could drink away shame, I'd be awash in a sea of brandy and regret."

The words were sincere enough, and yet, I suspected Tait was still lying. "You have produced evidence that suggests none of your amours had the opportunity or motive to see Evelyn harmed. That is reassuring and makes searching for her—or her remains—simpler. How much money did she take with her?"

Tait rubbed a hand across his forehead, the personification of world-weary ennui. "Interesting question, and I am not sure how to respond. Evvie had generous pin money, and I suspect she hoarded half of it. Five years of domestic economizing might have made for a sizable nest egg."

And that nest egg would have been in cash and coins. "Were you inclined to seek forgiveness for your peccadilloes with gifts of jewelry?"

Tait's smile was wan rather than charming. "Aren't we all?"

Some of us tried offering sincere apologies followed by reformed behavior. "She took her jewelry box?"

He nodded. "Left behind silks, embroidered dancing slippers, every letter I'd sent her, the poem I'd written commemorating our betrothal... Took her grandmama's pearls, coin meant to maintain our home, and her sewing basket. How can you live with somebody for years, love them to the best of your bumbling ability, and know them so little?" Real bewilderment, and possibly a trace of humility, colored his words.

"You've had time to ponder that question."

"I've read her diaries," he said, sitting back and resting an arm along the top of the bench. "Or tried to. They are heavy going, my lord. Evvie wasn't merely hurt. She was enraged, devastated, furious, in the sense of the Furies of old. I became the symbol of her childlessness, her endless sense of inferiority to her sisters, her resentment of her own gender—Papa Hasborough had no sons, you know. The Bard was right about a woman scorned."

"The line isn't Shakespeare's," I said. "The sentiment comes from old William Congreve, 'Heaven has no rage like love to hatred turned, nor hell a fury like a woman scorned.' From *The Mourning Bride,* which is a tragedy, if I recall aright. Can you estimate the value of the jewels and coin Evelyn took with her?"

"The coin might have amounted to several hundred pounds, my lord. Her pin money was ample, this is a sizable household, and she ran it most efficiently. She liked to brag to her sisters about that pin money. The jewels..." He rose and stretched. "Nothing all that precious. Evvie was fond of semiprecious stones. Amethyst, jade, turquoise, opal, peridot, lapis lazuli... They went well with her fair coloring, and she took good care of them. Gold settings, of course, given that she was blond—is blond."

He left the gazebo, and I followed him down the steps.

"Some days," he went on, "I talk about her in the past tense—she was blond. Other days, she's present tense—she is a difficult wife. Tell me which to use, my lord, for I genuinely don't know what is appropriate."

I was mentally sketching a picture of two young people, both spoiled, both canny enough to be at bottom, insecure. Doting sisters or a fawning mother were not indicative of reliable affection from the world at large. A week socializing in Mayfair, watching far more wealthy and attractive people wield far more power, would have brought that lesson home to them both.

They'd married a bit desperately, while pretending their match was splendid from every perspective, and then no children, no grand entertainments, no passionate connubial romance... just crops planted and harvested, quarterly assemblies, and village gossip, while the rest of the Hasborough sisters married real money, and Evelyn began to hoard her pin money.

"Do you have an inventory of the jewelry?" I asked as we strolled in the direction of Tait's home.

"I should, for insurance purposes, but I never put in a claim, of course. A wife cannot steal her own baubles. Never wrote Evvie's obituary. Never gave her clothes to charity. Evvie is having her revenge, does she but know it."

"Find me the inventory, if you please, and a copy of any document that disposes of Evelyn's estate."

"A wife doesn't have an estate."

Some wives did. My wife certainly would, were I ever so fortunate as to have one. "What happens to her widow's portion if she dies before you do?"

Tait halted at the bottom of the steps that led into the weedy garden. "I'm not sure. That's a question I promise myself I'll research, but then neglect to follow up on. I think, in the absence of children, my family's contribution comes back to me with any interest accrued, and the Hasborough contribution is divided between Evvie's sisters."

Who apparently had all married well and did not need the money. "Have a look at the settlements and find us a definitive answer," I said. "I'd also like to examine Evelyn's diaries."

Tait trotted up the steps into the garden proper. "Those are personal, my lord."

"Precisely, and yet, she left them behind. If she wished for you to find her, perhaps without admitting that even to herself, then the clues to her destination are most likely in those diaries."

He stopped, opened his mouth, shut it, and resumed walking. "Oh, very well, but you mustn't say a word about this to Hyperia. She thinks I'm a fine fellow, and I'd like to keep her opinion of me in good repair."

"I have promised you discretion, Tait. Question my assurances again, and we shall have words."

He guffawed, though I'd meant the warning in earnest.

～

The pretty housekeeper showed me to Evelyn Tait's apartment, then hovered by the door as I stood in the middle of a celadon, cream, and pink sitting room. The color scheme was old-fashioned and feminine, while the appointments were more sturdy than elegant. Culled from the lumber rooms, perhaps.

"I'm told Mrs. Tait liked the view of the village," the housekeeper said. "The church spire gleaming white above the maples, the creek winding along the thoroughfare. A peaceful scene."

Tait had referred to the woman only in generic address. *My housekeeper will show you to Evelyn's rooms.*

I cracked a window, which took some effort. "You are Mrs....?"

"Ames, my lord. Agatha Ames." She turned a stoic eye on an arrangement of hydrangeas gone brown with age and on cobwebs gathering at the corners of the windows.

"Your tenure and Mrs. Tait's did not overlap?" The carpet was overdue for a beating. The mantel was dusty. The globes of the modest chandelier still held a half-dozen white candles, but the glasses themselves were in want of cleaning.

"I've been at my post about a year, my lord, since last year's Bartholomew's Fair. The footmen recall Mrs. Tait with respect and affection. They say she wasn't too high in the instep and always paid on time. Didn't begrudge a fellow a longish half day and always sent them home to see family in summer."

A lovely testament to domestic tranquility, and yet, even as a new bride, Evelyn had had her own apartment. That vanity was indulged in most frequently by wealthier couples.

"Where might I find her diaries?"

"Through here."

The bedroom had even more of a neglected-museum-display quality, the bed hangings fading in irregular swatches from purple to pink, the folding mirror over the vanity dusty and speckled.

"I've told Mr. Tait we need to take these rooms in hand," Mrs. Ames said. "He won't hear of it. Won't allow us to put away the bed hangings, though they're already ruined. Won't see the carpets taken up, or even permit me to do a thorough dusting. I will close the window you opened because we're not allowed to air the apartment either."

Interesting. "Why not?"

She drew a swirl in the dust on the vanity. "He comes up to these rooms late at night. We hear his footsteps. The boot-boy thought it was a ghost the first time he heard somebody moving around in here, but ghosts don't leave footprints in the dust that exactly match the soles of Mr. Tait's boots. I had to show the lad that the sizes were precisely the same."

Either Tait was consumed by guilt, or he honestly missed his wife. "The dressing closets connect her apartment to his?"

"Yes, my lord. I put Mrs. Tait's clothes in the cedar chests, and I didn't ask permission to do that. I haven't been reprimanded for it either. I moved the diaries into a drawer of the escritoire, which so far has kept them from the mice." The word *mice* received an emphasis worthy of a reference to the Corsican Monster.

"Then you do look in on these rooms from time to time?"

"I'm the housekeeper. I'm supposed to *keep* the house, but he insists... I'm sorry. I ought not to criticize my betters. If Mr. Tait treasures his wife's memory, then he shouldn't let these rooms fall into ruin. I dust the portrait out of common decency, and he hasn't objected to that, or maybe he hasn't noticed."

Mrs. Tait's likeness occupied the usual place of honor above the bedroom mantel. Afternoon sun illuminated a young lady with classic Saxon coloring—flaxen hair, blue eyes, fair complexion—and a subtle smile. She wore a heavy pearl choker—her grandmother's, perhaps—from which the usual demure blue and white cameo descended. Her earrings were more pearls, as was the bracelet about her wrist. More strands of pearls had been draped about her neck.

Tait had liked her willingness to overdo the jewelry, or recalled it fondly in hindsight.

Her dress was a billowy azure affair depicted as having the same luminous quality as the pearls, and her décolletage was more daring than a debutante would risk, and yet befitting of a young matron in the first flush of her marital dignities.

Despite all the finery, the word that came to mind as I beheld the errant Mrs. Tait was *plain*. One could not accuse her of an oversized nose or prominent ears, nor had she crossed eyes or a pronounced jaw. She was simply... unremarkable. With appropriate attention to fashion, she might be said to approach handsomeness, but her gaze lacked warmth.

Evelyn Tait, even in jewels and satins, looked sturdy, plain, and well aware of her limitations.

Mrs. Ames extracted a trio of bound volumes from a lockable drawer of the escritoire. "She always strikes me as a woman in waiting. As if the sittings for her portrait can't be over soon enough, but until they are, she will endure the boredom and tedium required of her."

A housekeeper's lot could be tedious in the extreme. "I'm told Evelyn Tait envied her sisters."

"I wouldn't know, my lord. We can't all be beauties or marry princes. Wherever Mrs. Tait is, I hope she's well and happy."

"As do I. You need not keep me company. I'll nose about a bit more and then be on my way. Has my tiger made a pest of himself?"

"Not at all, my lord. We're always happy to pause in our labors to pass the time with a neighbor. Somebody put the manners on that boy, and Cook says he has a splendid appetite."

Good work, Atticus. "Growing boys and all that. Thank you for your time, Mrs. Ames, and I will close the window, so you needn't bother."

"Thank you, my lord." She curtseyed and withdrew, and I closed and locked the door behind her. I would take the diaries with me. Better for the housekeeper if she was unaware of that plan. I closed the parlor window lest I forget, though the stale air in the bedroom offended me on Mrs. Ames's behalf.

The dressing closet was cedar paneled. Opening the door at the far end presented me with a mirror-image chamber redolent of bay rum. John Tait's dressing closet was full of gentleman's attire, tall boots, hat boxes, and the like. I closed that door and did the usual tapping on the wainscoting and testing along the walls.

I found no hidden compartments, no loose floorboards, nothing to suggest another set of diaries, a hidden cache of letters from a doting swain, or a stash of lover's tokens, more's the pity. The ideal outcome, from my perspective, had Evelyn eloping with a devoted swain and welcoming the prospect of an annulment. Tait could tell all and sundry his wife had been declared dead, and clothe himself in a widower's honors rather than a cuckold's shame.

Such fictions contributed to the peace of many a village, and I respected them for their pragmatic kindness.

I made a final inspection of the only space Evelyn had been able to call her own in the entire rambling manor house and did a quick sketch of the portrait over the mantel. The impatience Mrs. Ames had alluded to didn't come through to me, but I saw no joy either. No sparkle, no mischief.

No hint that despite her majestic bearing, Evelyn Hasborough Tait had delighted in a brisk Roger de Coverley and loved a good joke.

I gathered up the diaries and made one more visual inspection of the whole apartment.

The rooms puzzled me. I saw no indications that a bold young wife had settled into these chambers. Evelyn's hairbrushes and combs had been arranged just so on the vanity, and the bedside table didn't boast even a *Book of Common Prayer*. No lingering scent of muguet reminded the visitor of the lady's presence. No colorful shawl hinted that she'd not always been a creature of fashionable pastels.

The rooms were sterile, a harsh word when applied to living beings, and yet, Tait apparently came to this apartment to commune with memories or to wallow in despair.

I departed silently, diaries in hand, and made my way to the stable without encountering my host or his housekeeper. As I waited for Atticus to tear himself away from the blandishments of the kitchen, I did note one detail about Evelyn Tait's apartment that had caught my eye.

The doors—to her parlor and to her dressing closet—had both locked only from the inside. John Tait had never been able to lock his wife in her rooms—one hoped he'd have never made such an attempt—but Evelyn had been able to lock him and everybody else out.

I found that odd, but what did I know of domestic marital arrangements?

∼

"You have to make His Grace see reason." Millicent Dujardin had found me in the conservatory, and clearly, she would not leave me in peace until she'd had her say. "Leander has been tossed about too much in recent months. He's only settling in at the Hall as well as he is because Lady Ophelia has exerted her influence over the staff. To uproot my son now... I refuse to do it, my lord."

Was Arthur intent on sending Leander away? If so, His Grace and I would have words—emphatic words—though Arthur and I had been in accord when the question arose as to where Leander and his mama should dwell.

The lad was Harry's by-blow, and we were as much a surprise to Leander as he was to us, though he was a welcome surprise. Very welcome.

"Millicent, explain yourself." I collected the diaries I hadn't yet read and patted the place beside me on the settee. "What exactly is Arthur proposing?"

She perched beside me on the edge of the cushion, as if at any moment, she might take flight and join the pair of swallows darting about the conservatory's rafters. The outside doors let in a slight breeze, but because the process of moving tender plants indoors had begun, the space was thick with potted greenery.

A good place to hide, usually.

"His Grace thinks Leander would enjoy seeing Paris," Millicent began. "I gather Mr. Banter's godson will join the gentlemen on their travels as far as Paris, and then at some point, Lady Ophelia will retrieve young George. His Grace and Mr. Banter will then journey on to Berlin or someplace yet more distant. The duke wants to include Leander as company for George, but the boys are at least four years apart in age, and... I won't have it. I am Leander's mother, his legal guardian, and the only authority he's known. *I shall not have it.*"

As far as the world was concerned, Millicent was the boy's governess, and the lad was Leander Merton Waites, of no specific connection to me or Arthur. Ducal households became repositories for all sorts of stray cousins, dotty elders, and common-law relatives. The boy's recent arrival at the Hall had occasioned a few puzzled glances, but Arthur's consequence was sufficient to keep the gossip down to a murmur.

"What exactly did Arthur say, Millicent?"

She rose and paced the distance between the potted orange trees flanking my settee. "I overheard His Grace and Mr. Banter speculating that George could use the companionship of another boy. His Grace mentioned that Leander was likely a bit lonely, too, and travel broadened the mind even at young ages, so perhaps Leander might accompany them. My son is not a diversion for some spoiled little squireling on holiday."

I didn't know Millicent well, but my brief acquaintance with her suggested she was a woman of fortitude and common sense and a devoted mother. The thought of parting from Leander clearly had her rattled.

"Firstly, Leander wouldn't go to Paris without you," I said. "Secondly, he won't go to Paris at all if you object. Thirdly, His Grace and Banter talk about everything. They are close. They are friends." They were an utterly devoted couple, but Millicent could puzzle that part out for herself. "His Grace knows, for example, that young George could well be Banter's son rather than a mere godson."

"That is none of my concern."

My sisters were forthright people disinclined to brooding. They were also the offspring of a duke and a duchess and generally well respected. Millicent's situation could not have been more different. She'd been raised in a humble parsonage, gone into service of necessity, and become one of Harry's many trysting partners. That neither she nor Harry had intended for a casual romp to become a passionate affair would be no comfort to Leander when he grew old enough to grasp such subtleties.

That Harry had been swept off his feet was some comfort to me, though.

"What exactly is your concern?" I asked, rising. "Arthur isn't wrong about travel being educational. Another mother might jump at the chance to see Paris and share the sights with her son."

"I am not another mother. I am... Leander's mother, and it's bad enough he never knew his father. I don't blame Lord Harry for that, I blame myself. Leander has lost his home. He lost what family we did have. Now we're here, far from Town and all that is familiar, and... His Grace proposes extended travel."

I was not at all keen on seeing Leander whisked off to Paris, with or without his mother. I'd be left at the Hall to manage the best I could in Arthur's absence, and that prospect was frankly daunting. I trusted the stewards and solicitors as far as their responsibilities went, but somebody had to give them direction, and that somebody would be me.

The idea that I could spend the winter growing better acquainted with my nephew had been a consolation.

"I'll speak to His Grace," I said. "I won't tell him he was overheard, but I'll sort out his plans for Leander." My first inclination was to urge Millicent to confront Arthur herself, while I happily brought up the rear guard. Arthur, though, was a-swoon at the prospect of travel with Banter, shy by nature, and ducal by inclination.

He might blunder, in other words, and if Millicent chose to take the boy off to John o' Groats, we had no legal authority to stop her.

"Arthur needs your permission to travel anywhere with Leander," I said. "We enjoy our nephew's company at your sufferance, madam. Have you made up your mind about Sunday supper?"

Lady Ophelia was agitating for Millicent to join social occasions at the Hall as a vaguely explained distant relation visiting the family seat with her son. A widow fallen upon hard times, perhaps, and forced to rely on the family patriarch for respite from an unkind world.

Millicent was a pretty blonde, well formed, and well-spoken. She was the daughter of a gentleman in the technical sense, and had life been kinder, she might well have married a gentleman, though she would have been an unusual choice for a ducal spare such as Harry.

Lady Ophelia's invitations were meant to be kind, but so far,

Millicent had resisted. I wasn't sure why, but had become increasingly concerned with her possible reasons.

"I would rather remain out of public sight," Millicent said. "As soon as I pretend that I'm other than Leander's governess, I lose every choice but those you and His Grace are willing to grant me."

Ah. Post-battle remorse. I was familiar with the condition. "You agreed to come here, agreed that a connection to Harry's family could only benefit Leander, but now you have regrets."

She brushed her hand over a pot of mint. "I have uncertainties. If I'm to be a widow, I need a late husband and a fairy tale to recite about our courtship and marriage. I'll need widow's weeds at least five years out of fashion. My late husband's name should be Harry so as not to confuse Leander. Or perhaps my husband is a sea captain, and we fear him lost, but aren't certain, except that sooner or later, somebody will say something to Leander in the churchyard, and he will be thrown into confusion yet again."

Leander knew only that his papa had been a brave soldier, fallen in service to Good King George, and that Arthur and I were paternal uncles.

"You've been building entire battlefields in Spain, my dear, to bend the aphorism."

She resumed her seat. "I haven't much else to do. The staff take excellent care of Leander, and he delights in new faces and new challenges. He's like his father in that regard."

Or he was like a normal boy with a normal complement of curiosity. "Sometimes, on the Peninsula, I'd be given a mission, and I'd march out smartly, or sneak out smartly by dark of night, eager to follow orders. Perhaps I was to report on French troop movements, or ascertain where the sympathies of a walled town lay. Invariably, I'd be in a hurry, eager to impress my commanding officers with speedy success."

She broke off a sprig of mint and brought it to her nose? "But?"

"But to quote one old sergeant, 'You cannot make a baby in one month with nine women.' If the French aren't moving their troops save for training maneuvers, if the walled town hasn't formed any firm allegiances, then a hasty report could well be a report in disastrous error. Sometimes the best course is simply to watch and wait, Millicent."

She tossed the sprig of mint into the pot from whence she'd taken it. "I dislike being helpless. At least in service, I had work to do and a wage to call my own. Here, I am of no use to anybody."

"Not so." I took the place beside her without asking permission. We were family, after all. "Leander would disagree with you vehemently, and as it happens, I have a question for you."

She drew herself up. "Ask."

What topic could possibly justify that upright, braced posture? "You've kept house for several families?"

"I have. Good people, gentry rather than peerage, and in Town, a couple of well-off merchant families."

"Is it usual for a wife to be able to lock her bedroom door from the inside?"

Clearly, that wasn't the anticipated query. "It... can be. In a fancy household, the wife's lady's maid confides in the husband's valet regarding any matter that might make a shared bed awkward."

What could she...? "Menses," I said, as if I'd come up with a great insight. "Headaches, that sort of thing."

"Exactly that sort of thing. If the couple don't want the whole household to know of such goings-on, and husband and wife are uncomfortable with a frank discussion—or the husband has no sense of his wife's bodily calendar—then a locked door communicates the situation clearly enough. I worked for only one family that resorted to such measures. Very formal people and up to four children when I was in service with them. Why that question?"

"Miss West has asked me to look into a matter of a missing wife, and my first priority is establishing whether the lady truly left of her own volition. She apparently did. Now I must determine where she went and if she's stayed away voluntarily."

"You'll be looking for the proverbial needle in a very large haystack, my lord."

"A needle that might not want to be found, and for good reasons. Like you, though, I am somewhat at loose ends, and an investigation distracts me from more worrisome thoughts."

She rose. "You'll talk to His Grace about Leander?"

I got to my feet as well, ready to resume my reading. "I will, and soon."

Millicent startled me with a hug. "Thank you. Harry was so fond of you, and now I know why."

The words stunned me, in a good way, but before I could react, the nearest door opened, and Hyperia strode through.

"Oh dear." She stopped short several yards away as I turned loose of Millicent. "Am I interrupting?"

"No, miss." Millicent bobbed a curtsey and dashed off, leaving an awkward silence in her wake.

Very awkward.

CHAPTER FIVE

I closed the conservatory door as Millicent's steps retreated down the corridor. "Arthur is threatening to take Leander to Paris. Millicent objects. I am to reason with my brother in the name of anxious motherhood."

Hyperia picked up one of the diaries. "Leander might enjoy Paris."

I gently pried the book from her hands. "Millicent might enjoy seeing Paris with her son, but she's like a spooked horse. Having once lost her composure—in this case, her home, her privacy, her means, and her profession—she's more easily rattled. Leander is settling in here more comfortably than his mama is." Much more comfortably, now that I thought about it.

I put all three diaries on a potting table and took Hyperia's hand. "Those are Evelyn Tait's journals. Tait gave me leave to read them, but I did not take that for permission to share them with anybody else."

Hyperia patted my knuckles and dropped my hand. "If those were my diaries, and I'd been concerned about their confidential nature, I'd have taken them with me."

Well, yes. A point I'd made to Tait. "Leaving them behind as a reproach to Tait and allowing strangers to read words written in anger are two different things. Then too, Evelyn apparently departed in high dudgeon. She might have simply forgotten them."

Hyperia ambled between the rows of potted citrus, and I walked beside her. On many previous occasions, she'd linked arms with me on her own initiative or taken my hand.

Not today, apparently. "What do you know of Millicent?" Hyperia asked. "Other than that she and Harry fell in love and had a child?"

The change of topic was a pathetic relief. "She was raised in a vicarage, and such were the family circumstances that Millicent went into service as a housekeeper. She had a series of employers from good though not exalted families, save for Lord Harry, of course, and posts among both gentry and cits."

We came to the open door that led to the terrace. Because the conservatory was on the eastern side of the Hall, the terrace was in afternoon shade. I stepped through, and Hyperia followed.

"Summer is over," she said, sniffing the air. "We'll still have mild weather for a time, but the days are noticeably shorter, and frost isn't far off."

Half my mind was on Evelyn's diaries, another half on Millicent's situation, but something in Hyperia's tone warned me to focus on the lady at my side.

"Is something amiss, Perry?"

She went to the balustrade, which overlooked a section of the deer park that rolled off toward the home wood. The forest foliage was golden, the undergrowth a palette of yellows, greens, and the occasional splash of red. The grass enjoyed the luxurious abundance of autumn, and by any standard, the day was beautiful.

"Healy is dunning me."

Healy West was Hyperia's brother, and no great fan of mine. In his eyes, I'd all but jilted his sister, left the military in disgrace, and failed to offer any explanation for either transgression. I'd informed him that siring children had moved beyond my powers, at least for a time, and he'd relented to the point that he was civil toward me.

Grudgingly civil. "Your brother is dunning you to return to Town?"

"That too."

"Dunning you to part company from me?"

"And from Lady Ophelia, who is not a good influence, and from your most unusual investigations, which are the subject of talk. He means well."

Healy meant to preserve Hyperia's chances of snagging a husband, despite her insistence that marriage held no attraction for her. I considered offering her polite platitudes and the sort of questions a friend should ask—*but what do you want, Perry?*—and decided on honesty instead.

"I don't want you to go. Selfish of me, but the truth."

She perched a hip on the balustrade, precisely the sort of informal, comfortable conduct I found endearing. I adopted the same posture facing her.

"You'll miss me?" she asked.

She was not speaking in the conditional. "Terribly. You've already decided to go?"

"Healy can't cut off my funds, but he provides the roof over my head, in Town and at Westview. I must rub along with him domestically from time to time, and he is my brother."

"Brothers and their foibles make the world a more challenging place. Did you tell him when you'd depart for Town?"

"I haven't replied to his letter yet."

Another great, obvious insight befell me. "Are you hoping I will talk you out of going?" I had told this woman I loved her, and I did, but grasping the subtleties of her mind would be a life's work, assuming I had the opportunity.

"Maybe hoping you'd try?"

Diffidence was not usually in Perry's nature. *Think, man.* "On the one hand, I fear to disrespect you by suggesting how you should proceed. On the other hand..." I moved closer and put an arm around her shoulders and to blazes with any chambermaids, godmamas, or dukes spying on us from the windows.

Perry rested her forehead on my shoulder. "On the other hand?"

"Tactical retreat has fooled many an enemy general."

"You're saying I should do the pretty in Town now that Parliament will soon be sitting again. Swan about Mayfair, placate Healy, and restore his sense of my biddableness."

Healy wasn't a complete fool. "He knows you aren't biddable. He's looking to test your loyalties, and you do love him, Hyperia."

She wrapped an arm around my waist. "I do, despite his dunderheadedness."

Another strategy was forming in my mind, one that would put Healy on the defensive and leave Hyperia freer to do as she pleased. The theory wanted testing, though, and possibly even discussion with Lady Ophelia before I aired it with Hyperia.

To say nothing of discussion with Arthur, head of my family, resident duke, and all-around brilliant tactician.

Who was leaving in a fortnight or so.

"We could elope," I said, though that wasn't the theory I'd been considering. "Off to Scotland with us."

"If I'm ever to marry, Jules, I want my settlements, and Healy would be under no obligation to turn them over if we eloped."

She did not dismiss the idea of eloping out of any fault with me. I took courage from that. "You can have every penny of your settlements. I'll match whatever funds Healy withholds and make sure all of Society knows of his penury. I am in line for a dukedom, Perry, much as it pains me to contemplate such a fate. Nobody would think our marrying that unusual." Belated, perhaps a crooked lid for a crooked pot, but a mere nine days' wonder to the casual observer.

In truth, a match between us would be unusual in the extreme, with Hyperia unwilling to take on motherhood, myself unable to perform the preliminaries to fatherhood, and the title demanding parenthood of us both.

Hyperia sat up. "We are discussing *marriage*, Julian, which strikes me as sending in the artillery when a few sharpshooters can handle the job."

The job of placating Healy did not require marriage, true enough. "You aren't haring off because I've been discreet about Tait's investigation?"

"No." She rose, and I stood as well. "Well, maybe a little. I like helping with your puzzles. I can't tear about the countryside as you do, but I contribute something, just as Lady Ophelia does."

That Hyperia regarded her part as so minor offended me mightily. Lest she swan away, I took her in my arms and spoke very close to her ear.

"I am a better investigator because you love me. I hold you in my mind and in my heart waking and sleeping. I consider many a conundrum by asking myself, 'How would Perry see this?' 'What would Perry tell me?' I tear about the countryside, as you put it, fortified by the thought that I can return to your side, tell you the whole of what I've been up to, and have your good counsel to help me sort it out. This business with Tait is onerous in part because we cannot tackle it together."

She nodded. "I do love you. I will miss you awfully, Jules."

"And I love you. I will invite you down to the Hall for Yuletide holidays, along with Lady Ophelia and a sister or two." My sisters would not leave me to face the holidays all on my lonesome at the Hall, and they needed to make Leander's acquaintance at some point too. "I can even invite Healy, and an invitation to a ducal seat will present him with quite a choice."

She shifted back enough to peer up at me. "I like that. Put Healy in a corner. I know your sister Ginny best of the lot, though they are all lovely."

"I'll start with her, but the sisters will decide who my holiday minder will be, regardless of any preferences I might express."

We moved, arm in arm, back to the conservatory.

"What of your mother?" Hyperia asked. "She seems to be least in sight here at the Hall."

"The duchess is something of an enigma to me. She was a detached sort of mother, at least in my case, and she does seem to prefer her spa towns and dower properties." Of which there were three, one in Town that rivaled even the duke's Mayfair residence for refinement and comfort.

"Invite her," Hyperia said. "Not an *invitation* invitation, but a letter explaining who will be at the holiday festivities and asking her to join in."

The sticky business of festivities needing a hostess and Her Grace being the logical party for the role passed through my mind, but that was a question for later in the campaign.

"As it happens, I have to trot up to Town myself," I said. "I left in a bit of a hurry and want some of my books about me if I'm to bide at the Hall."

Hyperia stopped with me among the citrus trees. "You will speak with Ardath Deloitte, won't you?"

Why did I bother to attempt dissembling before such a noticing mind? "I might." Also Lina Hanscomb, if I could scare her up. "I regret to inform you that I cannot leave for Town until Monday, though."

She patted my chest. "Such a pity. Your delicate constitution must vex you terribly."

It did, though my health was far less delicate than it had been a year ago. "We're to enjoy Tait's company for Sunday supper, if you'll recall. Lady Ophelia was importuning Millicent to make up numbers, but I doubt she will oblige."

"I'll recruit another suitable parti. One of the local widows, perhaps."

"Not Mrs. Probinger, please."

Hyperia smoothed my lapel. "She took an interest in you when you were searching for Viscount Reardon?"

"Not that sort of interest, but her presence might still be awkward."

Hyperia gave me a long, skeptical look and stepped back. "When you've found Evvie Tait, or found out what became of her, I will expect a report. Perhaps not a full report, but a report of some sort."

"I will delight in delivering it—when I've completed the investigation."

Hyperia sent a pointed look in the direction of the diaries on the potting table, then headed for the door.

"I'll see you at supper, Jules. I must have my carriage dress aired and pressed if we're to leave on Monday, and then there's packing to do, lest I make somebody work unnecessarily on the Sabbath."

She departed through the same door Millicent had used, though the comment about airing her carriage dress gave me something to think about.

Millicent, former housekeeper, mother without benefit of matrimony, and discreet guest, likely *had no carriage dress*. If she'd owned such a garment at one time—hemmed for sitting, sturdy fabric for the vagaries of travel, fashionable within those limitations—she'd long since pawned it.

Millicent very likely had *no wardrobe* suitable for even informal Sunday supper at a ducal residence. Upon reflection, I thought it likely that she remained in the guise of a governess because she had no other costume and no funds to obtain same. We'd assigned her a chambermaid, of course, but those duties and the duties of lady's maid were vastly different.

"We've been treating her like a servant, not like family," I muttered.

My discussion with Arthur acquired some urgency, and yet, I took up the last of the diaries, repaired to the settee, and resumed reading the journal of a very angry young woman.

∽

A Battle of the Nations had been fought in the kitchen prior to Sunday supper, with Mrs. Gwinnett, our cook, attempting to make His Grace's final company supper as memorable as possible. Hyperia and Lady Ophelia argued for humbler fare, and staff loyally supported both camps depending on the hour.

The result was a beef roast that would have been the envy of any ambassadorial chef and side dishes and desserts worthy of the great Carême himself, though fewer in numbers than Mrs. Gwinnett would have preferred.

While the food was impressive, I was more interested in the company. Arthur occupied the head of the table, Lady Ophelia the foot. Hyperia and I had one side to ourselves, and opposite us sat Mr. John Tait, looking obnoxiously splendid in his Sunday finery, and a Mrs. Euphemia Ingersoll. She was a recent arrival to the surrounds, a widow with a small child, though I put her age south of thirty.

She was soft-spoken, willowy, and had a pleasant laugh. Not quite a retiring lady, but certainly a quiet presence. Not a beauty either—good complexion, smooth blond chignon, regular features—but when she smiled, she was quietly attractive in the manner of a woman who had nothing to prove to anybody.

I liked her, in other words. Tait, by contrast, acted as if he barely recalled being introduced to Mrs. Ingersoll in the churchyard, then proceeded to aim nearly all of his conversational sallies in her direction.

"You must lend us your little Merrin," Lady Ophelia said. "We've a five-year-old boy visiting in the Caldicott nursery, and a playmate would enliven his days considerably."

"Merrin hasn't found many playmates yet," Mrs. Ingersoll replied. "She's only four, but a precocious four, if I do say so myself. A fiend for her letters and a shameless mimic. Divine services are a tribulation to her when the weather's fine, but she does enjoy the singing."

"Divine services," Lady Ophelia remarked over a serving of raspberry fool, "can be a tribulation to all of us when the weather is fine.

Your Grace, don't frown at me so. You will wrinkle prematurely. Julian is smirking at his dessert, and Hyperia thinks I'm outrageous. Mrs. Ingersoll knows of what I speak, being a mama herself. Mr. Tait, a drop or two more of that wine, if you please."

Tait obliged. Arthur steered the conversation away from odd little visitors to the nursery and back to harvest and his upcoming travel.

"You're taking Osgood Banter along?" Tait asked.

"Or he's taking me," Arthur replied. "I fear my artistic education pales compared to his."

"The single ladies in the shire will go into a collective decline," Lady Ophelia observed. "Fortunately, Julian will be on hand to console them." She simpered at me.

"On that note," I said, "perhaps I can interest the ladies in a constitutional about the garden when we've finished our sweets. The chrysanthemums are in good form, and I'd like to stretch my legs after such a feast."

Hyperia took up the chorus, and we were soon arranged in a polite promenade. Arthur offered his arm to Lady Ophelia. Tait paired up with Hyperia, leaving Mrs. Ingersoll to do the pretty with me.

"Tell me of this little fellow in the ducal nursery," she said, donning a wide-brimmed straw hat. "The village gossip is astonishingly thin when it comes to the doings at Caldicott Hall."

I accepted a parasol from a footman and escorted the lady onto the terrace. "Give it some time. Once the local goodwives have established your bona fides, you'll be inundated with talk." I opened the parasol and passed it to my companion, who rested it against her shoulder as we descended into the garden.

We moved along comfortably arm in arm, she being on the tall side and happy with a sedate pace.

"My bona fides might take years to establish," she replied. "They are protective of the Caldicotts in the village. I catch references to you having served too well on the Peninsula, and His Grace having lost both brothers for a time, but nobody parts with details.

Be grateful for that, for the loyalty you and your family have earned."

She wasn't asking for those details, and I wondered who had been disloyal to her. "Was your husband military?" Britain, indeed the whole Continent, was awash in war widows.

"Nothing so noble. Just a merry fellow who drank himself into an early grave. We grew up on the same London street, and he's buried in that very neighborhood. I hear you are off to Town on the morrow."

Her late spouse had been a merry fellow apparently not worth more than a passing comment. We all grieve differently. I was not one to mention Harry if I could avoid it.

"I will escort Miss West back to Town," I said, "and take care of some errands before preparing for a winter at the Hall, my first in some time, and I will be biding here without His Grace."

She paused by a pot of forget-me-nots, a cheerful splash of blue that had somehow been made to bloom far later in the season than usual.

"The silences are different when you're alone," she said, gaze on the flowers. "In a house the size of the Hall, you and your brother could rattle around for weeks and not see each other, but when he's gone, and you know he's gone, the rattling around has an emptier feel, even if you and he aren't particularly close."

That was the sort of observation Lady Ophelia might have made. Personal, insightful, unexpected.

"The officers' mess worked on the same principle," I said, resuming our progress. "Between meals, you went there to read, to clean your firearms, to write a letter home, because somebody else would be sitting at the next table engaged in an equally solitary task, and solitary together was preferable to solitary alone."

"And yet," she said, "I avoid the company of certain widows. Bad of me, but one must look forward at least some of the time. Merri—I call her Merri more as a statement of optimism than fact—keeps me looking forward."

"Mrs. Probinger is a cheerful soul," I said. "Practical, well-liked, has a lovely garden." She was also among Tait's erstwhile paramours, one of those facts I wished I'd never encountered, for her sake. Mrs. Semple came to mind as another cheerful soul, but she was also a busy soul and prone to managing.

"I've made Mrs. Probinger's acquaintance. The vicar's wife has been conscientious about introductions, and I do feel as if I'm getting to know some of my neighbors. Was Lady Ophelia serious about having Merri visit the nursery? One doesn't want to presume."

Lady Ophelia had been half serious, half stirring up trouble. Her invitation gave Mrs. Ingersoll an excuse to call on *me* after Arthur's departure. I didn't exactly dread the prospect—the lady was restful company—but neither did I appreciate the meddling.

"The boy in the nursery is a family connection." I stopped at the lavender border, which had yet to be pruned, and plucked a few sprigs for my lapel. "Leander is five, recently retrieved from London, and likely to spend the rest of his childhood calling the Hall home. An occasional playmate would enliven his days considerably." *He delights in new faces and new challenges...*

Before welcoming any guests to the nursery, though, I would of course confer with Millicent.

Mrs. Ingersoll tucked her parasol under her arm, took the lavender from me, and situated my nosegay in my buttonhole. "Better."

This bit of familiarity brought the lady close enough that I caught a whiff of her scent, a subtle, summery honeysuckle that clashed with the brisk fragrance of the lavender. As I submitted to her fussing, I caught Tait's eye across a bed of purple asters.

His expression was hard to read, but his focus was purely on the lady. Perhaps he was one of those tiresome fellows perpetually smitten by novelty. His courtship had been notably quick and his succession of lovers distinguished by the brevity of his affairs.

Hyperia said something, and Tait bent his head closer to hers.

"Would you like to try the maze?" I asked, though I knew its secrets of old.

"Some other time, perhaps. I suspect mazes were invented by governesses who wanted to keep their charges within shouting distance, while avoiding the exertion of chasing after the little darlings the livelong morning."

"My own mother might agree."

Up on the terrace, Lady Ophelia was in earnest conversation with Arthur. His Grace's expression was that of a gentleman graciously attending a guest, but his posture bore some tension. He wasn't accustomed to being lectured, poor lad.

"I suspect my brother could use an interruption," I said. "Do you mind?"

"I excel at the polite interruption." She flashed me that sweet smile, and we made straight for the terrace.

"I vow I am impressed," Mrs. Ingersoll announced as soon as we'd ascended the steps. "His Grace has forget-me-nots blooming in autumn. This is a horticultural feat, and I must know how it has been accomplished."

Arthur prosed on enthusiastically about the head gardener being a genius, and the conservatory having a corner prone to chilly drafts, and whatnot and whatever. Mrs. Ingersoll gave the duke her rapt attention, Lady Ophelia ceded the conversational field, and Hyperia and Tait soon joined us on the terrace.

"Might I offer you a lift to the village, Mrs. Ingersoll?" Tait asked after the assemblage had agreed that the time for parting had arrived.

"The day is pleasant for walking," that lady replied. "I do appreciate the courtesy."

"You can walk anytime," Lady Ophelia observed. "Take pity on the man, Mrs. Ingersoll. He's clearly determined on his chivalry."

And sometimes I admired her ladyship's gift for graciously interceding. "Before you leave, Tait, I have some items to return to you. Perhaps you'd join me for a moment in the library?"

We extricated ourselves from the company of the ladies and moved in silence to the privacy of the library.

CHAPTER SIX

"I've read them all." I passed over Evelyn's diaries. "She was heartbroken by the time she left you."

Tait accepted the three volumes. "One knew as much, my lord, and I wasn't exactly flourishing either. How will you proceed from here?"

Tait could apparently switch from doting swain to disgruntled, abandoned husband in a moment.

"Having given the matter some thought, I will move forward on the assumption that Evelyn is alive, and that attempting to trace her flight from your side is a pointless endeavor." Coaching inns kept records, but the identities of ticket purchases were impossible to confirm.

"What does that leave?"

The very question I'd spent much of the night considering. "She took her jewels, and pawning or selling them would best be done in London. If nothing else, the diaries attest to loyal correspondence between Evelyn and her sisters. She doubtless sought assistance from one of them, made the rounds of the shops on Ludgate Hill, and decamped for parts unknown when she was flush with cash."

"That's why you're off to London—to interrogate jewelers?"

"In part. I will also pay calls on Ardath Deloitte and Lina Hanscomb, if that lady bides in Town."

Tait set the diaries on the sideboard, poured himself a tot of Arthur's finest brandy, and downed the drink at one go. His presumption astonished me, but then, we were discussing the fate of his wife and possible collusion by her siblings.

"Evvie's sisters don't care for me, but I can't see Ardath abetting Evvie to the tune of abandoning me altogether."

What Tait did not know, or what he chose to ignore, was the volume and regularity of Evelyn's correspondence with her sisters. Her journals recorded nigh daily sendings and receivings of mail among the four ladies, with occasional epistles noted from cousins, old friends, and former neighbors as well. Based on those diary entries, Evelyn had been frank regarding her marital frustrations.

Margie condoles me on Mr. Tait's bad behavior. Counsels patience.

Ardie is wroth with Mr. Tait for his caddishness.

Babs threatens to call Mr. Tait out if he doesn't soon outgrow his foolishness. I would gladly serve as her second.

Pages and pages of same, and yet, castigating Tait for misbehaving years ago would serve no purpose, nor was it my place.

"For all Ardath knew," I said, "you had given Evvie permission to take the waters before the weather turned disobliging. The excursions to Ludgate could have been presented as outings to the modistes, and the purchase of a coach ticket to Bath was, in fact, a coach ticket to York."

Tait eyed the decanters. "I've set you to chasing a loose pig about on a farm lane?"

"You've set me a challenge. Mrs. Semple professed to have no idea where Evelyn bided, but I, too, have a sibling whose fate is shrouded in uncertainty. I can assure you, Tait, on my best day, ten years hence, I will not be able to discuss that situation as calmly as

Mrs. Semple appeared to deal with the prospect of her missing younger sister."

Tait poured himself another half a tot. "You think she knows something."

I hoped she did, another conclusion gained while tossing and turning. "I suspect she knows enough not to worry overmuch. A letter once a quarter, word through mutual acquaintances, *something* allows Mrs. Semple to be at peace regarding Evelyn's fate." That was the sole insight I'd gleaned after pondering my interview with that lady. A hunch, a theory, an educated guess, nothing more.

"I am not at peace," Tait said, finishing his second drink. "I am increasingly not at peace."

Rather apparent to the casual observer, but what had rattled him? The genial squire had been by turns voluble and quiet at the meal, and his composure was all but deserting him now.

"You've endured this long," I said. "Let me see what I can discover in London. I'll send word if I'm not returning directly to the Hall."

"Please do. As much as I worry that Evelyn has met a bad fate, I'm also unhappy at having to set you on her trail."

He wasn't half so unhappy as the woman who'd written those diaries. "See Mrs. Ingersoll home. She's pleasant company and a sensible creature. You will hear from me soon."

"Right. Eyes front, forward march."

Tait attempted to do just that, but his arm caught the stack of diaries on the sideboard, and they tumbled to the floor. He and I reached for the same volume at the same time and nearly bashed our heads together, but with some dithering, we managed to put all three books into Tait's keeping.

I escorted him to the front door, where final farewells were being made. Tait's coach and four waited at the bottom of the steps, while Arthur, Hyperia, and Lady Ophelia offered good-byes.

I bowed over Mrs. Ingersoll's hand, and she curtseyed. "A pleasure to have made your acquaintance, my lord."

"Likewise, ma'am."

She leaned close, and I thought she might presume to kiss my cheek—country manners could be appallingly informal—but she merely nudged a sprig of lavender closer to its mates and allowed Tait to escort her down the steps.

When the coach horses were trotting along the carriageway, Lady Ophelia was the first to speak.

"That man must enjoy making a cake of himself. I declare, if he's not pouting, he's flirting. Hyperia, I know you consider him a friend, and perhaps we're not seeing him at his best, but he's honestly rather tiresome."

She took Arthur by the elbow and left me and Hyperia on the terrace.

"I agree that John was not at his best," Hyperia said as the coach neared the gateposts. "He was distracted, but I suppose that's to be expected. I liked Mrs. Ingersoll."

"So did Tait." I should not have made such an ungentlemanly observation, but Tait's behavior suggested that at least one puzzle had a simple explanation. He was more than ready to move on with his life, if not with Mrs. Ingersoll, then with some eligible parti.

"Don't be catty, Julian. He's lonely."

Mrs. Ingersoll was lonely, too, but she wasn't swilling brandy, making sheep's eyes, and losing her dignity as a result.

"I will be very lonely when you return to London."

Hyperia swiped my boutonniere right out of my lapel. "Good."

She left me on the step, and I remained there as the dust slowly settled over the drive. Some fact or observation about the meal was trying to gain my notice, some detail that had slipped past me at the time...

Try as I might, I could no more lay mental hands on what bothered me than I could have collected the dust raised by the departing coach. I refused to go back into the house, fearing I'd leave a precious mote of truth wafting about on the autumn breeze. Instead, I took myself around back to the garden walks.

Tait had been unsettled throughout the meal, off-stride, though his manners had certainly been up to the challenge of a ducal table. Lady Ophelia hadn't mauled Tait too badly, and Hyperia had been uniformly pleasant to him.

Mrs. Ingersoll had been all that was polite, as had Arthur and I.

I appropriated a few more sprigs of lavender, and rather than tucking them into my lapel, I pinched the flowery heads to release the aroma and…

The scent of honeysuckle. That was the detail I'd noticed. On Mrs. Ingersoll, the fragrance had been pleasant. On John Tait, something of a surprise. When we nearly bumped heads in the library, I'd caught a whiff from his person, and the note was the same as that worn by Mrs. Ingersoll.

Well, well, well.

Coincidence possibly, but I'd washed my hands in Tait's breakfast parlor, and that soap had been scented with lemongrass. Honeysuckle was a bit unusual. Either Mrs. Ingersoll had gifted Tait with a few bars from her own stores, or the gentleman had had occasion to wash his hands—or perhaps his entire person—while very recently under Mrs. Ingersoll's roof.

Naughty, naughty, John Tait. Naughty indeed.

~

Escorting a lady on her travels is usually a thankless undertaking. When I'd last performed that service for Godmama, I'd at least been able to ride inside the coach with her. Godmama, being a widow and family friend of very long standing, could be private with me in a closed conveyance for hours at no risk to anybody's reputation.

Hyperia was not a widow, and thus I faced the prospect of riding up top with John Coachman or covering the distance to Town in the saddle. My presence was necessary to handle coin, give orders to hostlers and porters, and generally ensure the lady's safety, but my company in any meaningful sense wasn't part of the arrangement.

And yet, I wanted to escort Hyperia wherever she pleased to go, and thus I was up early on Monday and prepared for a trying day.

"Wait twenty-four hours," Arthur said when I entered the breakfast parlor to find His Grace dining in solitary splendor. "Wait at least until noon. Nobody makes good time on muddy roads."

His suggestion was accompanied by the steady patter of a purposeful autumn rain on the parlor windows.

"Better to start early, while the roads are still passable. The rain will keep traffic to a minimum, and that helps too." I dished myself out a serving of omelet from the sideboard and speared a few slices of ham as well. The fare at many coaching inns was to be avoided if at all possible, and the traveling coach would be well stocked with cold sustenance.

"What's the rush?" Arthur asked, pouring me a cup of China black as I took the place at his right hand.

"I want this business with Tait concluded, and the next steps of the investigation lie in Town."

"He seems an agreeable sort." Arthur had placed the jam pot beside his own plate. His Grace of Waltham was a fiend for raspberry jam, and the strawberry preserves never lasted long in his presence either.

"Tait is very good at being agreeable to ladies," I replied. "Too good, in fact. I suspect he and Mrs. Ingersoll were intimately agreeable as recently as last night, and yet, her presence at your table came as a surprise to him. You will please not pass my speculation along to even Lady Ophelia."

"Her ladyship comes to her own conclusions without any help from us." Arthur appropriated two slices of toast from the nearest rack, and though both were already buttered, he commenced adding more. "She'd travel up to Town with you, did you ask it of her."

Meaning I could travel inside the coach, with her and with Hyperia. "Leander is partial to her ladyship, and she to him. A day in the elements is nothing for a former soldier."

Arthur topped his buttered toast with generous portions of jam.

"A former soldier who twice came home more dead than alive had best be careful of his health. You are my heir. I will not forgive you if you are carried off by a lung fever you caught playing the gallant for Miss West."

We were private for the nonce, and I had made Millicent a promise. "Speaking of carrying off... Is there any truth to the rumor that you've considered taking Leander to Paris as company for young George?"

Arthur shook the butter knife at me. "Listening at keyholes, your lordship? Wellington might have appreciated that skill, but I'll not have it."

"Then be more careful when you and Banter assume you have privacy. Millicent got wind of your schemes, and she disapproves of uprooting the boy."

"We'd uproot her, too, of course. I trust she understands that much?"

"So she can be your unpaid governess for two lively boys who are not close enough in age to be true confreres. I'll not have it."

Arthur contemplated his toast, which he would manage to eat without spilling so much as a crumb on his plate or a drop of jam on his cuff.

"What are we to do with her, Jules? When Leander's patrimony became clear, I thought the conundrum resolved, but Leander's mama is proving to be a riddle unto herself. I am leaving you here to sort out that situation, and that doesn't feel fair to me."

Arthur was asking me, not for advice, but to take on a matter squarely with his purview as patriarch, a matter more delicate and complicated than the daily correspondence.

"She needs pin money," I said, starting on my omelet. "She needs the keys to Mama's sewing room and two seamstresses to work at her direction. She needs a lady's maid assigned exclusively to her, one of the younger ones, even if the maid mostly sits on her tuffet and squints at her mending. She needs access to our accounts at every shop in the village, and she needs time."

Half of Arthur's first piece of toast met its fate. "You are right. Millicent deserves indicia that she is as much our family as her son is. Spot on, Jules. Anything else?"

I sipped my tea and enjoyed the novel pleasure of advising my titled brother. "Write to Leander and include a few lines to Millicent in every epistle. Warn her that you are sending Leander a sketch of this or that or a set of Hessian tin soldiers. Treat her like his mama and as you would one of our sisters."

Arthur embarked on his second piece of toast. "Our sisters would never hide in the nursery, Jules."

You don't know that. I thought of Evvie Tait, so bitterly and frequently disappointed in her spouse, in her empty nursery, in looks no amount of heirloom pearls could make anything other than plain and stout.

"When the ladies lose patience with us, they become unpredictable."

"I defer to your greater experience, but I can assure you Miss West is not losing patience with you. She got a letter from her brother earlier in the week, and he's doubtless agitating for her to play hostess for him once Parliament resumes. That man needs a wife, but he's too selfish to settle down."

Polite society muttered the same about Arthur—erroneously, of course. "West would rather Hyperia settled down, though not with me."

"Then Healy West is not merely selfish, he's a selfish ass. You ate the last of the toast, you plundering Visigoth."

"I ate the two pieces you left for me. You drank the last of the tea."

Arthur scowled and picked up the newspaper, and I wanted to weep. He and I should have years to bicker at breakfast, but he was leaving me for France. If there was one place I would never set foot again, it was bloody, bedamned, beautiful France.

"Tait is a member at the Highlander," Arthur said from behind the financial pages, "and I believe he was accepted at the Contrarian.

He's not much of one for time in Town. Does his boots and hats by mail order, says Tatts tends to be overpriced."

"You've made inquiries?" Not that I was investigating Tait, of course.

"I mentioned to Vicar that I was to entertain a man with whom I was only passingly acquainted, and Vicar obliged with a few facts. Mrs. Vicar would have had the truly useful information, but I leave her to your kind offices. I wish you'd wait a day to travel, Jules. Coach accidents can be fatal as can a putrid sore throat."

"My will is in the safe. Look after Hyperia and Atticus, if anything happens to me." Lady Ophelia would look after them without my having to ask.

Arthur folded down the newspaper. "The boy, I grant you, is in need of constant supervision, but as for the lady, she, firstly, can look after herself, and secondly, looking after is usually a spouse's prerogative."

"You know why she and I ought not to marry."

Arthur set aside the paper. "I do not care a boot-boy's curse for the succession, Jules. We have enough personal wealth to manage without all the ducal properties. Life is short. I've nearly lost you too many times to demand that you sacrifice what's left of your three score and ten to the dictates of a dukedom neither of us did anything to deserve."

Travel was apparently already broadening the mind. "I see."

"You think I'm in high spirits because I'm going off on holiday, and you're right, but I've also been the duke, and it's a blessed lot of tedium for not much return. I'm telling you, travel up to Town when the roads are dry."

In other words, tarry with Hyperia at the Hall for as long as I could.

"I appreciate the sentiments—all of them—but we will depart as soon as Hyperia is ready."

As it happened, Hyperia presented herself in the breakfast

parlor, within the quarter hour. The coach was brought around to the porte cochere less than an hour after that.

A groom held Atlas's reins, an oilskin tarp protecting the saddle still in place. That saddle would be cold and wet within the first mile, and when Atlas tired, I'd tie him to the back of the coach and enjoy the bone-racking paces of a series of hardmouthed rented hacks.

"Ride inside with me," Hyperia said. "When the weather clears up, you can exile yourself to the elements."

"Hyperia…" A gentleman would start the journey in the saddle and finish it in the saddle.

"Please, Jules. I promised I would not interrogate you about John Tait, and you can promise not to interrogate me."

Whatever could she…? "Is there a reason I should be interrogating you, Hyperia?" I abruptly suspected there was. I feared there was.

The rain beat down, cold and miserable a few feet away. The offside leader stomped a hoof, and the footmen finished lashing our smallest trunks to the boot. The rest of Hyperia's baggage would follow at a modest pace, accompanied by Atticus and a groom or two.

"No reason for anybody to interrogate anybody, Jules. Will you ride inside?"

"Yes, until we find dry roads." Which we might never do, literally or figuratively. I instructed the groom to take Atlas back to his cozy stall, and if a horse could look grateful, mine did.

I not only sat beside Hyperia on the forward-facing seat, I tucked an arm around her shoulders, and she gave me her weight. Within a few miles, Hyperia was dozing at my side, or pretending to, and thus did we pass most of the journey to London.

My darling, precious, dearest Perry had lied to me—she knew something relevant. I was sure of it. Had I once again been cast alone and starving on the freezing slopes of the Pyrenees, I could not have felt more desolate.

∼

"Won't you come in for a cup of tea, Jules?" Hyperia asked when we'd arrived in her brother's mews.

I stood on the alley's slick cobbles, cold drizzle making the whole scene dreary—drearier—and bowed over the lady's hand.

"Thank you, no," I replied, keeping her gloved fingers in mine. "I'd like to get John Coachman out of the wet, and Healy will want you to himself for a bit."

Hyperia chose to let that euphemism pass. Healy wanted his sister away from me, not quite the same thing as delighting in her presence himself.

"You'll call before you leave town?"

The question had doubtless cost Hyperia some dignity. "I will call before I leave, I give you my word. When I return to the Hall, I will write, though I might resort to subterfuges involving Lady Ophelia's aid. I will send my sisters around on reconnaissance when they are in Town, and I will invite you and your rubbishing brother down to the Hall for the Yuletide holidays."

A slight, pleased smile was my reward for that recitation. "You've thought about this."

Mile after mile, I'd thought about telling Tait he could take his handsome, beleaguered self to Coventry, for all I cared, because this distance between me and Hyperia was intolerable.

"Lady Ophelia will enjoy regular correspondence from you as well, I trust?" I asked.

"Very regular."

I surrendered her hand and felt as if I were going off to war after a particularly lovely leave, but of course, that sentiment was disproportionate to the moment. I'd often been eager to return to my military duties, for all I loved my home and family. I was in the grip of foreboding now rather than eagerness.

"Jules, when His Grace and Banter take ship..." Hyperia glanced over her shoulder at her brother's house. "Don't brood. Don't let the doldrums overtake you. Winter is hard enough with all the cold and darkness, but I'll worry about you."

Hyperia was fretful, too, a small consolation. "Lady Ophelia will not allow me privacy, much less brooding." Except that the plan was for her ladyship to head to Paris later in the autumn to retrieve young George and bring him home. I would, sooner or later, face weeks of relative solitude at the Hall.

A prospect I might have once relished instead filled me with misgivings.

Drat this wretched, sopping, stupid day.

Hyperia crossed the alley, opened the garden gate, and motioned me through. The garden was not private enough—too many windows overlooked it—but what we said was less likely to be overheard.

"Jules, about John Tait... I know my friendship with him troubles you, and I can't help that. I think you should know that, though we once—"

I held up a hand. "Perry, please, not now. What you tell me may color my regard for Tait in ways that make objectively investigating his circumstances more difficult." If Hyperia had allowed Tait a lover's privileges—privileges I might never know or be capable of enjoying with her—then further dealings with Tait loomed as nigh unbearable.

"Perhaps later, then," she said, "when you make your final report, however redacted. I want no misunderstandings between us, Jules."

"Sometimes silence is understanding enough. At this point, I have no confidence that I'll locate Evelyn Tait any time soon." Or ever.

Hyperia brushed a glance over me that gave away nothing. If she was exasperated with me, well, so be it. I was coping with frustrations of my own, thank you very much.

"I'd hoped an investigation would take your mind off His Grace's departure," she said. "I was wrong, wasn't I?"

I was not a toddler to be distracted with a picture book while waiting for my supper. "I do enjoy the puzzles, Hyperia. You aren't wrong about that. It's more the case that..." How to put this? "The night before battle, soldiers write letters home to be sent in the event of their deaths. They clean their weaponry, enjoy a tot of whatever decent libation they've been saving for a special occasion. One cannot exactly contemplate a battle not yet joined, but one can't forget it either. I'm in that same mental posture. France has stolen one brother from me and made a good effort to steal my wits, my life, and my reputation too. I do not trust France to give me back my surviving brother."

"You have your reasons," Hyperia said, "except that we are not at war, Arthur is exceedingly sensible, and Banter is endlessly protective of him."

Damn Healy West for precipitating this whole, awkward parting. "I am protective of you, Perry. I want to take you in my arms and never let you go, much less see you dutifully pouring tea for your brother. Promise me *you* won't brood."

This smile was brighter. "Ladies don't brood. We grow thoughtful."

"Perry, if you find yourself growing too thoughtful, send for me. Arthur's Mayfair house has pigeons that fly home to the Hall, and you are free to use them. I'll leave word with the staff to that effect. I'll meet you in the park, at Hatchards or Gunter's. Healy is your brother, not your commanding officer, and he's certainly no authority over me."

"Pigeons." Hyperia's tone was pleased, and I was relieved to think I'd offered her some reassurance she hadn't been able to ask for. "I'd forgotten about the pigeons. Bless the pigeons, and bless you for reminding me of them."

We stood beaming at each other in the mizzling rain, my boots getting wet, Hyperia's bonnet feathers going droopy.

"I love you," I said quietly and without touching her. That I must be so restrained broke my heart and made me furious. "I will call before I leave Town, and that is a promise."

"I love you," she replied just as softly. "Neglect to call, and I will be wroth with you."

She'd worry, in other words. "I have my orders, Miss West." I touched a finger to my hat brim—I did not blow her a kiss—and executed an about-face. I waited by the garden gate until my lady was safely under her brother's roof, then I waved the coachman on and turned my steps for Ludgate Hill.

A few hours of daylight remained, such as that commodity had been in evidence at all, and I wanted Tait's situation resolved with all possible haste. The walk across Town would give me time to think and time to recover from a farewell that had left my heart aching and my temper uncertain.

CHAPTER SEVEN

"Her Grace favored us with a call a fortnight past," Mr. Grabel said. "Your dear mother is a careful customer. Has excellent taste too."

I had begun my circuit of the shops with Grabel's establishment precisely because a Grabel had been attending to Caldicott jewelry for at least four generations. My christening rattle had been fashioned under Grabel's direction, and should I find myself in need of an engagement ring, I'd bring my custom to this elegant little establishment situated just off Ludgate Hill.

Mr. Grabel's business was about at the midpoint between the Old Bailey and the churchyard of St. Paul's Cathedral, symbolic of some moral subtlety or other. I'd always liked his shop, which sought to impress with quality rather than overwhelm with quantity. A few tastefully lavish pieces were displayed on beds of velvet. A few portraits indicated the lofty fate of other works.

"If you can think of an appropriate Yuletide token for Her Grace," I said, examining a trio of ruby bracelets reposing on gold cloth. "I am all ears."

Grabel, bald, bearded, and with the merry blue eyes of an aging elf, went to his ledger book. He licked his fingers and turned a few pages.

"Her Grace asked about..." He peered at an entry. "A watchcase for a small boy. She said he is too old for a porringer, too young for sleeve buttons, cravat pins, and such, but a pocket watch or standish might catch his fancy."

The duchess might well have been shopping for Leander. Arthur had doubtless informed her of the whole situation, and regularly reporting to Her Grace on my nephew's progress would now fall to me.

"I suppose a penknife will become my responsibility." But what initials should I have engraved on this little commonplace? Was the child Leander Merton Waites? Leander Merton Caldicott? Leander Merton Dujardin, after his mama's nom de guerre?

Another discussion to have with Arthur before he left.

"A penknife is a nice place to start," Grabel said. "Nacre or ormer works well for an inlay. Even gold inlay on wood has a nice look. A folding penknife would be a bit different and more safely carried in the pocket."

"I'd rather he kept sharp objects stashed in his desk or in the standish Her Grace contemplates. As it happens, though, I'm here with a different topic in mind."

Grabel closed his notebook. "Is his lordship taking a bride?" The question was rendered with a conspiratorial twinkle that made me want to turn right around and return to the chilly, damp afternoon outside.

"Not at present, but I have been asked to trace the movements of a bride who came to London five years ago. She would have brought a quantity of jewels with her and been looking to pawn the lot."

Grabel stared past my shoulder. "I avoid the pawning, my lord. Always, sadness attends such a transaction. For pawning, you are better off asking Herr Lucas or Mr. Stottlemeyer. They are discreet, their clientele is varied, and their businesses are well established."

"Discretion is of the essence in this case."

Grabel's gaze returned to me. "Ladies pawning jewels are always in need of discretion, and sometimes they need a fast coach and passage to Calais too. Then one meets the husband and wishes the lady Godspeed."

I could not see Evvie leaving the ambit of her sisters' support, at least not early in her flight. "The difficulty was financial rather than a matter of the lady's bodily safety."

Evvie's diaries had never once referred to Tait threatening her with physical harm, nor had she considered him verbally vicious outside the context of their mutual sniping, though his actions had wounded her sorely.

"Can you give me a name, my lord? Families of means tend to patronize the same shops down through the years."

To insist on confidentiality would have insulted him. "She was Mrs. Evelyn Tait at the time, née Hasborough, of the Sussex Hasboroughs, hailing from near Climpton Parva. One of four girls."

He held up a finger. "We shall consult the oracle. Oma!"

I had seen Oma when I'd been a small boy, and she'd struck me as impossibly old then. She shuffled forward from the back of the shop, no taller than my breastbone, stooped and stringy with age, her face as wrinkled as a hedge apple in winter.

"Lord Julian, you have done some growing up."

"The tallest of the lot," I said, feeling foolishly proud. "You are looking well, madam."

"I look old, and this one,"—she jerked her chin at her grandson—"expects me to keep his books despite endless interruptions. Why have you bothered me this time, Heinrich?"

"Hasborough. Sussex gentry. His lordship has a question or two."

She eyed me up and down. "They are all married, my lord. Don't waste your time. Great, strapping females they are too."

"I'm not looking to propose to the lady. Do you recall to whom the Hasboroughs gave their custom on Ludgate Hill?"

Her gaze turned thoughtful. "Look in at Stottlemeyer's. He has many Sussex families among his customers. Not the titles—not the big titles, anyway. He'll pawn, reset, or break up jewelry upon request. Not too proud to work with the semiprecious if that's a lady's fancy. Does good work. Doesn't take all year to do it."

A pointed look at Mr. Grabel accompanied that last observation.

"*Danke*, Oma," Grabel said.

"You are welcome," she said, tidying a display of watch chains laid out on purple velvet. "You should close early, Heinrich. My bones tell me the cold comes, and when the cold comes, the customers stay away. Good day, my lord."

She shuffled out with no more ceremony than that, and Heinrich seemed relieved.

"Oma has a better eye for the jewels than I ever will, and she has kept more secrets than you can imagine. Royal secrets."

"Not a burden I'd wish on anybody. Where can I find Mr. Stottlemeyer?"

"Across the street, three doors up. He'll not close early. We none of us will. If we closed early on every gloomy day, we'd have no custom."

"You've been a great help, and I will be back to discuss my nephew's needs. I like the idea of a penknife, but must consider some details first."

That Leander was my nephew was a disclosure of sorts, but such was Grabel's tact that he showed no reaction.

"We are always happy to see a Caldicott come through our door, my lord. Best of luck with your inquiries."

I put my hat on and wished I'd thought to bring an umbrella. "Thank you, and thanks to your grandmother."

I had a hand on the door latch when a quavering voice called out from the back of the shop. "Emeralds for Miss West, my lord. Nothing less than emeralds will do. Emeralds for royalty and romance, and they'd suit you now as well."

I hurried out into the rain and closed the door firmly behind me. Emeralds, long associated with the goddess Venus, were said to aid in fertility.

Opals for me, perhaps, for hope and love, but adorning myself in emeralds would have been turning folklore to a desperate end, and I wasn't that far gone—yet.

∼

"And why does my lord inquire about such old business?" Stottlemeyer asked. He was big, blond, and elegantly attired, a monumental sort of man who nonetheless had shelves and shelves of delicate work on display.

Too much, in fact. When pearls and citrines, lapis lazuli, and turquoise all competed for attention, when cameos, chokers, bracelets, necklaces, combs, and rings winked from every compass point, the effect was busy rather than dazzling.

Not much in the way of diamonds, rubies, sapphires, or emeralds, though, suggesting clientele of less-than-lavish means.

I took one look at Stottlemeyer's impassive features and decided on a subterfuge—an obvious subterfuge—so that sensibilities could be preserved all around.

"The lady inherited her grandmother's pearls," I said. "A hoard of them, in fact. Ropes and bracelets and chokers and combs... and her sisters have asked me to discreetly attempt to trace the heirlooms. If they were sold, the sisters are interested in buying them back and would be most grateful to whoever could broker those transactions."

Stottlemeyer weighed my deceptions and apparently found them adequate. Given his reputation and his trade, mine were doubtless among the simpler lies he was told in the course of a day.

"Have you a date, my lord?"

I informed him of the window of weeks following Evelyn's departure, and he disappeared through burgundy brocade curtains behind his watch counter. The shop was thankfully deserted—the rain was coming down in earnest—and I pretended to admire the inventory.

Initials polished away from the back of a mirror and replaced with Stottlemeyer's maker's mark, a monogram artfully made over into a flourish of rosettes on a watchcase, a pair of bracelets that looked to have been cut down from a single necklace... So many sad stories, or perhaps, so many people earning coin from baubles that had brought them only fleeting happiness.

Stottlemeyer reemerged from his sanctum sanctorum, his gravitas worthy of an undertaker. "I did not accept any pearls for pawning or resale in the month you cite, my lord."

Maybe Evelyn had kept her granny's pearls out of sentimentality. "What about opals, turquoise, amber, lapis lazuli, and the like? She was partial to showy pieces and had fair coloring. She also had considerable stature and wasn't given to fashionable understatements."

Stottlemeyer gave himself away with—oddly enough—a movement of his ears. Some people swallowed upon receiving a mental start, some raised their eyebrows, some shifted their feet, some parted with a *hmmph*, or a *well, well, well...* Stottlemeyer's ears moved.

Great stature and pearls clearly touched a chord in memory.

"A moment, my lord."

He disappeared again, and again I waited, longer this time.

When he emerged from between his velvet curtains, Stottlemeyer looked, if anything, slightly vexed. His annoyance suggested he could not offend the brother of a duke, but neither could he compromise his reputation for discretion.

In other words, he knew something relevant. "I can tell you again, my lord, I accepted no opals, turquoise, amber, lapis, or the like for resale or pawning in the month that interests you."

Firstly, unless Stottlemeyer had been suffering a protracted bout of Walcheren fever, he'd have accepted some or all of those jewels into his inventory in the course of any given month. Secondly, he was choosing his words with exceeding precision.

I produced a gold sovereign and set it on the nearest glass display case. "For your trouble and for your time. The Hasborough sisters are determined that I find those pearls."

He recognized the name, for the first time meeting my gaze. "They were good customers."

Past tense, which simplified Stottlemeyer's dilemma. Upon marriage, a woman would tend to patronize the shops her husband favored, whether for jewels, gloves, or candles.

"And you gave good service, which is why, five years after her nuptials, Evelyn Hasborough came to you for some discreet transactions." I reconsidered his words, few and brief as they were. "You accepted no jewels from her, either for pawn or purchase, but did you *reset* a few pieces for her?"

To spend money disguising jewels that were likely headed for liquidation struck me as something between overabundant caution and illogic.

Stottlemeyer's blond brow furrowed. "Not reset."

I had no idea what convoluted code of honor he was adhering to, but coin had loosened his hold on silence. I put another sovereign on the display case.

"You did something so that the pearls at least became unrecognizable."

The two sovereigns disappeared into Stottlemeyer's pocket, his movements as deft as a sleight-of-hand artist's.

"She had only the pearls left," he said. "She'd taken the rest to Lucas. Some he bought, some he offered to resell for her. Nice pieces —all of my pieces are nice—and he offered her fair terms. She went to him because she was concerned that her husband might think to inquire of me, not that I am in the habit of disclosing particulars to husbands in disgrace. She said her man was too lazy to ask questions of every jeweler in Town, and she trusted her pearls only to me."

The Hasborough ladies had made a good, worthy impression on Stottlemeyer. "I'm only interested in the pearls."

"I broke them down," Stottlemeyer said. "Those long ropes became bracelets, combs, rings... She kept the choker with the cameo, because I told her that would fetch a good price as is, but the rest... You could fill a whole jewelry case with the results, my lord."

What a phenomenal memory Stottlemeyer had when he was inspired to use it. "What would you say her jewels were worth?"

He wrinkled an aquiline nose. "Lucas has standards. He doesn't deal in trash or trinkets. If he has paste, it's excellent paste in a first-rate setting. Good pieces only, and the people patronizing his shop have means. Not vast fortunes, but means. They have come up in the world enough that haggling is beneath them. The lady would have come away with several hundred pounds, my lord. Lucas does not price his items to move quickly. Some ladies prefer to see their used goods in the shop window."

I applied my imagination to such a scenario. "Because the gentleman who gave them the piece will be humiliated by the display?"

Stottlemeyer nodded. "*Ja*, and because then all the ladies will see that a particular locket initially on offer at Garrard's has been consigned to my own humble window. The careful gentleman will avoid that locket if he seeks a gift for a woman he truly esteems. In the eyes of the best Society, the locket has come down in the world, you see."

Enough subterfuge and posturing for a military campaign. "Interesting, and not something I was aware of previously. I will convey my findings to the relevant parties, and thank you for your time. You have been most helpful."

"Glad to be of service. I don't suppose I can interest your lordship in a snuffbox? We have quite a selection."

"Thank you, no. I don't indulge." The rain was letting up, too late for my poor boots, and the afternoon was shifting toward evening. "If you happen to come across any of those pearl pieces, would you let me know?"

I set my card and a third sovereign on the glass counter. Stottlemeyer took only the card.

"I thought I'd seen the last of those pearls about a year ago, my lord. Every few months, some maid would come along and leave another piece with us for reselling—never pawning. That stopped last autumn, and I concluded that Miss Evelyn had found other means or exhausted her store of pearls."

I retrieved the sovereign. "You recently saw another item from the set?"

"A month ago, the choker. The largest, most valuable remnant of the originals. I didn't recognize it at first because the cameo had been removed, but the pearls themselves were carefully graduated in size, and I use a particular kind of silk to string my necklaces."

I was very sure that my feet moved and my eyebrows rose. "Who brought it in?"

"A chambermaid sort of person, nondescript, and she retrieved the funds in the usual fashion, with the chit we gave out when we accepted the piece. Discretion is assured when no names or directions are involved."

"Anything memorable about the maid?"

Stottlemeyer smiled, and the dignified proprietor became a genial fellow who'd gladly share the snug with you on a winter night.

"Not a damned thing ever distinguishes such maids, sir. Plain of face, plainly dressed, neither old nor young, hair tucked up in an old straw bonnet, eyes downcast, black gloves, jet reticule. I've seen a thousand such maids, and I hope to see a thousand more."

Had I made progress with this discovery? I'd have the length of London to ponder that question. "Thank you again, Stottlemeyer. I am much indebted to you."

"If my lord ever needs a snuffbox..."

"I will shop your establishment first."

He bowed, I departed, and I was wandering through St. James's before I realized that yes, I had made progress. Considerable progress. That steady trickle of jewelry established a few important facts.

Evvie Tait was not in service. She was living off the proceeds of her married years and had recently sold the last major asset in her possession.

If she was supporting herself in such a fashion, she was likely without male protection, whether in a bigamous union or in some other irregular arrangement.

She was able to communicate with somebody trustworthy in London closely enough to receive coin in exchange of her goods, and that arrangement all but eliminated the possibility of flight to the Americas or the Continent. Perhaps Evvie was hiding in London itself, which was notoriously easy to do.

Most significantly of all, Evelyn Tait was apparently alive. Would her husband rejoice or despair to learn she yet lived?

~

I ate a cold and solitary supper in the Caldicott House library, not wanting to put the staff to avoidable bother. I had my own dwelling in London, now shuttered and locked, though I maintained a small staff there as a gesture in the direction of my independence.

How had Arthur maintained his sense of independence against the tide of ducal obligations and regalia? Because he surely had, splendidly so.

"You nigh onto wrecked your boots, guv." This observation was offered by young Atticus. When I traveled, he transmogrified into my self-appointed general factotum.

"Did you knock, young man?"

"Aye, but when you get into your brown studies, the Archangel Gabriel could dance a jig afore you, and you'd not notice. You finished with that tray?"

Half a sandwich remained, and I wasn't yet sated. "My compliments to the kitchen." I appropriated one of the two slices of gingerbread and slathered it with butter. "You may take the tray."

Which would boast not a single crumb by the time it arrived belowstairs.

"Your trunks are in your room, the big 'un and the little 'un, and the fires are lit in your bedroom and sitting room."

I bestirred my tired mind to consider a small boy attempting to get around to some point known only to him. "My thanks. Are you situated among the footmen?"

"I have me regular cot, which isn't very close to the fire, mind, but the room is snug enough, and I can have all the blankets I please. Place gets to stinkin', though, with all them fellers farting and whatnot through the night."

I could not divine the direction of Atticus's thoughts. "Try sleeping in an infantry barracks when cabbage soup has been on the day's menu, my lad. I'm sending an express to the Hall. Have you any correspondence to add to mine?"

"Who would I write to?"

To whom would I write when Arthur had decamped for points distant? Dispatches to Her Grace weren't quite the same as prosing on to a brother.

"Lady Ophelia would doubtless like a report, you having been recruited to the ranks of her minions, after all."

"I'm your minion first, guv. Told her that in plain words."

Bless you, my child. "Use the paper and pen at the desk. Tell her we arrived safely with all our luggage, and his lordship is missing the Hall already."

Atticus peered at me through dark bangs growing overly long. "You are?"

"In a manner of speaking." I missed Hyperia, though she bided but a few streets away. I missed the Hall. I missed... Well, yes, Godmama. A bit.

Atticus would soon know, if he didn't already, that a former boot-boy did not perch at the ducal desk and print an epistle for the sake of practicing his letters, but I was grateful for his company.

"How do you spell infernal?"

"H-e-l-l-i-s-h."

"That ain't right, guv. Infernal begins with in, and that's i-n, unless you mean like a coaching inn."

"I-n-f-e-r-n-a-l."

As in, I was infernally frustrated to think of Hyperia dragooned back to the family fold. Before I knew it, Healy would entertain offers for her hand, all unbeknownst to Hyperia herself.

I had a thousand questions for her as a result of the day's interviews. Where did Tait go for his jewelry? Where did spinsters and widows lodge in London that was both affordable and decent? What did Hyperia know of Ardath Deloitte and Lina Hanscomb? How should I approach those ladies if I wanted to be taken into their confidence?

Soft snoring soon accompanied my thoughts, Atticus having apparently concluded his letter and repaired to the sofa facing the hearth. The dinner tray—devoid of leftovers—sat on the desk.

The clock struck midnight, and my breakfast with Arthur could have been a lifetime past. I banked the fire, sealed up the various bits of correspondence I'd completed, and tucked Atticus's epistle into my letter to Arthur.

Atticus, too, had put in a long day, and the thought of rousing the lad so he could repose among the flatulent footmen had no appeal. I slipped off his boots and draped an afghan over him. In sleep, he looked seven years old, an observation that would appall him. I blew out the candles and left him to his dreams.

The fires had been lit in my rooms, true, but the chambers bore the lingering chill of unoccupied winter quarters. Running the warmer over the sheets helped, but as I drifted into the outer reaches of sleep, contentment eluded me. I had much to be grateful for, and in the past year, I had overcome many difficulties.

I'd told Tait that marriage was not the sum of a well-lived life, but if I had to watch the woman I loved be courted by a lot of swaggering swains handpicked by her meddling brother, I might well lose all the ground I'd gained.

And then some.

CHAPTER EIGHT

I set a snare for Ardath Deloitte, and she stepped right into it.

The mechanism was simple: I sent a note begging for the favor of her hospitality at eleven o'clock and citing Mrs. Semple's kind suggestion that I pay such a call. I wanted to interview Evelyn's youngest sister free of possible interruptions from other visitors, hence the unsociably early hour.

Thirty minutes before the appointed time, I stationed myself in the alley behind the capacious Deloitte domicile. The air was nippy, the breeze pushing dead leaves about on the blond cobbles. Autumn had arrived in London, and the scent of coal smoke was everywhere.

A boy came running through the garden gate to confer with a groom. The groom sent the boy back to the house and disappeared into the stable.

The team was apparently being put to harness. I loitered discreetly twenty yards off, waiting to see for whom the carriage was being prepared. The pair of grays backed into the traces were spotless and elegant—grays were a vanity, always more work to keep clean—and calm. My money was on the lady taking flight, and I would have won that bet.

Mrs. Deloitte did not enjoy quite the grand dimensions of her oldest sister, but she was majestic enough, particularly when sweeping along in a red merino cloak with a fur collar and an enormous fur muff about her hands. More vanity—the morning wasn't *that* cold. She reminded me of somebody, probably Mrs. Semple, though a difference in age and individual features obscured the likeness.

A footman trotted along beside her, opening the garden gate in time for her to gain the alley without breaking stride.

I slapped on a smile and marched forth smartly. "Mrs. Deloitte? Lord Julian Caldicott, at your service. I hope you received my note?" On crested stationery and sealed with my signet ring pressed into the signature Caldicott lavender-scented purple wax.

Consternation flashed through blue eyes, but the lady recovered quickly. "Note? My lord, you have me at a loss." Her tone was puzzled rather than disdainful, which boded well for my mission.

"I do apologize. I'm sure my footman said he'd delivered it into the hands of your underbutler, but notes go astray all too often. I will presume, then, on the good offices of your sister Mrs. Margery Semple, who promised she'd write to you on my behalf."

Mrs. Semple had made no such promise, but I'd read Evelyn's diaries, and the sisters were loyal and frequent correspondents. Mrs. Semple held the rank of senior general. If Mrs. Semple advised Evelyn to go up to Town for some shopping in retaliation for Tait's flirtations, Evelyn had packed her bags accordingly.

"You're acquainted with my sister?" Mrs. Deloitte unbent so far as to remove a gloved hand from the muff and offer it to me. She had Evelyn's coloring—fair complexion, blond hair—but her features were more delicate, and the result was more attractive.

I bowed, she curtseyed, and the footman found it expedient to make a great production out of crossing the alley to ensure the gate was properly latched.

Good Lord, was the lady given to assignations in alleys? "I have had the pleasure of a lengthy visit with Mrs. Semple and invited her to call at Caldicott Hall if she was of a mind to. I believe she will favor us with a visit before His Grace takes ship for the Continent."

I was flaunting my consequence shamelessly—Arthur's consequence, rather—because I was dealing with gentry married into the merchant classes. Consequence often mattered more in such circles than it did in the peerage itself, though, by rights, I ought to have had a mutual acquaintance provide an introduction in person.

I hadn't time for such niceties, and besides, Mrs. Deloitte had attempted to avoid me when my stated mission was to find her missing sister.

An encouraging blunder on the lady's part.

"I do recall Margery mentioning something about a call from you," Mrs. Deloitte said. "Unfortunately, my lord, this is not an opportune—"

"I need only a moment of your time. Perhaps I might escort you to your destination? In the alternative, I can come back this afternoon when you've completed your errands." I was not, in other words, somebody she could put off, short of resorting to rudeness. If she showed me a bit of patience, by contrast, she could boast of a ducal *connection*.

"If you promise to be brief," she said, "we can chat in the conservatory. John Coachman, if you'd walk the team, I'll be back shortly."

The coachy nodded from his perch and gave the grays leave to walk on.

The conservatory was relatively warm, also private, and the location spared Mrs. Deloitte from offering me tea or any other excuse to linger. One might call the choice of venue rude. She took off the figurative gloves as soon as the door had closed behind us.

"If I recall Margery's letter, she said you were poking about in search of Evelyn. Has John Tait finally recalled that he has a wife?"

And this was the sister whom Tait believed was *least* set against him? "I am searching for Evelyn, but I made it plain to Mrs. Semple that my intention is primarily to pass along a message to her: Tait is willing to pursue an annulment if that's what Evelyn wants. I will not reveal your sister's whereabouts if she's determined on her privacy. Tait, for his part, would like to know that Evelyn is well and happy rather than moldering in a pauper's grave."

His life hasn't been easy. I left that startling sentiment unvoiced because I doubted it would aid Tait's cause. Perhaps I was sensing what Hyperia perceived more clearly: John Tait was neither widower, nor husband, nor bachelor, nor youth. He was a masculine anomaly, and for him, that status had become unbearable.

Not knowing if he'd precipitated his wife's death had become worse than unbearable.

"John has waited years to suffer this attack of conscience where Evelyn is concerned," Mrs. Deloitte said, pacing away from me. "He's probably spent all of Evelyn's money, and now he needs to remarry."

Possible. "The house is in good repair, considering it lacks a lady's hand, and his acres appear to be thriving. Besides, I was given to understand that Evelyn's sisters will benefit from her death to a greater degree than Tait would."

Mrs. Deloitte smiled, and I understood why Evelyn had felt so plain in comparison. "My lord, do my circumstances suggest I am in want of funds?"

"Circumstances can be deceiving, but were you in want of funds, you'd be hastening me to complete my investigation, to find a record of Evelyn's death. So far, you've offered insults to Tait—deserved, very likely—and nothing that would help me to find your sister."

Mrs. Deloitte began picking off dead leaves from a struggling potted rose. "I know nothing that would assist you to find Evvie. I pray for her nightly, and if John is in misery, perhaps that's divine retribution. He was a thoughtless husband to my sister. Evvie is no great beauty, but she was smitten with Tait and with all his charming ways."

Ardath's tone suggested she had been a little smitten, too, hence her bitterness now.

"You were jealous of her," I said gently, "once upon a time, and when Tait paid attention to you, you were flattered. That must have been confusing to a young woman barely out of the schoolroom, and Tait should be pilloried for his cavalier behavior. It occurs to me, though, that Evelyn could negotiate favorable terms from him, if he pursues an annulment. If he simply waits another year or two to petition the courts to have her declared dead, she gets nothing."

Sometime between nightmares, I'd realized that Evelyn might have given her pearls to her sisters for safekeeping, and the sisters had slowly run through Evelyn's treasure chest because Evelyn was no longer extant to need the funds.

Ardath Deloitte, as the sibling dwelling in London, was the most likely beneficiary of the pearl hoard, if so.

"The courts take forever to declare anybody dead," Mrs. Deloitte said, giving up on the rose and moving on to an anemic fern. "Years, sometimes."

She was making more of a mess rather than tidying anything up.

"That's not always the case. The courts require that one wait seven years to petition to have somebody declared dead, but in the absence of any evidence supporting Evelyn's continued existence—I've found none worthy of a judge's notice—the petition could be granted quickly. Evelyn would be left with nothing."

I wasn't quite lying. I believed Evelyn was alive and soon to run out of funds. Tait's timing had been better than he'd known in that regard.

Or Evelyn might have expired of bad eel pie at a lesser coaching inn and been buried in some obscure churchyard. I hadn't found a single soul who'd laid eyes on her after she'd left the marital home, after all.

"We always felt sorry for Evelyn," Mrs. Deloitte said, brushing pieces of dead plant from her gloves. "She was very much in Margery's shadow, and Margery was slow to attract an offer. Mama was growing desperate. Evelyn was so... so robust and always willing to ride out with Papa, or go shooting with him. Evvie was the son he'd always wanted, but she wasn't a son, and she wasn't pretty, and she had a temper... She got all the pearls because we felt sorry for her."

"The pearls were to be a shared legacy?"

"The will was vague, but Margery said the pearls flattered Evelyn, and pearls are boring, so my sisters and I agreed. I don't regret it."

"Would it surprise you to know those pearls have gradually been resold over the past few years?"

She ceased fussing with her gloves and stared at me. "How can you possibly know that?"

"I did not know it—I only suspected—but you confirmed my theory. Evelyn left behind five years' worth of diaries, she left behind poetry Tait had written to her, she took none of his love letters. She took mostly coin and jewels. In her shoes, I'd have gone through the money first, and when that was gone, I'd start selling my jewels. I'd sell them in London, where the best prices could be fetched and where I had trusted allies."

A maid came in, carrying a full watering can. She saw us, set the can down, curtseyed, and hastily withdrew.

"My lord, I love my sisters, all of them, and I even have some sympathy for John. He was young, spoiled, and had nobody to tell him how to deal with a wife, or so my husband claims. I nonetheless know nothing of Evelyn's whereabouts, and that is the God's honest truth. I wish you the best of luck in your search, not for John's sake, but for Evelyn's. Now, if you'll excuse me...?"

She wouldn't risk abandoning me in the conservatory, but neither would she be home to me if I called again. That's how much luck she wished me as I sought to find her sister.

I picked up her enormous muff. "I'll see you to your coach," I said, gesturing to the door that led to the garden.

We returned to the alley as the carriage turned in from the street and the horses plodded up the cobblestone way.

"Is John paying you?"

The question surprised me and should have offended me. "What does that matter?"

"If he can afford to pay you, he can afford to support a new wife, can't he?"

"Not necessarily, but as it happens, I do not accept coin when doing favors for my friends."

The coach came to a halt, and a footman hopped down from the boot to tend to the steps. He opened the door, but stepped back when I offered my hand to Mrs. Deloitte.

She accepted my courtesy—she had little choice—but I did not immediately aid her to enter the coach.

"My brother died under uncertain circumstances, behind enemy lines, possibly from natural causes, possibly in unspeakable agony. I don't understand what he was doing in enemy territory, why he surrendered without a fight, or whether he was acting under orders or on his own initiative. The questions never leave me for long."

She snatched the muff from my free hand and put a foot on the step. "I'm sorry to hear that, my lord. If you wouldn't mind, I must be on my way."

"If you are haunted by a similar uncertainty regarding Evelyn, you hide it well."

She climbed into the coach. "Perhaps I do. Best of luck, my lord."

I fired my last shot. "Do you know anything of the whereabouts of Mrs. Evangeline Hanscomb?"

"Lina Hanscomb? Lord, no, I haven't heard that name for years. You'd best ask Margery what's become of Lina. She will know if anybody does. She might also know who John's flirts were here in Town and what has become of them. *Good day*, my lord."

I closed the door under the disapproving gaze of the footman, and John Coachman sent the horses on at a brisk, noisy trot.

I left Mrs. Deloitte's alley and wandered quiet streets and lanes rather than major thoroughfares. I needed time to think. Mrs. Deloitte had been lying some of the time, telling the truth some of the time.

Lina Hanscomb, for example, lived one street over.

Any bride new to London, as Mrs. Deloitte had once been, firstly and above all else used preexisting acquaintances to gain a toehold on the social whirl. Mrs. Hanscomb had married well, considering her antecedents. Ardath Deloitte had been more than passingly familiar with her sister's best friend from school, and thus, her professed ignorance of Mrs. Hanscomb's whereabouts had been a blatant lie.

I'd call on Mrs. Hanscomb directly, before the two women had a chance to confer.

As I retraced my steps and rehearsed opening lines, I was plagued by the sense that when Mrs. Deloitte claimed not to know where Evelyn was at present, she'd been telling the truth.

What on earth was I to make of that when the maid who'd interrupted us in the conservatory had been very plainly attired, neither young nor old, and very plain of face indeed?

*

"My lord." Lina Hanscomb curtseyed and came up smiling. "We have a mutual friend in Miss Hyperia West, though she and I have been out of touch in recent years. She was a great admirer of yours at one time."

Mrs. Hanscomb's opening salvo put her in a class above Ardath Deloitte as a verbal sparring partner. She'd troubled to educate herself about my reputation and my past, which the Hasborough sisters apparently had not.

"I continue to count Miss West among my dearest friends," I replied, bowing over the lady's hand. "She's recently returned to Town, in fact, if you are of a mind to renew your acquaintance."

"Perhaps I shall. London is so dreary as winter closes in, and all the talk is of bills, votes, and budgets. Do have a seat, my lord."

She'd received me in a formal parlor remarkable for the quality of the furniture. The sideboard, tables, mantel, picture frames, and mirror frame were all of mahogany, and in every case, the dark wood was relieved with intricate walnut inlay. A pattern of vines, leaves, and roses unified the whole and perfectly balanced the aesthetic between heavy and refined.

The carpet, curtains, and upholstery established a palette of cream, forest green, and burgundy, a departure from the pastels common in the typical peerage parlor. Red roses on the sideboard added a graceful accent and further underscored that somebody had good taste. Whereas another woman might have demanded a bouquet of two dozen blooms, Mrs. Hanscomb's posies numbered seven.

"Your note mentioned that you're searching for Evelyn Tait," my hostess said as a footman set a silver tea service before her. "How can I be of assistance?"

"I'm not sure you can help me, but I'm in the no-stone-unturned phase of the inquiry. Plain tea will do for me. You and Evelyn Tait were close. What sort of person is she?"

Mrs. Hanscomb made a pretty picture navigating the tea tray. She was of medium height, sable-haired, and going pleasingly matronly about the middle and the bosom. Her green eyes were shrewd and her bronze afternoon attire the epitome of understated fashion. Even her dress blended well with the room's appointments.

"Evelyn was a good friend," Mrs. Hanscomb said, an interesting place to start. "She could be moody, cross, and low-spirited, but she was also loyal, funny, and refreshingly bold, by schoolgirl standards. She taught us all how to smoke cigars—she'd learned from her father, apparently—and she talked me into taking a trouser role at one of our spring theatricals. I hadn't even that much daring in me at the time. She knew all the songbirds by their tunes and could imitate most of them, though ladies aren't supposed to whistle, are they?"

"She sounds like an original." The term was invariably a compliment—when applied to pretty women.

"She should have been, but those sisters of hers..." Mrs. Hanscomb passed over my tea, two iced cakes tucked onto the saucer. "They made Evelyn's life a purgatory."

Well, well, well. "I thought the Hasborough siblings were a close-knit and devoted quartet."

Mrs. Hanscomb fixed her own tea—also plain—and took a tea cake for herself as well. "To the rest of the world, they were, but the family had no son, and thus the property was destined to go to a cousin. Evvie was supposed to marry him, but he had other plans and, being five years her senior, was in a position to act upon them. He's an absentee landlord who rents out his manor house and lives very affordably in the South of France."

"Thus marrying well became imperative for all four sisters."

"Isn't marrying well always imperative?" She sipped her tea, and I did likewise. "Evelyn was the plainest of the sisters, and like the lowest hen in the pecking order, she suffered for it. They were always pinching her cheeks and ordering her about. 'Must you stand so tall, Evelyn?' 'The curling tongs are your friend, Evelyn.' 'Get back upstairs until you've fashioned a proper coiffure.' 'Evelyn, why can't you at least attempt to move with some grace?' Her father died two years before her come out, and a good deal of Evelyn's joie de vivre went with him."

Had Evelyn Tait been a man, her height, strength, and boldness would have been admired. "Did she care for Tait at all, or was he merely the choice her family insisted she accept?"

The tea was hot, strong, and smooth. The cake delicately flavored with cinnamon, a lovely combination. I also found the conversation interesting. I'd concluded that Evelyn was spoiled and headstrong and that she'd expected too much of her spoiled, headstrong husband.

The tale wasn't that simple, and shame upon me for thinking it so.

"That's the odd thing," Mrs. Hanscomb said, munching her tea cake. "John and Evelyn were well suited. He thought her slightly ribald humor was wonderful, and she liked his determination to do well by his acres. They could talk endlessly of plow designs and pig breeds. She didn't mind that he lacked a substantial fortune. He didn't care that Evelyn was no great beauty. She was roaringly healthy, didn't put on airs, and rode like a dragoon."

A hoyden, except that hoydens were supposed to be pert, saucy, little pocket Venuses whose great fortunes won them Society's fond indulgence.

"Would her sisters have done away with her for the money they'd inherit?"

Mrs. Hanscomb put down her tea cup. "Gracious. When I speculate in such directions, Mr. Hanscomb tells me that I've been reading too many Gothic novels."

"But you have speculated?"

She finished her tea cake and selected another. "Evelyn was initially so happy to be a wife. Her letters positively gushed with joy. For the first six months, she was rhapsodic. John was the perfect husband, a brilliant farmer, and beloved by his neighbors and retainers alike."

"A fairy tale."

She held out the plate of cakes to me, and I realized I'd eaten both of mine. I took one more.

"What you call a fairy tale is the ironclad promise made to every girl on her way out of the schoolroom. She will find a wonderful man. He will esteem her greatly. She will delight in managing his household and bearing his lovely, healthy children. She will pass blissfully through the remaining portion of her seven ages and depart life with a heart full of gratitude for all the contentment and affection she's known."

"I hope that fairy tale is coming true for my sisters." And, in some way, for Arthur too. What sort of future did Hyperia hope for, if not one with a husband and children?

"The fairy tale hasn't come true for you, has it?" Mrs. Hanscomb spoke gently, kindly even.

While I wrestled with the urge to smash my tea cup against the elegant mantel, I admitted that Hyperia and Mrs. Hanscomb would get on swimmingly. Both ladies looked life straight in the eye.

I took refuge in the stated purpose for my call. "Evelyn's marital joy apparently dimmed, did it not?"

"Precipitously. John developed a wandering eye, or Evelyn did, and simply keeping his house was no challenge at all for her. She grew stout—she was never a sylph—and the nursery remained empty. Her letters became shorter and fewer and often consisted of little more than some recipe for a decadent sweet that she'd come across. She never invited me to visit, though we'd promised each other we wouldn't drift apart."

"She pushed you away?"

"Or she couldn't bear to admit that I was happy and content while she grew bitter. I don't know as that development pleased her sisters, but it certainly gave them something to gossip about."

"You stayed in touch with her sisters?"

"Ardath is a neighbor, and Barbara and Margery both come up to Town from time to time. Our paths cross."

Never an occasion for wild rejoicing, apparently. "Ardath Deloitte claimed not to know what had become of you. I was to inquire of Mrs. Semple as to your whereabouts."

Mrs. Hanscomb frowned at her tea. "Ardath regularly borrows from my staff when she's entertaining formally, and I am free to borrow from hers."

"But you don't?"

"The need has not arisen. I suspect Evelyn's sisters are part of the reason that matters between Evelyn and John grew so troubled. Margery, in particular, dispenses advice as if she were the oracle of Sussex. She tried to tell me that flirting with my husband's friends would ensure I wasn't taken for granted by my spouse."

I could see the matronly, serene Mrs. Semple handing out just such a nostrum, and in a few instances, her guidance might even have been sound.

"If Evelyn flirted with John's friends, and John was busily flirting in retaliation with everything in skirts, I can see where the marriage went into the ditch."

"The question," Mrs. Hanscomb said, "is whether Margery sent it there on purpose. John and Evelyn were happy. Margery and her husband are cordial at best, and Ardath's spouse is too fond of his imported brandy. I can't speak for Babs's situation, but sibling rivalry can become diabolically complicated."

So... it... could. "I have reason to hope that Evelyn is still alive," I said. "Tait is willing to pursue an annulment, and he's willing to leave Evelyn in peace wherever she is. He's spent the past five years alternately hoping she'd return and fearing that he inadvertently caused her demise. I can't see that the status quo is serving either party optimally, hence my willingness to search for the lady."

Mrs. Hanscomb rose and used a pitcher on the sideboard to top up the water in the vase of roses. "If Evelyn had one quality that outshone all the others, it was determination. She was determined to prove her sisters wrong—she *would* find a husband who appreciated her. She *would* be happy. She *would* get back to the life in the shires that she loved. To blazes with turning down the room with gouty widowers who saw her as an unpaid governess for their children and a robust nurse for their dotage."

I stood as well, manners demanding that courtesy. "You miss her." The realization came as a relief. The Hasborough sisters might have ulterior motives regarding Evelyn, but Lina Hanscomb, secure in her place in the world, had the luxury of honest feelings.

"I miss Evvie sorely, and I worry about her, though she warned me that she might do something drastic. She was in Town visiting Ardath, five years ago nearly to the day. Evvie told me that matters with John had reached an impasse, and it was time for bold measures. I had no idea what she alluded to. She disappeared shortly thereafter —supposedly returning to Sussex, though she didn't—and the conversation made more sense in hindsight."

"Tait was never told that she'd made it as far as London."

"Perhaps he never asked. Evelyn was determined, as I said, but her determination was often driven by pride. John could be just as stubborn, and one shudders to think of the children they'd have had."

Except they'd never been so blessed, as the platitude went.

"Where should I seek her?" Mrs. Hanscomb would have given that topic considerable thought.

"I don't know. Evelyn was a creature of the shire, but strangers stand out in small villages and even in market towns. A port city always has a lot of new faces coming and going, but I can't see Evelyn ever being very far from good old English agriculture."

"Did she have any other close friends?"

"Not to speak of. We were a twosome at school, and while we were friendly with other girls, Evelyn did not exert herself to be likable, and I was of the same bent. One good friend is sometimes all one needs."

I had learned much about my quarry in the course of our discussion and about those with a motive to make Evelyn's life difficult. My belief that Evelyn would turn to her sisters for aid was shaken, but not destroyed.

Other than her own means and native wit, how else would she establish a new life in a new venue, except with the support of her siblings?

"How did Evelyn spend her idle time?" I asked, simply because this was another blank spot in my understanding of her.

"When she couldn't be in the saddle, she liked to read. Her father had been inclined to literature, the sort of fellow with a handy quote for any occasion. She and he would read the same books and write to each other about them. Evelyn was something of an herbalist and could sketch plants, animals, and landscapes with superior competence. She had a good singing voice—contralto—and had a vigorous command of the pianoforte."

Evelyn had had her own approach to ladylike accomplishments, in other words, but no outstanding passions that would shed light on a preferred place of escape. No yearning for the sea, no longing for the romance of the Highlands, no pleasant memories of summers spent on the Dales.

"Please find her, my lord. Even if all you do is tell her I've missed her, and I'd keep her confidences, please find her."

Hyperia would appreciate such a forthright plea, while I found it burdensome. Searching for Tait's embittered, flighty wife had been a chore undertaken at Hyperia's request. Finding a woman treated ill by her siblings and spouse, one with a loyal friend who yet worried about her, put the inquiry on a different and more personal footing.

"I will give the investigation my best effort," I said, "but searching the whole of England for a trail that went cold five years ago is a daunting prospect."

My hostess saw me to the door and asked to be remembered to Miss West, and then I was back out in the elements, no closer to discovering Evelyn Tait's whereabouts than when I'd started my day. I was, though, closer to Evelyn herself, and thus I next turned my steps in the direction of Hatchards bookshop.

CHAPTER NINE

I had missed bookshops terribly when I'd served in uniform. On leave, I'd made it a point to stop by Hatchards and place large orders, and I thus became something of a regimental lending library. If I left camp to impersonate a shepherd in the hinterlands, all and sundry knew my books were to be freely borrowed in my absence.

Books were civilization to me, proof of learning and laughter, full of wisdom and entertainment. That I'd stopped reading for pleasure after Waterloo had alarmed even me, even in the dull and melancholy state into which I'd fallen. Eventually, I had managed poems—short poems—but I had yet to tackle lengthy works of fiction.

The afternoon was turning blustery as I entered my old haunt, a familiar sense of foreboding dogging me. What had changed here, where I had spent so many pleasant hours? What was the same? Could I still enjoy the treasure trove that was a well-stocked bookshop, or had that pleasure died on the battlefields along with my youth and innocence?

The scent hit me first—vanilla and leather, though most of the inventory wasn't yet bound. Customers could see to their own binding or order the process to suit their individual tastes. Arthur preferred brown calfskin for most of the library at Caldicott Hall. For my books, I'd chosen the more durable goatskin, usually dyed red.

"Good day, sir. Welcome to Hatchards." The clerk was too young, too serious, and unknown to me. "Might I assist you to find something in particular?"

I wasn't ready to shop. I was still noting where a fern had replaced a chair, or a set of shelves was full of bound volumes that had once housed only magazines.

"I'll browse for a time first. Is Mr. Aiken still employed here?"

The young man's expression brightened. "Of a certainty. Shall I fetch him for you?"

"No need." Comfort enough to know the old fellow was still bustling about, muttering to long-dead authors and conversing in Latin with ancient poets. "I'll find my own way."

I wandered among travelogues, biographies, agricultural authorities, French plays, Restoration comedies, and the Bard and his contemporaries. Fashion had a few shelves all to herself—that was new—as did art history, language manuals, dictionaries...

Aladdin's Cave of Wonders hadn't held half so much treasure.

As much as I'd fought to regain European markets for London's merchants and to overthrow an emperor ruling by conquest rather than divine right, I'd fought for these books and what they represented. I found a chair and sank into it, unnerved to have stumbled upon that insight.

Napoleon would have burned the lot of them, or hauled every tome in England back to France for the delectation of his bloodthirsty populace. He'd plundered Alexandria, Rome, and half the world in between. But for Lord Nelson's seamanship, *l'empereur* would have sacked London as well.

Hatchards' lovely books thrown in the flames, Twinings a ruin, Tatts a shambles...

"Upon my word, Lord Julian Caldicott, I bid you welcome!"

Lean, gray, and always coming undone somewhere, Mr. Flavian

Aiken charged toward me with an outstretched hand. I rose in time to intercept his overture and to endure a hearty clapping on the back.

"My lord, you are a sight for these old eyes, indeed you are. Come for more Catullus, have you? You are looking well, sir, if I might venture such an observation." Aiken ceased thumping me and lowered his voice. "One worried for you."

I focused on a black leather edition of *Horse-Hoeing Husbandry* by Jethro Tull, blinked severally, and swallowed.

"The Catullus was much appreciated. Very much appreciated. Clever enough to be interesting and ribald enough to inspire mirth." Aiken had sent me a bound volume *as a homecoming token, if your lordship will forgive the presumption*, and I had needed the mirth desperately.

Catullus had pulled me through some dark hours, as had Sappho, Donne, Shakespeare, Virgil... I'd read novels and histories at war. I'd retraced my way to peace through poetry, verse by verse.

"Have you come to renew old acquaintances, my lord, or are you in search of a particular tome?"

"Some of both. My sisters have set me to browsing on behalf of one of their friends. She's not yet thirty, adores life in the shires, has a strong interest in agriculture and herbals and a good sense of humor. A vigorous woman with a solid literary foundation and who also is an accomplished equestrian."

I might have been describing half the young women in England, but it was enough to have Aiken looking thoughtful.

"She'd like Mrs. Burney and Mrs. Radcliffe, I'm sure."

"She's doubtless read their every word."

"*Sense and Sensibility*? Very popular with the ladies, as is *Pride and Prejudice*."

I hadn't cared for either tale, mocking as they did nearly every character however high- or lowborn. Criticizing Merry Olde and her social crotchets was easy, and the author's primary strength seemed to be criticizing with elegance and wit.

"You get a lot of orders for those?"

"Indeed, we do, and not only from the ladies. Young fellows can offer books as gifts in these modern times. If the curate or the schoolteacher wants to impress a lady with both his devotion and his learning, a gift of literary merit does the job. The happy couple can pass hours in earnest conversation about turns of phrase or themes or character motivations. Courtship-by-book is quite the latest rage."

"You make me feel old." Would Hyperia like to be courted with books? "What of poetry? Does nobody read the poets anymore?"

"They do, though the classics are no longer ascendant. Mr. Wordsworth's *Lyrical Ballads* continues to have a following, and his more recent *Poems, in Two Volumes* has found favor with many. I don't know whether writing poetry that appeals to the masses improves the masses or compromises the poetry, but there you have it."

"Come now, Aiken. How can more people reading poetry ever be a bad thing? And it's not as if Wordsworth is penning cant and slang, is it?" Though as to that, cant and slang, when pressed into the service of rhyme, could be brilliant and hilarious.

"You have me there, my lord. By Jove, I have missed you. Never one to retreat into platitudes." He pushed his spectacles up his nose, which emphasized their crookedness. "Your young lady might enjoy Arthur Young's *Tour in Ireland* or his *Farmer's Tour Through the East of England*. Before he got all political, Mr. Young had a sharp eye for all things agricultural. Shall I fetch them for you?"

"Please." I owed Aiken something in return for his welcome, and nothing would please him so much as inspiring a purchase of books.

I wandered the several floors of the shop, noting where inventory had moved or disappeared—very little French language verse, for example—and found myself beholding Charles Lamb's *Tales From Shakespeare: Designed for the Use of Young Persons.*

Leander wasn't ready for even the simplified Bard, but Atticus might enjoy the more bloodthirsty works when his vocabulary improved.

I left the shop half an hour later, having arranged for three books to be sent around to Arthur's townhouse. I'd found no insights into Mrs. Evelyn Tait's personality or preferences, but I'd found a warm welcome, and at the moment, that mattered to me more.

My investigation was not yet at a dead end, and oddly enough, Mrs. Ardath Deloitte had pointed me in the direction I ought to take. I would circle back to Sussex and chat up Mrs. Semple again. Who had flirted with John Tait's unhappy wife? What efforts had Mrs. Semple made to find her prodigal sibling? And I would confer in person with Lady Ophelia.

Whatever was true of my godmother, she never forgot a scandal, and the Taits' acrimonious separation was a scandal, if not quite a tragedy—yet.

                ∽

"You again." Healy West sneered the words at me while the butler absorbed himself with taking my hat and walking stick.

"If I am unwelcome," I replied pleasantly, "you need only say so. I won't be staying long, and I did promise your sister that I'd call before quitting Town. A gentleman ought to keep his word, don't you think?"

I was betting that the presence of the butler would prevent Healy from tossing me out on my ear. Healy could snub me with impunity on a deserted bridle path, but when his rudeness had an audience, word of his behavior would soon spread all over Mayfair.

"See that you don't," he said. "Stay long, that is." He marched up the corridor, leaving me in the company of the butler, Deering, who'd known me since I'd been in shortcoats.

Old Deering looked pained in the extreme. He'd known Healy West since that fine fellow had graced his christening gown.

"My apologies on behalf of your employer, Deering." West could have indicated his displeasure with me more discreetly—by note or with a cool welcome. The petulance on his part before domestic staff was badly done.

Deering sent a puzzled look at Healy's retreating back. "I'll let Miss Hyperia know you're here, my lord. Would you care to wait in the family parlor or the formal parlor?"

"The family parlor." I chose the more private option, the family parlor having no windows on the street. Healy was annoyed enough that I'd called at all. No need to taunt him by publicizing my presence.

"Very good, my lord. Shall I send in a tray?" The question was a show of support, because the requisite two polite cups meant a longer visit.

"No need. I will journey down to Caldicott Hall when I depart these premises. The traveling coach is stuffed with refreshments."

He left me outside the family parlor, a place where I'd once been welcomed as a close friend. I made myself comfortable, half closing the curtains on the garden windows. The morning sun was bright, and the less I saw of bright sunshine, the happier my eyes were.

The room was vacant somehow. No worn pair of slippers sat by the swept hearth. No sewing basket occupied a windowsill. Neither magazine, nor books, nor correspondence suggested anybody had spent a pleasant hour in what should have been one of the most comfortable rooms in the house.

I was contemplating closing the curtains altogether when Hyperia arrived.

"Jules." She left the door half open. "A pleasure to see you."

I bowed, though Hyperia hadn't curtseyed or offered her hand in welcome. "Likewise, always. You're looking well."

My dearest Perry looked ruthlessly composed. She wore a day dress of rust brown, a color that should have flattered her, except that this morning, the darker hue left her washed out.

"Healy was rude to you, wasn't he, Jules?"

Some unwritten rule said that gentlemen kept their differences from the ladies, but this was Hyperia, and I was keeping enough from her thanks to Tait and his missing wife.

"Your brother disapproves of me, but he stopped short of turning me away. I'm at something of a loss to know why he continues to hold me in dislike."

She stalked across the room and drew the curtains open. "He thinks you're courting me."

Good. I turned my back to the morning sun. "I've explained to him that procreation is beyond me, and you've been made aware of that limitation." I should have blushed to admit my failing aloud, except that I was angry with Healy West, angry with John Tait, angry with Evelyn's prevaricating sisters, and I'd soon be out of patience with Evelyn herself.

"You *told* him? Jules, that's private."

"Hyperia, the curtains..."

She yanked them closed all the way. "Sorry. I hadn't considered your eyes. What business is it of Healy's if you and I are friends?"

"I don't typically declare my love for mere friends, Perry, and Healy is no fool."

She glanced at the door, waved me to a corner of the sofa, then took a wing chair at a right angle to my seat.

"Healy is up to something," Hyperia said. "I don't know what troubles him, but he's cross with the staff, out until all hours, then closeted with the solicitors for half the afternoon. I dine alone at every meal, and yet, he all but insisted I return to London. I thought I knew my brother, but he's become an increasingly unpleasant enigma."

I did not want to hear this, though Hyperia's confidences were always safe with me. "Shall you return to the Hall with me?"

She traced the brocade pattern on the chair's upholstery. "I daren't. Healy was wroth that you escorted me to Town."

"Have you any notion why his animosity is so intense? He believed that I jilted you, so I shared the relevant particulars with him, but today he was barely civil to me." The old scandal—that I was a traitor of such shameful iniquity that I'd traded my brother's life for my freedom—might fuel his distaste, but Wellington himself had acknowledged me before polite society.

Who was Healy West to question the Duke of Wellington's judgment when it came to my military career? Who was I, for that matter?

"Has Healy been unlucky in love?" I asked. Nothing soured a young man's disposition as could Cupid misfiring an arrow.

Hyperia stared at the carpet. "Possibly. Parliament is back in Town, and yet, Healy isn't socializing. He inveigled me home by claiming to need a hostess, except that he apparently doesn't."

"He needed you away from me." Why? Unless Healy was, indeed, thinking of marrying Hyperia off. "Does he object to me courting you, or are all suitors off-limits?"

Her head came up. "Healy well knows my views on childbearing, Jules."

The syllogism completed itself easily enough. "And he knows I cannot inflict that fate upon you. Ergo, you might well marry me in some sort of friendly union of mutual, passionless convenience."

The notion broke my heart, but to see Hyperia marched up the church aisle into the arms of another would shatter me utterly.

I had no use for being shattered utterly. France had taught me that, at least.

"That's..." Hyperia rose and paced before the empty hearth. "That's ridiculous, but logical. Logical for Healy. A white marriage. All the ducal consequence, no more spinster sister cluttering up the house. Ye gods, I wish women over the age of one-and-twenty could dwell someplace like the Albany, all of us in congenial proximity, but independent and unbothered by our wider family."

She had a point. Ladies could and did live in such arrangements—in bordellos and convents—and never in as great a degree of luxury as the bachelors at the Albany enjoyed. Where on earth could Evelyn Tait be biding?

"Write to Lady Ophelia," I said, getting to my feet. "She might know if Healy's gambling losses are overwhelming him, if he's made bad investments, or if he's been deemed an unsuitable parti for next year's crop of heiresses. You know your brother, and if you sense that something is amiss with him, then something is amiss.

I'll interrogate her personally when I'm back at the Hall this evening."

Something had been amiss with Harry prior to his last disastrous mission. His mood had been off. I'd surmised that he'd been keeping something from me, and thus I'd followed him when he'd left camp by dark of night.

"I'll miss you." Hyperia took my hand in both of hers. "I've been missing you when you bide only a few streets away. I take it Evelyn Tait isn't lurking in Ardath's attic?"

I considered our joined hands. "Ardath claims not to know where Evelyn is, and I shouldn't even tell you that much."

Hyperia slipped free of my grasp. "Why not? I might have a material contribution to make to this inquiry, Jules, but you insist on keeping this distance. Ardath Deloitte puts on airs. She was the spoiled youngest sister, with a few pretensions to beauty. Because all of her older sisters were married off, she knew she could have a second or a third Season, and she enjoyed herself accordingly."

Information I'd not had, but it explained one small puzzle. "Then she has reason to hate John Tait, because her flirtation with him is why she was married to Deloitte after a very short courtship. Tait ended her reign in Mayfair, if a reign she had."

"Flirtation?" Hyperia resumed her seat. "Ardath and John flirted? Surely that was nothing more than friendliness on both of their parts. I can't imagine John truly crossing such a line with his wife's sister."

Botheration and perdition. "You will please not mention my admission to anybody, especially not Tait, and I really must be going."

Hyperia was back on her feet. "You really ought to tell me what you've found out so far about Evelyn, Jules. I am sure I do know something useful, except I have no idea what that might be because you insist on being so blasted closemouthed."

"Not closemouthed, Perry, please. I am endeavoring, with limited success, to treat Tait's situation confidentially."

She glowered at me. "You didn't treat the situation at the Makepeace house party confidentially. You didn't treat Viscount Reardon's disappearance or Leander's contretemps confidentially."

I wish I'd never agreed to investigate Evelyn Tait's disappearance. "Tait esteems you greatly, and he's concerned that his reputation remain untarnished in your eyes. Even something as unimportant as misconstrued friendliness with Ardath might reduce your respect for him, and he doesn't want that."

"John is a good man. He's not a saint. I of all people know that. I'm not a saint either."

I put a fingertip to her lips lest she go on to admit that they had been unsaintly together while I had frozen my manly humors to bits in the Pyrenes.

"Let's leave it at that," I said, tracing the outline of her upper lip. So soft, so stubborn, and so dear. "Please, for the sake of my dignity, let's part on a less acrimonious note."

She caught my hand, then caught me close and commenced kissing me like a woman intent on proving a point. Gently at first, then with increasing ardor, until I had both arms around her and was returning fire with everything in me.

God in heaven, Hyperia felt *good* pressed close to me. Alive, lovely, eager for shared pleasure... I was so involved in the sensation of her tongue tracing my lips that when arousal stirred to life, I simply went on kissing her.

Hyperia found her self-control before I even thought to make the attempt, so enthralled was I with her means of parting on a less acrimonious note. We stood in a loose embrace, panting and, in my case, dazed.

I was dimly aware that the door was only half closed, though Healy was more than welcome to find us *in flagranti osculum*.

"Jules?"

"Hmm?" She bore the wonderful fragrance of jasmine. Her shape was wonderful. Everything about Hyperia West was wonderful.

"Would a marriage between us truly be passionless?" She glossed a hand over my falls, where—to my shock and delight—I harbored nascent evidence contradicting all claims to passion's absence.

I gathered her close. "I don't know, Perry. I honestly don't know. I've been told to give it time, that the situation can right itself eventually, but it's been a year, and... I just don't know."

I was equally uncertain if she wanted the situation to right itself—she who had a near terror of childbirth—or if she preferred the alternative. An affectionate eunuch of a husband would never threaten her with motherhood.

"Should I apologize for kissing you?" she asked, stepping back.

"Never. Should I apologize for kissing you back?"

"Not if you value your life." She was very certain on that point.

"Then I will wish you good day and expect you to maintain a loyal correspondence with Lady Ophelia, despite Healy's disapproval. In a pinch, my sisters can also be relied upon to get word to me of any urgent developments. And don't forget the pigeons."

"Right. Pigeons. I won't be telling your sisters that I miss you."

I had been missing Hyperia, too, not only in my heart, but also in my mind, in the part of me that delighted in puzzles and investigations, but delighted equally in Hyperia's unique perspective on life and on me as I went about my inquiries.

"When I have found Evelyn Tait, you and I will contrive a means of spending some time together, and Healy can go to blazes."

She smiled, albeit the expression was a bit forced. "Agreed. Away with you, Jules, and promise me you'll be careful."

I bowed and took my leave, pleased with the kiss, troubled with the discussion, and vexed at Healy West. Hyperia had not seen me to the door, as a cordial hostess would have. I consoled myself with the thought that she'd needed some privacy to compose herself, but the argument was weak, and I knew it.

Damn Healy West and all siblings who took it into their heads to meddle.

"I didn't expect you back quite so soon," Lady Ophelia said as Leander wrapped his arms about my waist. "Child, your uncle merely nipped into Town. What is all the fuss about?"

I picked up the boy and perched him on my hip so that he and I were eye to eye. "You missed me?"

He nodded and mashed his nose against my neck. "Mama said you were a soldier. My papa was a soldier."

And his papa had died. Ergo, I was an unreliable quantity. "I'm not a soldier anymore, Leander. I will never be a soldier again now that I'm Uncle Arthur's heir. The next time I go up to Town, your mother might let you come with me."

He speared me with the look of a child inclined to fixate on details. "Will you ask her?"

"When next I see her, I will." I didn't hold out much hope of an affirmative answer, given the uncertainties swirling about the boy. Why was I chasing Evelyn's Tait's cold trail when I might have been seeing Leander more firmly situated?

Leander put his hand on my cheek so that I could not look away. "You *promise*, Uncle Julian? Promise you'll ask Mama if I can travel to Town with you?"

"I promise I will ask." I put the child down—he was a solid armful—and he immediately seized my hand.

"Mama said I could show you my soldiers, Uncle Julian. I set them up over by the fireplace. We're trooping the color."

Lady Ophelia was looking troubled, the nurserymaid hovered by the window, and I did not want to play soldiers. The journey from Town had been dusty and bone-racking, and I wanted to track Arthur down before supper.

If he hadn't planned on taking a few pigeons with him on his travels, he would by the time we'd finished our next conversation.

"Come see my soldiers, Uncle Julian." Leander pulled on my hand, and while I was aware that he'd been through much and was likely at a fretful point in his day and had been worrying at length about *me,* I also didn't care for such demanding behavior.

"Be a good uncle," Lady Ophelia murmured. "Give the lad twenty minutes now, and the rest of his day will go more smoothly."

Twenty minutes. How many times had I intruded on my father's morning paper or quiet stroll about the garden and kept him captive for twice that long? I claimed to want children, and then I begrudged my nephew twenty minutes.

"Very well," I said, taking a seat cross-legged on the carpet and hauling Leander into my lap. "What is this trooping-the-color business, and are those the Coldstream Guards prancing about at the edge of the rug?"

Leander explained to me that a parade of regimental flags was an exercise to assist illiterate soldiers to learn which emblems went with which regiment and also a fine day out *for the toffs*. The first part was dubious lore, the second part entirely true. When the regiments in all their parade finery marched past the monarch, half of London turned out to enjoy the spectacle.

I made a few comments, about the order of the procession and ladies' hats spooking the drum horses as French cannons never had, and soon half an hour had passed. In the ducal nursery, Leander had an embarrassment of amusements, including Hessian mercenary figures, mounted cavalry, and French hussars.

"You have spent hours with your soldiers, haven't you?" I asked, rising.

"My papa was a soldier."

The nurserymaid's expression was determinedly blank.

"Many men were soldiers, Leander, and ladies followed the drum, too, but Old Boney has been buttoned up on a miserable island far out to sea. He's not coming back ever again."

Leander scrambled to his feet, but made no grab for my hand. "He came back once already. We had the Hundred Days and Waterloo. Waterloo was a great battle where Wellington won everything."

"Wellington nearly lost everything, my boy. I was there."

Leander looked puzzled. "Did you save the day?"

"I... survived. Many others did not. Weather had a lot to do with who won." That and the last-minute arrival of Blücher's reinforcements. "The French set themselves the task of charging across a veritable bog, and that's nearly always a bad tactic."

"The Jacobites charged across a bog at Culloden, and Good King George's army *slaughtered* the traitors." Leander stuck out a foot and swept the entire 95th Rifles off their feet.

Maybe I wanted only daughters. "Your grasp of history remains rudimentary, but we have time to address the situation. Your nurse is giving me pointed looks. Is it time to wash up for supper?"

"Yes, my lord. Time and past. Master Leander, please wash your hands."

Leander dropped to his knees and began resurrecting his sharpshooters. "Mama's not here. I don't have to wash my hands until Mama is here."

His tone was dismissive, taunting even. *Bratty.*

"Good heavens." I scowled at my nephew with a severity that was only partly feigned. "You have disobeyed a direct order from your first lieutenant, Private Leander. A very serious offense."

Leander rose and tried for a smile. "Beekins isn't a first lieutenant."

"She is the immediate authority charged with keeping you safely and constructively occupied. You disrespect her or disobey her at your peril, young sir. Recruits have been court-martialed for less. An apology is in order."

Leander peered at me, probably in hopes that I was teasing, though I was not.

"Sorry, Beekins."

I did not relent. "And?"

"And it won't happen again, and I'll wash my hands now."

So he did know how to apologize, and he grasped exactly what his offense had been. "Well done. Enjoy your supper. I'll tell you more about Waterloo when I visit tomorrow, provided Beekins gives you a favorable report."

Leander trudged over to the wash basin and began scrubbing his paws.

"I mean that, Beekins," I said. "If that boy gives you trouble, thwarts your authority, or shows ungentlemanly inclinations, you will please inform me." *As the twig is bent, so is the tree inclined.* Old Mr. Pope had been right about that much.

She watched him using a brush on his fingernails. "He's a good boy, my lord, but he's bored, and his mother spends less and less time with him. He's a smart lad and ready for his letters, but it's not my place to say what's to be done with him."

"You have ideas."

Leander rinsed his hands and shook them vigorously, sending water droplets all over His Majesty's forces.

"I'm just the nurserymaid, my lord."

Meaning, she'd likely been minding children since she'd turned seven years old. "Think about what would improve Leander's situation, Beekins, and you and I will speak at greater length when we have privacy."

She favored me with a hint of a smile. "Yes, my lord. Lady Ophelia will likely speak to you on the same topic."

"I appreciate the warning. Please remind the boy what towels are for, and I will see you on the morrow."

I left the nursery suite with an unbecoming sense of relief. I'd thought of Leander as a sweet boy to whom life had been unfair. No father, a mother reduced to subterfuges and desperate measures in the midst of penury, uprooted from all he'd known...

Now Arthur was preparing to take ship, the lad's mother was playing least in sight, and I had business that frequently took me away from home and hearth. Perhaps Lady Ophelia had some notion what could be done to give the boy a sense of stability and purpose, because I hadn't the first clue.

CHAPTER TEN

Supper was a quiet affair. I was tired, Arthur was preoccupied, and Lady Ophelia declined to entertain us with her usual font of small talk.

"Julian, you have yet to give me the news from Town," she said when Arthur had excused himself.

"I was barely in Town. I dropped Hyperia at her brother's doorstep, chatted up Ardath Deloitte and Lina Hanscomb, popped by Hatchards, and came home." As a younger man, I would have packed a lot more activity and a lot less sleep into a one-day excursion in London. "Leander troubles me."

"He's a Caldicott male. They have a natural inclination to be troublesome."

Something was bothering my dear godmother. "The world does not know he's a Caldicott male, and what is the point of raising him here at the Hall if not to favor him with the family connection?"

Her ladyship rose before I could hold her chair. "This discussion begs for a glass of Arthur's calvados. I favor it in autumn."

I offered her my arm when we reached the corridor. "I'm not

imagining that Leander is..." Testing the limits of his freedom in the nursery, certainly. "Unsettled?"

"The poor child is coming undone. You had sisters to keep you in line. Older brothers, dedicated retainers. He hasn't even a regular playmate. Beekins does what she can, and Millicent has been trying to be both regularly present in the nursery and regularly absent. She's spending every spare moment in the sewing room."

I took that as progress, though toward what goal? "What does Millicent say about her son's lack of respect for Beekins?"

"I haven't asked her."

"Ah." Another job for the soon-to-be-acting duke. "She continues to absent herself from even family meals, Godmama."

We reached the library, which was not quite cozy, despite roaring fires in both hearths. The night had turned blustery, the wind moaning down the flues and subtly stirring the curtains.

"I love autumn," Lady Ophelia said. "All two weeks of it. How did you leave matters with Hyperia?"

I poured us both drinks, rearranged some fire screens, and offered Godmama a seat in a reading chair. I took its twin, a perch upon which I'd read many a verse of Milton and Shakespeare and even a few of Mrs. Radcliffe's tales.

"Healy West has taken me into dislike," I said. "Hyperia reports that her brother is acting oddly, and I haven't time at the moment to investigate his grievance. I realize I am the subject of gossip, but I've been back in England for a year, I keep as much to myself as I can, and West understands that I meant his sister no insult by leaving her free to pursue other attachments."

"Except she's not free, is she?" Her ladyship sipped her drink, and by firelight, the youthful beauty she'd had in abundance was more in evidence. Lady Ophelia could be a flirt, a gossip, a curmudgeon, or a doting godmother, but seeing her in repose reminded me that she was also a widow—twice over—and a woman who'd buried two children.

"How do you bear it, my lady?" The question was out, all unpremeditated and awkward.

"Bear what? My life is generally an unbroken procession of delights, save for when you or one of your ilk vex me."

"I've lost one brother before his time. You've lost much more, and yet, you claim to be happy. If Arthur should come to any harm... I don't want to be the rubbishing duke. Not when the role has been filled so recently by men so much more able than I."

She was quiet for a moment while the fire crackled and wind soughed. "When Harry sang you the same lament—that he didn't want to be the duke—how did you console him?"

Insightful question, because Harry *had* sung the same lament, in every imaginable major and minor key. "I told him he wasn't the duke yet, and he might never be the duke, but if the title befell him, he would execute his duties in his own style. That being the duke allowed him that much freedom."

"And you were right—he was whining for nothing, as it turned out. Banter will guard Arthur's safety vigilantly, Jules, and you need not worry about Hyperia. She won't marry some vapid viscount to pay her brother's gambling debts."

That her ladyship should so easily divine my fears was unnerving, also comforting. "Healy has gambling debts?"

"Most young men about Town do."

"He's not entertaining, and he is out at all hours, then meeting at length with his solicitors."

"Perhaps Healy is preparing to go courting."

I tasted my drink, which I, too, associated with autumn—apples, pears, warm spices, and a pleasant heat. "I want to go to bed and sleep until noon, and I want to charge right back to London and get to the bottom of Healy's odd behavior."

"You miss your dear Perry."

"Dreadfully. Tait has asked me to keep the less savory aspects of his situation from her notice, and she feels the distance keenly." *As do I.*

Her ladyship's gaze went to a portrait of the late duke over the mantel. The shifting shadows from the fire gave His Grace a spectral air, though he was a jovial ghost, as ghosts went.

"When my first husband died, I realized that much of our conversation had been argument. We indulged in reasoned debate, bickering, philosophical disputes, spats, squabbles, and everything in between. After he was gone, I saw what a great honor he'd done me, engaging me like that, as an equal and a partner in conflict. I have never found his like in that regard, and I miss him still."

"You're saying a little absence might be salubrious? I spent years on the Peninsula missing her, my lady."

"But did she spend years missing you?"

"I haven't asked her." Had she sought comfort in John Tait's arms? None of my bloody business. "I wish I'd never agreed to look into Tait's problem. Everything I've discovered thus far says he brought the difficulty on himself. He was a fine husband for the first six months following the nuptials, but by the end of the first year, his stock was plummeting in his wife's eyes."

"Reality intrudes, alas. What will you do about Leander?"

"Have you invited the Ingersoll child to visit the nursery?"

"I did, and Mrs. Ingersoll politely declined." Her ladyship fished in a skirt pocket and produced a single page twice folded.

I scanned the words, written in a hand worthy of a Swiss finishing school. No girlish flourishes, no blots or dashes. Invitation much appreciated, et cetera, but household matters at a fever pitch as is always the case this time of year, and perhaps later...

"*Are* household matters at a fever pitch?" I asked, tucking the epistle into my breast pocket.

Lady Ophelia finished her drink and returned her glass to the sideboard. "Julian, she's a village widow, barely gentry, and new to the area. Summoning her daughter to play with the Caldicott by-blow is hardly flattering to anybody."

I was abruptly more than simply tired. I was weary to my soul and lonely to my bones. "He's just a boy trying to cope with a world in tumult, for pity's sake, and the Caldicotts claim a dukedom, last time I checked. What sort of mother denies a lonely child the comfort of even a single afternoon with a playmate?"

"A sensible mother if the playmate isn't the right sort. You'd best resign yourself to dealing with Leander's irregular antecedents for the duration of his earthly sojourn, my lord. He's neither fish, nor flesh, nor good red herring, and he hasn't a father on hand to smooth his way."

I rose out of manners and from the sure conviction that I was at risk for spending the night dozing in the chair like the snoring dodderers gracing every club in St. James's.

"Leander has me." And I was determined to be enough.

"He has *us*, you hopeless man. He has us." She took my drink from my hand, finished my calvados, and put the glass beside her own. "What will you do about Tait's situation?"

Oh, him again. "Who set her cap for him besides Evelyn, Godmama? To whom did he send poetry besides her?"

"Now that is interesting. According to my recollections, amply aided by my journals, he provoked speculation regarding his intentions toward the Frampton girl—the oldest girl, not the one who's out now—and he made sheep's eyes at Miss Juniper Holland."

The name was vaguely familiar. "She married some German prince?"

"Indeed, and she's swanning about Hanover, claiming cousinship with all manner of royalty, but then, the German states are awash in princes and princesses. Miss Frampton married a wealthy Scot and hasn't been seen in London since her nuptials."

Two dead ends to go with a veritable collection of same. "What of the fellows who paid attention to Evelyn Hasborough? Surely she had a gallant or two?"

"She raced Jasper Thick in the park and won, and they were notably chummy after that. Thick was bosom bows with Henry Wendover, and I recall seeing the trio at Gunter's. Both Wendover and Thick escorted her to services a time or two, but neither fellow had much of a fortune."

I no longer carried a copy of DeBrett's in my head, but I did recall a few pertinent details. "Thick's brother is an earl."

"With five healthy sons."

Still, to marry into any titled family would have been a coup for the likes of Evelyn Hasborough. "What of the other fellow... Wendover? Bought his colors, didn't he?"

"Decorated, mentioned in the dispatches, and brought home a Spanish bride. He's an MP for some obscure hamlet, thanks to his uncle, the viscount."

Wendover would also have been a desirable connection for Evelyn, but she'd settled instead for John Tait, perhaps of necessity.

"Might Evelyn and John have anticipated the vows?"

"What has that to do with anything, Julian? Young people are supposed to try each other's paces. If it doesn't go well, they can tell everybody the settlements proved unworkable, and no scandal attaches. I vow the French still hold a portion of your intellect captive."

My intellect, my health, my dreams. "I've not moved in Society for years, Godmama. Allowances must be made."

"Not by me, you lout. Off to bed with you, and stop fretting. Things tend to look better in the morning."

No, they didn't, but that I had somebody to offer me platitudes was reassuring. "I will miss you when you decamp for Paris, madam."

"Then come with me."

Had she jabbed me in the ribs with her elbow, I could not have been more unprepared for the blow. "I loathe the thought of setting foot in France. Going to Belgium for the Hundred Days, hearing French spoken on every hand... I can't go back, my lady. That much freedom is yet mine to claim."

She took up the candle snuffer and made the rounds of the sconces, though the job belonged to the footmen.

"Give it time, Julian. You've come a long way, and I have faith that you, too, might someday consider your life a procession of unbroken delights."

I might, ages and ages hence, but today was not that day. "Shall I light you up?"

"I am not yet ready to surrender to the arms of Morpheus, but you look thoroughly knackered. Off to bed with you."

I trudged up the steps to my apartment, which was blessedly cozy and quiet. I drifted off to sleep, though my dreams were plagued by visions of Healy West refusing me admittance to his house and Leander pitching his toy soldiers out the nursery window—foot, horse, and cannon, one by one into the abyss.

∼

Things did not look better in the morning, but they looked manageable. My plan was straightforward: I'd shake the truth of Evelyn's location out of Margery Semple, confer with Evelyn herself, and leave that lady's husband to deal with any particulars.

Once I'd resolved the Tait situation, I'd sort out Healy West, Millicent Dujardin, and my darling nephew. Somewhere in the middle of all those undertakings, I'd bid Arthur farewell for who knew how long.

"Julian!" The duke himself hailed me from the stable yard. He swung off his steed—exercising Beowulf was another duty I'd take on soon—and handed the reins to a groom. "Beautiful morning for a hack."

His Grace was in suspiciously good spirits, suggesting that he'd encountered Osgood Banter in the course of his outing.

How lovely for them. "Your Grace." I bowed. "Nice weather indeed."

"Rain by nightfall, no doubt. How goes the battle?"

Arthur had an ability to appear caught up in his myriad duties—harvest was well under way, travel preparations were ongoing, solicitors were a weekly fact of his existence—while he yet remained apprised of details that should have been beneath his notice. He was much like Wellington, who'd been prodigiously dignified even on the day of battle, but who'd yet had a sense for how the common soldier was faring. Wellington had kept his infamous army in rum and rations, harrying Parliament for supplies almost as diligently as he'd harried the French across Spain.

"If by battle you refer to my efforts to locate Evelyn Tait, I'm making progress."

"Lady Ophelia tells me Healy West has been less than gracious toward you."

The groom who'd taken charge of Beowulf was spending biblical ages loosening the girth, running up the stirrups, and picking out the horse's feet.

"Let's walk, shall we?" I gestured to a path leading in the direction of the stream that ran before the Hall and wandered from thence to the home farm and the home wood.

"You are not to dash my spirits, Julian," Arthur said, striding along beside me. "I forbid it."

"I'll dash you in the creek if you think to give me orders, Your Grace."

"That's better. You should inquire of Banter regarding West's situation. They were friendly, once upon a time."

The ground became boggy indeed. "*Friendly?*"

"Not like that. Get your mind out of the bedroom. *Friendly* friendly. Osgood Banter is well-liked, gets along with everybody, the darling of the hostesses, and so forth. He has charm."

Charm was apparently cause for puzzlement. "They were friendly, but they aren't now?"

"They are polite now, in the manner of men who are avoiding each other, as if a debt has been forgiven or a drunken confidence ignored. Banter won't say much about it, which inclines me to believe West has somehow made a fool of himself."

"I'm off to call on Margery Semple now, and then I should make a report to John Tait. If Banter will be in residence tomorrow, I'll call on him then." Assuming I wasn't haring back to London in search of Evelyn Tait.

"I don't care for Mr. Semple," Arthur said, picking up a flat rock and skipping it across the stream. "He's on the board of aldermen, on the vestry committee, has an eye on the commission of the peace. His fingers reach into many a pie, but he doesn't seem to be able to make his business prosper."

"Such are the times. What is his business?"

"Dry goods, though he owns a farm that he lets out."

Dry goods covered anything other than hardware and fresh produce. "One doesn't let out prime acres."

"Ask Tait about that, if it's relevant. I'll invite Banter for dinner tonight. Spare you the distance."

I actually liked the hours I spent on horseback, provided the weather was halfway obliging. Still, I'd be in the saddle a fair amount even without a jaunt over to Bloomfield.

"If Banter is free, that would suit."

Arthur skipped another rock. "He's getting free, thanks to you. If Osgood hasn't expressed his gratitude, then I'm expressing mine."

His Grace referred to a little situation involving a misplaced hound, a hopeless bully, and an ambitious spot of rural blackmail that I'd recently been able to foil.

"I did what was asked of me," I said. "Luck was on my side." Eventually, I'd had some luck, thank providence.

"When I'm traveling..." Arthur picked up three stones and began to juggle them. "Will you still poke your nose into puzzles and mysteries?"

"If asked to do so, yes."

"You will be asked. You're getting a reputation for untangling sticky situations discreetly. Vicar mentioned as much, and if he's hearing about it, then talk of your investigations has spread to many interesting corners."

"I am not daunted by a bit of talk." I was no longer *as* daunted by talk, rather.

"Good." His Grace neatly caught all three rocks. "These inquiries have a cheering effect on your demeanor. Lady Ophelia agrees with me."

I did not agree with him. "Arthur, will you do me a favor?"

He was at once on his dignity. "You don't have to ask, Julian. Name the deed and consider it done."

I watched sunlight play on the stream where I'd waded and frolicked as a boy. "Teach Leander how to skip stones. Show him that you can juggle. Do it before you take ship."

Arthur tossed the rocks one by one into the water. "Leander's a bit young for skipping stones and juggling. He might grow frustrated."

"Show him, all the same, that His Grace of Waltham can and does skip and juggle rocks."

"Why?"

"It's important." I punched Arthur on the arm and departed, my throat unaccountably tight. Papa had taught me to skip rocks, too, or taught Harry while I'd watched, but the juggling... That had apparently been a gift reserved for Arthur, and it was a gift I wanted to see passed on to my—our—nephew.

"Good hunting!" Arthur called after me.

I waved without turning back. My oldest brother's life at long last was becoming an unbroken procession of delights, and I was delighted for him. Absolutely delighted.

༄

"My lord, what a surprise." Margery Semple curtseyed politely and welcomed me into the same parlor where we'd had tea on my previous visit. "A pleasant surprise. I wasn't aware you'd come back from London already."

Why should she be concerned with my comings and goings? "My business in Town was concluded, though I must say not very satisfactorily. Shall we be seated?"

The pug was nowhere in evidence, though the same pressed flowers and embroidered samplers graced the walls. *He that hath knowledge spareth his words: and a man of understanding is of an excellent spirit.* Proverbs, though I knew not which chapter or verse, and more than a little annoying, in my present unexcellent and baffled spirits.

Mrs. Semple gestured me to a wing chair and ensconced herself in a corner of the sofa. She hadn't rung for tea, though when last I'd called, I'd been invited to return at my whim and pleasure. Clearly, Ardath and Margery were in the habit of exchanging express dispatches.

"I called upon Mrs. Deloitte," I said, taking my seat, "but she professed to have had no warning from you regarding the purpose of my inquiry or my need to consult her."

Mrs. Semple brushed her fingers over the fringe of a pink pillow. "I certainly did write to her, my lord. We are all most concerned for Evelyn. Have been for years. I hazard that Ardath was behind on her correspondence, and another letter from me was hardly cause for her to catch up. Either that, or my letter went astray. The king's mail is reliable, but not perfect."

Plausible excuses, of course, except that Sussex mail was routinely delivered to London within twenty-four hours, and no snowstorms, deluges, civil disturbances, or acts of God had troubled the stage routes in recent days.

"Not only was Mrs. Deloitte unforthcoming," I said, "but when I asked her what other London gentlemen had caught Evelyn's eye before Tait proposed, she expressly commended me to consult with you. You, on the other hand, expressly commended me to consult with Mrs. Deloitte, claiming she knew Evelyn far better than you did, particularly during the relevant period. What am I to make of this confusion, Mrs. Semple? Must I continue flying back and forth between you two sisters to confirm your mutual ignorance? Did either of you know Evelyn at all?"

Mrs. Semple set the pillow aside. "My lord, you must understand that during her London Season, Evelyn was bearing up as best she could. Tall women are at a disadvantage socially, and Evelyn was the tallest of us all. She was no sylph either and preferred an active life. She was not the sort of young lady who attracted gallants and followers. She preferred books to fashion, biscuits to *bons mots*. Her settlements were generous by the standards of the shire, but not by Mayfair standards."

A lovely little sermon that dodged my question. "So you were well aware of how she was going on in London?"

Mrs. Semple rose, though I'd been present all of five minutes. "I have three sisters, a dozen nieces and nephews, six children of my own, and a husband who expects an orderly, peaceful household. Yes, I knew of Evelyn's situation, but no, I did not dwell in her pocket. If my lord will excuse me, today is market day, and Mr. Semple is bringing company home for supper. To see you is a pleasure, but perhaps you'll send a note beforehand if you intend to call again?"

I remained in the chair for a moment, exercising the petty power of a man even a woman of her formidable dimensions could not haul bodily from the house. When I rose, I remained by my seat rather than oblige my hostess by scurrying off like a chastised dog.

"Then you maintain that Evelyn had eyes only for John Tait?"

"If she had other suitors, Ardath would know. I can send that query to her in a letter, or I'm sure on a second visit—provided you give her some warning and call at the usual hour—she'd be happy to entertain you."

Evelyn had been on let's-go-for-an-ice terms with an earl's brother and viscount's favorite nephew. She'd made a spectacle of herself racing in Hyde Park in their company. Margery Semple would have been well aware of such connections, and yet, *she was lying to me.*

"Where is your sister, Mrs. Semple?" I put the question gently, because I had no intention of galloping back to London just to see Mrs. Deloitte once again fleeing through the figurative postern gate, as Mrs. Semple was now intent on fleeing should I attempt to call again.

"My lord, I do not know where Evelyn is. I honestly, absolutely do not know, and neither does Ardath. We have racked our brains and cudgeled our memories and even considered consulting that odious man Evelyn married, but I have told you all I know, and now I must ask you to leave."

Why? Why receive me graciously, send me chasing wild geese through Mayfair, and now refuse me a cup of tea?

"Are you afraid for her?"

Mrs. Semple drew in a sharp breath and marched for the door. "Of course I am afraid for her. She is my sister, and I wouldn't put the dirtiest deed past that husband of hers. I very much fear he's wasting your time, my lord, or worse, using your good offices to obscure a heinous crime indeed."

I accompanied Mrs. Semple to the front door, donned my hat and spectacles, and cast about for a way to leave on a less acrimonious note.

"Evelyn has some money left," I said. "The last of the pearls—the choker—was sold only a few weeks ago. She shouldn't be out of funds quite yet, but she will be soon."

"Perhaps, if what you say is true, Evelyn has bought passage to a new life in a new land."

"After five years of biding in Merry Olde, close to family and familiar haunts? I can't see that making sense."

Mrs. Semple opened the door. "None of this makes sense, my lord. John Tait sounding the alarm after all these years, you poking your titled beak into matters that do not concern you. I vow Evelyn is causing nearly as much upheaval in absentia as she caused when present and accounted for."

Resentment colored that observation, resentment and bewilderment.

I bowed and took my leave, mentally drafting the report I'd make to Tait. My interview with Mrs. Semple confirmed that Evelyn's sisters were colluding to make my job harder, with each sister insisting I waste my time discussing some particular with the other sibling who professed bottomless ignorance.

As I climbed into the saddle and turned Atlas in the direction we'd come, a silver lining presented itself—Evelyn had *chosen* Tait. If she'd wanted to exploit her appeal to men from titled families, she could have.

She hadn't bothered, which suggested that at one time, Evelyn had truly been in love with John Tait. I found that conclusion somewhat cheering, though I could not say why.

CHAPTER ELEVEN

"My housekeeper is unwell," Tait said, welcoming me personally into his abode. "Some intestinal matter, or so I'm to believe. One doesn't inquire too closely when the ladies are indisposed." His signature smile was nowhere in evidence, and grooves bracketed his mouth.

"Is anybody else in the household ill?" I harbored an intense, personal aversion to dysentery, which had carried off a good number of Wellington's soldiers.

"No other casualties, thank heavens. Will the library do, my lord? The formal parlor is being aired, and the informal parlor is very informal at the moment. Harvest keeps us all busy, and domestic standards suffer accordingly."

"I enjoy libraries. They can say a lot about an entire household."

Tait showed me to a largish room with French doors that opened onto the back terrace. Afternoon sunshine slanted onto a carpet only slightly worn. The hearths were swept, though the andirons could have used a blacking, and the sconces were polished. The chairs were comfortably cushioned, albeit no longer in the first blush of youth, and the books were rather fewer than I expected a library to have.

Was I seeing evidence of financial hardship, or merely life at a busy, venerable country manor?

"Evelyn had most of the books put into storage," Tait said, glancing around at half-empty shelves. "She said the collection was largely tripe, and she was gradually creating a worthwhile selection. She was right too. My mother bought boxes of books at estate sales. Didn't want the village folk to think us unlettered."

"Evelyn enjoyed books?" I noted Mr. Scott's verses, Mrs. Radcliffe, Mrs. Burney, Mr. Swift, and myriad others both witty and entertaining. Mr. Wordsworth had earned his place, as had Restoration playwrights, the Bard, and Mr. Burns. Moliere was represented, and I was surprised to see a fair amount of classical literature in both Latin and Greek.

"Evelyn enjoyed books very much. Should have been one of those lady authors who pokes fun at polite society while pretending to set store by decorum and gentility. She started writing a novel, in fact, right after we were married, and I was amazed that she had the..." Tait fell silent, glanced around at the half-empty shelves, and linked his hands behind his back. "This ancient history is neither here nor there, my lord. I apologize for maundering on. Do have a seat. Shall I ring for a tray?"

Tait's manner was different somehow. Perhaps harvest was taking a toll on his energies, but his attitude was also less cocky, to use one of Lady Ophelia's words.

"I haven't had luncheon," I said. "A cup of tea would be appreciated." True to Arthur's prediction, morning's cerulean skies had given way to a few wispy clouds from the west. I wanted to conclude my business and get home, lest those clouds join together and make a sopping-wet fool of me later in the afternoon.

Tait tugged the bell-pull twice and led me to a pair of wing chairs before an empty hearth. "You've been to London."

I'd sent him an epistle sketching only plans—a call on Ardath Deloitte, a call on Lina Hanscomb.

"I've been to London, and if Margery Semple has her way, I will wear out my saddle traveling back and forth to Town while learning nothing of Evelyn's whereabouts. I did, though, talk with some shopkeepers on Ludgate Hill."

I acquainted Tait with the fact that the jewelry hoard had gradually been liquidated over the past few years, the last of it being sold only recently.

"This finding," Tait said, tapping a finger against the arm of his chair, "weighs against the notion that Evvie has taken up a bigamous union with a dashing sea captain."

An interesting conclusion to draw from the evidence. "This finding weighs against Evelyn having *died*." Sea captains, dashing or otherwise, could be impecunious, gone for years on end, or poor managers of their wealth. "It's possible somebody stole her jewels and has gradually been turning them to cash, saving her favorite piece for last by coincidence, but not likely."

Tait rose and paced before the empty hearth. The landscape holding pride of place above the mantel was an idealized, or perhaps historical, rendition of Tait's manor house, a pair of matched chestnuts in harness to a curricle racing up the drive. The season was summer, given the blooms rioting about the fountain, and the manor was flanked by stately oaks twice the size of the specimens I'd seen.

The mantel itself was bare, save for three… ah, Evelyn's diaries were stacked on one end. Tait hadn't returned them to the mausoleum upstairs.

"I've been reading them," he said, following my gaze. "Truly reading them. Evvie was an excellent writer, and she spared nobody's blushes in those pages. I tell myself I'll read just one more month, but the candles gutter, and I realize… I'm sorry, my lord. I want to hear what you have to say, but I am a bit fatigued. The mind wanders." Tait sank back into his chair, and further conversation was suspended by the arrival of the tea tray.

Either Tait or his kitchen had taken pity on me. A plate of ham and cheese tarts was among the offerings, along with sliced apples and every soldier's fast friend, a stack of shortbread.

"Don't stand on ceremony," Tait said. "I haven't much appetite." He poured out for us both and left me to fill a plate for myself. "Evelyn was miserable. Her diaries either make that plain to me in a new way, or remind me of matters I've worked hard to forget. We were so happy, and then..." He swirled his tea, a stout China black, no skimping or reusing the tea leaves.

"What happened, Tait?" I asked between tarts. "For better than six months, you and Evelyn were in love and doubtless in lust, and then it all curdled. What changed?"

He glanced at the diaries. "I don't know. Whatever it was, Evelyn didn't refer to any one incident explicitly, but I fell from grace in some way. Any friendly exchange on my part with another woman became rank infidelity. I realized at some point that Evelyn always had time to listen to the curate's woes, but never time to stand up with me at the assemblies, and then I started noticing how often she smiled at the curate, and... What a farce. If Evelyn were here now, I'd ask her what the hell happened to us, because I surely do not know."

I wanted to treat his claim skeptically. Tait had much to answer for under the heading of clodpated husbandly maneuvers. I had to admit, though, that I also sensed genuine bewilderment in his words.

One minute, he'd been a new husband enjoying all the privileges of his station, the next, he was nearing thirty and hoping to be neither cuckold nor widower. The world had shifted on me in similar ways. One minute, I'd been following my brother through the starry night, half on a lark, half fretting that he was up to foolishness. The next minute, French officers had materialized from the ether like demons rising from hell, and my life had never been the same.

"Evelyn's sisters claim to honestly not know where she is," I said, by way of moving the conversation forward. "She hasn't gone far from London, though, I can tell you that."

"Tell me that how?"

"Because sending any sort of valuables through the mail is to be avoided at all costs. You've probably received bank notes sent by halves, packages that were obviously opened, coins wrapped in stockings."

"I have, and I've sent them too. You think Evelyn is biding near Town?"

"She would not bide in Town," I replied, "because in the parts of London Evelyn could safely frequent, she'd risk being recognized, and she'd run through her coin too quickly. I suspect she's not far from Town, and somebody loyal to her can make the journey without too much effort."

Tait made the sort of face inspired by the taste of sour milk. "Margery seldom travels of late. She can't, what with being the brains behind her husband's limited mercantile success, the manager of his rented acres, and the mother of his six children. Semple isn't an idiot, but he's prone to fits of imagination, and grand plans don't see the bottom field marled."

"What of Ardath?"

"Ardath loves Town, loves being the wealthy merchant's gracious wife, though Deloitte's business isn't what it was now that the European markets are open to us again. Ardath never once came to see Evelyn after our marriage, and she hasn't visited Margery, that I know of, either."

I finished the last of my tarts and started on the apple slices. "How would you know where Margery Semple goes?"

Tait smiled with a hint of his former self-assurance. "The households were cordial at one point. Margery wouldn't spare me the time of day now, but Margery's cook and my cook remain friendly. The Royal Mail hasn't a patch on the village market day for relaying news."

True enough. "Evelyn will soon run out of funds, if she hasn't already. I am coming to think that her sisters have either betrayed her or lost her confidence. I believe them when they say they don't know where she is. Margery has implied that you are a murderer, and Ardath took the position that you were never good enough for Evelyn."

Tait winced. "Ardie said that?"

"She said you'd probably run through all of Evelyn's money, and you needed to remarry to repair your fortunes."

"She has learned to be nasty, then. A pity, but marriage to Deloitte hasn't been quite the featherbed she expected. He inherited some grand properties, but they're the kind that require cash and an army of servants to be kept presentable. Evvie tried to warn her, but Ardath saw a lot of gilded mirrors, pink marble, and exotic hardwoods. Deloitte looked the part, and he was offering to lay it all at her feet."

This was not the recitation of a self-absorbed bumpkin. "You and Evelyn discussed this?"

"When we weren't arguing or locked into a fuming silence, we were utterly compatible, my lord. Evelyn was no beauty, but she had beautiful endowments of common sense, humor, industry, and pragmatism. Also a formidable temper."

That last part seemed to amuse him. "You were fond of her."

"I was... head over ears isn't quite fair, but she made quite the impression on me. By the time I proposed, I realized I wasn't God's gift to Mayfair's heiresses, and I was surprised that Evvie hadn't any other offers. She was generously dowered, a talented manager, not too high in the instep... I counted myself fortunate to have won her hand."

"How generously was she dowered?"

Tait named a lump sum, to be invested in the cent-per-cents as the bride's portion of the dower funds, plus an annuity from some great-auntie that Tait dutifully added to the dower funds year by year, and the income from a tenant property Evelyn's papa had been able to free from the entail.

"She gets the property outright when she turns eight-and-twenty," Tait said, "and she was looking forward to that. Said my husbandry of the land needed modernizing, and she'd show me how to go about it."

"What happens if Evelyn doesn't survive to turn eight-and-twenty?" A hazy sort of dread was taking up residence in my guts. The sort of dread I associated with large numbers of armed French soldiers in much closer proximity to British forces than they were supposed to be.

Tait helped himself to a piece of shortbread. "If Evelyn dies without issue, the funds are distributed between me and her sisters, and the property is sold with the proceeds divided likewise. My family contributed to the dower funds handsomely, so a quarter of the total coming back to me isn't unreasonable. Why?"

I hesitated to share my theories, and a week ago, I would not have. Tait wasn't the same man he'd been a week ago, though. Whether reading Evelyn's diaries had affected him, or harvest-time fatigue dogged him, or the reality of Evelyn's possible death had reached him, he was a more worthy individual.

Sadder and wiser, perhaps.

"Who benefits, Tait? If Evelyn dies, who benefits?"

"I do, along with her sisters. I don't need her money, while Semple and Deloitte well might."

Or, more worrisomely, *her sisters* might and probably did. "How old is Evelyn?"

"She turns eight-and-twenty next month," Tait said. "Seems impossible that I've known her for a decade, and yet, she has become a stranger."

"Then she is soon to inherit that tenant property, and should she expire, her sisters stand to inherit a very pretty penny."

Tait stared at me. "Are you saying they've done away with her?"

"I'm saying they have a motive to do away with her. So do you, but I wasn't aware that both Mrs. Semple and Mrs. Deloitte might be in need of funds. Now I am."

I wanted to reread the diaries. I'd skimmed them previously, looking for names of people or places that might shed light on Evelyn's options. I sought to look for motives now and potential enemies rather than friends.

"Evelyn's sisters loved her," Tait said, rising. "Love her, rather. They bickered and spatted and complained about each other, but theirs was a loving family."

I stood as well. "People change, Tait. The Ardath you knew has become bitter and spiteful. Margery Semple is trying to raise six children and play the wife of a prosperous merchant on insufficient means. Evelyn loved you madly. You loved her too. You aren't that man anymore, and who's to say what Evelyn's sisters have become in the past ten years?"

"They aren't murderesses." He sounded uncertain of his own conclusion.

"I hope they are not, but the sooner I find your wife, the happier I will be. When you finish with the diaries, I'd like to read them again."

"You can take them now, my lord."

"When you finish with them will be sufficient, Tait. I suspect Evelyn left them behind for reasons, and you will glean more from them than I will." He'd put off truly reading them for five years, and now that he'd plucked up the courage to embark on the task, I wanted him to see it through.

"I glean a lot of heartache and a lot of grief in those pages."

"But that is not the whole story."

I bade him farewell before he could ask me what my next steps were. I'd confer with Lady Ophelia, chase down Jasper Thick of let's-go-for-an-ice fame if necessary, and then... what? I was haunted by the sense of missing something obvious—in the diaries or about the diaries, perhaps—but I was damned if I knew what. The library books, chosen for both edification and entertainment, were another clue I could not decipher.

I climbed back into the saddle, my head full of thoughts and forebodings. By the time I was once again on Caldicott property and riding around the village green, I'd formed a new theory of the situation.

Perhaps Evelyn had relied on her sisters to facilitate her escape from a frustrating marriage, but then her sisters had demanded coin in exchange for silence regarding her whereabouts. Evelyn, having very little coin left, had once again decamped, and this time even her sisters knew not where she dwelled.

That scenario fit the personalities as I'd encountered them, absolved all concerned of murder, and explained what information I had.

I could spin theories all day, though, and still not know where on earth Evelyn Tait, with her dwindling funds, might be biding. I was pondering that conundrum when I spotted Mrs. Ingersoll coming out of the chandler's shop. She hadn't seen me, which was fortunate, because my plans now included ambushing one unsuspecting widow.

~

"Mrs. Ingersoll, good day. Might I be of service as your porter?"

"My lord." She nodded and kept walking rather than stop and curtsey, and I fell in step beside her. "Greetings." She passed over her package and a woven basket of sundries. "If you will forgive a brisk pace, I'm on my way to the vicarage to retrieve Merri. Errands go more peacefully when she's otherwise occupied, but I don't want to impose on Mrs. Vicar's patience unnecessarily."

The parcel smelled of tallow rather than beeswax. The sundries included three skeins of blue yarn, an orange, a child's slate, a small box of chalk, and a potted plant that gave off the aroma of basil. I added the candles to the plunder in her bag and marched along smartly.

Even for a woman with some height, Mrs. Ingersoll covered ground quickly.

"You could leave Merri with us up at the Hall for an afternoon.

Young Leander is desperate for company his own age. Send a note, and we'll dispatch a maid to fetch her, or I will come myself."

Her pace slowed as we crossed the green. "Kind of you. Lady Ophelia did invite Merri to come play with Leander, but Merri had been cross with me just then, and I wasn't in the mood to bestow a special outing on her. I should have leaped at the invitation, I know."

She should have. For a widow new to the area to be given not only a seat at the duke's Sunday supper table, but also a chance to ingratiate herself further with the household... Though I well understood the folly of rewarding naughty behavior.

"We'll send another invitation on another day, and perhaps Merri will be better behaved. Did she ever know her father?" A personal question, but within the bounds of village nosiness.

"No."

"It must be hard when a child has only one parent and that parent has only one child. One would be protective of the other, of course, and devoted, but resentment might come into it too."

"Well, yes, but more to the point, Merri is lonely, and thus I have castigated myself for denying her an excursion to the Hall. I do want my child to be happy."

It is not good that the man should be alone... What of the woman? The children and the elders?

I seized village nosiness by the horns and posed another question. "Did I mistake the situation, or was John Tait acting a trifle lonely at Sunday supper?"

She smiled somewhat grimly. "Mr. Tait is lonely and troubled. I understand better now why that's the case. I'd mistaken him for a bachelor, you see."

All of my newfound compassion for Tait went straight into the nearest horse trough. "Did he misrepresent his circumstances the better to toy with your affections?" If so, I'd plant the man a facer, at least.

Mrs. Ingersoll laughed, a hearty boom of merriment at odds with her tidy dress and prim manner. A maid scrubbing the steps of the posting inn smiled at the sound, and a horse dozing at the smithy's hitching rail lifted its head abruptly.

"Toy with my affections? Not that, my lord. Never that. One marriage was enough for me. I understand Mr. Tait has set you to searching for his missing wife. Best of luck, but I told Mr. Tait that on no account should he look for the lady in hopes of a more permanent relationship with myself. I wish the missing Mrs. Tait a long and happy life wherever she is."

We crossed the lane circling the green and approached the gate to the vicarage. "Tait might not have meant to deceive you. All and sundry in the area know of his missing wife, and he likely assumed you'd been told."

"Give him the benefit of the doubt if you must, my lord."

"He might well be a widower. Even he doesn't know what's become of his missus."

"That is doubtless a hardship."

A hardship, and yet, Tait had nonetheless let himself flirt—at the very least—with Mrs. Ingersoll before he'd mentioned his errant wife.

"Please assure me he did not trifle with you."

She stopped at the gate. "Why interest yourself in such a tawdry topic?"

"What two people choose to do when private isn't tawdry, madam, if both consent on equal footing. If Tait lied to you and took that degree of advantage, he deserves a serious thrashing."

Her smile was mischievous. "I agree, but though I allowed Mr. Tait a few discreet liberties—he's a fine kisser, should anybody ask—he did not transgress quite as far as you suggest. People speculate about widows, and I'm prepared for that, but they also speculate about Merri. Is she legitimate? Does she look like her father? I have no patience with such questions aimed at a child, and I would not risk bringing an illegitimate baby into the world for all the kisses and flattery in England."

"Of course not." She reached for the woven basket I'd been carrying, but I kept hold of it. "Where shall I leave it?"

She looked me up and down. "On the porch of the MacDavies' cottage. I've let the property through the end of the year."

A humble abode owned by the blacksmith. "I bid you good afternoon, Mrs. Ingersoll. Is there any particular day of the week when having Merri visit at the Hall would be more convenient?"

"Market day is Wednesday. A market day to myself would be... I'd much appreciate it."

"We'll send the pony trap for Merri before noon on Wednesday, or the closed carriage if the weather is inclement. Leander will be in transports to know he's to have a playmate."

Mrs. Ingersoll put a hand on the latch. "He's an only child?"

"He is." As far as I knew.

"They face special challenges, as you've noted. I meant what I said, my lord, about searching for Mrs. Tait. I have no interest in seeing her peace disturbed. Not on my account. Find her for Mr. Tait if you must, but he's not to use affection for me as justification for setting you on her trail."

Even the self-possessed Mrs. Ingersoll was not in a position to dictate motives to grown men.

"Tait has *suffered*, Mrs. Ingersoll. He has been snickered at behind his back for years, accused of murder by his wife's family, and left to marinate in guilt and loneliness that eclipse what even the most dunderheaded husband deserves. He came to marriage young, with no father or uncle to guide him around the most tempting obstacles. His wife, by all accounts, could be a difficult woman, and yet, he has managed her portion and his acres conscientiously for the duration. Perhaps he set me to find his wife not because he's smitten with your charms, abundant though they doubtless are, but because he has reached the limit of what he can bear."

Or—most likely—a combination of the two.

"You defend him?" She was puzzled rather than angry. "You plead that it's impossible to be both in love and sensible?"

Her phrasing had a familiar ring. "Is that a quote?"

"More like an eternal verity, my lord, at least where certain men are concerned."

She was determined on her pique, and I was determined to give her another perspective to consider. "Tait allows nothing in Evelyn's rooms to be touched. He counted himself well favored to have won her hand. He blames himself for her departure and describes a union that in its early days was blissful. I do not presume to understand marriage as an institution, much less the Taits' version of it, but I can comprehend why John Tait yearns—and deserves—to find out what happened to his wife."

I expected a curtsey and a brisk farewell. My outburst had surprised even me, though I'd spoken the truth. Tait was going a bit mad, flirting with widows, haunting Evelyn's rooms, avoiding her diaries for years, then reading them obsessively.

"And what if his wife doesn't want to be found, my lord? Even you admit John Tait was no paragon as a husband."

"Should the lady make that clear to me, then I will inform her that Tait is willing to pursue an annulment. The absence of children and the lengthy separation weigh in favor of such a petition, and little scandal would attach to either party after all this time."

I was doing an execrable job of protecting Tait's privacy in this discussion, though given that my lapse was mostly a defense of Tait, I forgave myself for the error.

"Mama! Mama, you're back!" A small girl burst forth from the vicarage, pelted down the steps, and climbed over the gate to fling herself into her mother's arms. "Mrs. Vicar said you wouldn't be long, but you were ever so long. Who's *he*?"

A pugnacious question, and I was reminded that Merri was an only child. She would guard her mama's affections jealously and fear any dilution of Mama's loyalty.

"Lord Julian Caldicott, at your service, Miss Ingersoll." I seized a little hand and bowed over it. "Your mother was kind enough to join us for Sunday supper, and I have issued an invitation for you to call at the Hall as well."

Mrs. Ingersoll set her daughter on her feet, and the child grabbed her mother's hand.

"We're to pay a call, Mama? What's the Hall?"

"His lordship dwells there, and yes, we are apparently to enjoy its hospitality. *I'll explain when we're home.*"

A look passed between mother and child that spoke of manners, lectures, and some topics, no matter how exciting or fascinating, being for private discussion only. That a four-year-old could decipher such maternal code impressed me.

Mrs. Vicar bustled out of the vicarage, and before she could inveigle me into taking tea with the ladies, I made my escape, pleading a desire to avoid the gathering clouds. Before I could retrieve Atlas from the livery, I had to deliver the shopping basket I'd carried for Mrs. Ingersoll.

I behaved myself, more or less, leaving the goods on the covered porch right near the door. I did, though, peek through the curtains to see a sitting room of very modest appointments. A braided oval rug covered less than half the floor. A whitewashed stone chimney looked to be open on both sides, possibly serving both the parlor and kitchen area behind it. Steps led up to what was likely a mere sleeping loft.

The lone chair in the parlor was a rocking chair, and what looked like a cedar chest sat beside it. The mantel was a rough-hewn beam, with a spill jar at one end and a mug of drooping Michaelmas daisies at the other. The only other appointment was a disreputable hassock, though I did note a dozen books on the built-in shelves beside the chimney.

No ongoing war justified my snooping, and I came away feeling ashamed. Either Mrs. Ingersoll was parsimonious by nature, or she was forced to exercise economies of necessity. That single orange among her purchases had likely been the week's sole indulgence.

If I was to step into Arthur's shoes in earnest, then the fate of widows in my parish was my concern. I made a note to inquire of Vicar if Mrs. Ingersoll might be aided in some way without injury to the lady's pride.

She apparently had no family to offer—

Between one step and the next, insight clobbered me. Mrs. Ingersoll might have no family. Merri was an only child. Leander had no siblings that I knew of.

But Evelyn Tait had *three* sisters. Thus far, I'd wasted my time with Margery and Ardath, neither of whom had so much as mentioned the third—Barbara. Lady Ophelia was aware of this sibling, and the next steps in my investigation became blessedly clear.

CHAPTER TWELVE

"Might your ladyship be inspired to write a short note to Miss Hyperia West?" I asked.

Godmama, pestle in hand, peered at me over half spectacles that made her look like a scholarly stork. "Julian, write to her yourself. You and she are of age, and dancing about decorum and prancing around propriety grow ridiculous."

Her ladyship had ensconced herself in, of all places, the Hall's herbal. The air was redolent of gardenias, a rich, cloying fragrance that her ladyship favored. Bunches of drying plants hung from the exposed rafters, and herbs growing in clay pots lined the windowsills.

"Healy West has taken me into dislike," I said, sniffing the bowl of leaves and stems she'd been mashing. "I am trying to step lightly with him for Hyperia's sake. Shall I do this for you?"

"You shall not. One must not be too forceful." She resumed her labors. "Hyperia is a grown woman, and if her brother needs sorting out—mine invariably do—then she is equal to the task. Hand me the lavender."

She'd filled a small bowl with lavender flowers. I passed it over and took up a lean against a cabinet that stretched from the countertop to the ceiling. The herbal was semi-sunken, with latticed windows at ground level. This arrangement meant most of the sunlight was indirect, which was said to be better for preserving scents and medicinal properties in plant specimens.

The afternoon had developed a sullen overcast, and a fractious wind was whipping the garden's remaining flowers. Blue and red salvia bowed and swayed at eye level. Chrysanthemum blooms dipped and bounced into one another.

"You might tend to the fire," Lady Ophelia said, shaking a few teaspoons' worth of lavender into her mashed greenery. "My hips suggest the temperature is dropping, and we'll have a proper autumn storm this evening."

I took up the poker from the hearth stand and rearranged half-burned logs in the parlor stove that filled the herbal with cozy heat. A coal fire in the herbal was forbidden lest the scent taint the delicate plant aromas.

I liked playing with fire, always had. "Banter might join us for supper."

"And in deference to the weather, he'll stay to enjoy the Hall's hospitality for the night. He and Arthur will retire at a shockingly early hour, and I will be left in your dubious company." Lady Ophelia sniffed her bowl and resumed mashing with a twisting motion of the pestle. "Are you asking me to look into Healy's West's circumstances? He was involved in a duel earlier this year. The other fellow was said to have disappeared to the Continent, which suggests the wounds were not mortal."

I closed the stove and stood, poker in hand. "How do you know these things?"

"I just do. Hand me the lemon balm."

By scent, I identified a dish of dark green foliage already mashed. "What are you making?"

"I'm not sure. Soap possibly, or a tisane or sachet. I experiment in the herbal when I need to think. Healy West and Gaylord Montefort got into a spat over a hand of cards. Words were exchanged, followed by the usual dreary excursion to Hampstead Heath. Montefort deloped, Healy did not, though let it be said the shots were fired simultaneously. Montefort hasn't been seen since. Typical masculine stupidity."

If Montefort had died, then Healy West would be guilty of murder in the eyes of the law and a good portion of society. A convicted felon's worldly goods were nominally forfeited to the crown, should the matter ever come to trial. My first thought was not for Healy, but for Hyperia, who needed no more scandalous associations in her life.

"Why interest yourself in such matters?" I added two fresh logs to the fire, cherry from the look of them, a beautiful wood that burned long and well.

"I don't interest myself. When you were in Spain, did you ever find yourself sitting down at the same table with your French counterparts? Neither of you bore the other fellow any personal malice, and, in fact, you shared a certain rare sympathy of outlook with one another." She left off grinding and mashing and put a cast-iron pot of water atop the stove.

"If you must know, Godmama, the unwritten rule of engagement among intelligence officers of all nationalities is to avoid violence. Violence complicates the mission, which is gathering information and surviving to report that information to one's superiors. Brute force is the less sophisticated tactic. If my path crossed that of a French intelligence officer or an agent for the Spanish Bonapartists, we were civil about it."

"Just so, and you might even, in an odd way, have compared notes. If the generals on all sides were hell-bent on having a battle nobody could win, then you intelligence officers could agree in your civil way that such a battle was rank foolishness."

Had she been lurking at my elbow during a certain conversation in Spain, she could not have summarized the situation more accurately. Battle—which would have been mutual slaughter for no purpose on that occasion—had been averted.

"What has this to do with Healy West?"

"His godmother and I were rivals at one time for the affections of a certain royal duke. I prevailed, of course, but a few years later, Lady Mary Pringle had set her sights on some Bavarian princeling. I aided the course of true lust. I was still occasionally humoring my royal duke, and Lady Mary had accepted defeat graciously. We exchange views from time to time, and sometimes what she has to tell me has no relevance to anything, but eventually, intelligence of all sorts has a way of proving useful."

One shuddered to think what the mistress of a royal duke might have considered fair game in such an exchange.

"Lady Mary keeps an eye on Healy West?"

"The boy's father asked it of her, and with good reason. Inheriting too young rarely goes as well as it has in Arthur's case. Have you instructed him to take some pigeons with him on his journey?"

"Yes, my lady. Immediately upon my return from London." The pot on the stove began to steam, and Godmama tossed a handful of her mashed mixture into the water. "My request, that you pen a note to Miss West, remains, but I also wanted to ask you about one Barbara Hasborough."

Her ladyship began tidying up, dumping all of her unused specimens into a dustbin and setting bowls and knives into the wet sink.

"The quiet sister," she said. "Supposedly sickly in childhood, not as tall as her siblings, but still quite robust. Did her one Season in the ordinary course, accepted the suit of a Berkshire baronet, and hasn't been heard from since. Why?"

Berkshire lay a few hours' ride from Town. "Because I suspect Evelyn Tait has been biding with dear Barbara and sending her sibling into Town occasionally to sell a piece of jewelry. Lina Hanscomb told me Barbara and Margery have both occasionally looked in on Ardath, but neither Margery nor Ardath so much as mentioned Barbara to me."

"And when two gabbling women are inexplicably silent on a

particular topic common to them both, a smart man takes notice. You're off to Berkshire, then?"

"Seems I am. I'll take the traveling coach and try to get there in a day."

Lady Ophelia stirred her steaming pot from which a complicated aroma rose. Sweet from whatever the gardenia scent was, brusque with the top note of lavender, and tangy with a hint of lemon in the finish.

"This jaunting about can't wait until Arthur has taken ship, Julian? I don't care for you haring all over creation for days on end, out in the elements at all hours, taking on troubles that have nothing to do with you. The war is over, Harry is dead, and you could find every missing wife in Merry Olde, of which there are many, and you won't bring him back."

"I know that." *Why did she have to turn her blunt speech on me now?* "Hyperia asked me to find Tait's wife, and I have reason to believe Evelyn is in peril."

"Those Hasborough sisters were all well dowered. Do you fear Tait will do Evelyn in if he finds her first?"

"I... do... not." *But I would take care that nobody followed me to Berkshire, and I would report my findings to Tait upon my return only if the lady gave me permission to do so, assuming I found her.*

"But you can't be sure. Very well, tilt at other people's windmills if you must. I will write to Hyperia after supper, and you can enclose whatever note you please before Arthur franks the mail in the morning. He always rises in such a good mood after Banter has spent the night. The two of them need to learn some discretion."

"Or we need to learn to appreciate Banter, because Arthur is as deserving of good moods as the next man."

The herbal was now pleasantly scented with a sort of general conservatory aroma. Botanical, fragrant, complicated... Not a perfume, exactly, but certainly appealing in soap or sachets.

"Be off with you," her ladyship said, brandishing her pestle at me.

"But get a good night's sleep before you decamp, or I won't be colluding with you to get your *billet-doux* to Hyperia."

"Thank you, Godmama. For everything." I kissed her cheek and left her muttering in French about impertinent young men and foolishness being the order of the day.

∽

A great, booming thunderstorm that started just after midnight kept me from a proper night's rest. I no longer jumped at a rumble of thunder as I once had, but neither was any noise that resembled cannon fire restful. The puzzle of Evelyn Tait's situation distracted me as well.

I was overlooking some connection, some fragment of truth sitting in plain sight, though mentally reviewing everything I knew brought me no insights. I still wanted to reread Evelyn's diaries, and I wanted to revisit her rooms.

"Ain't never been to Berkshire," Atticus said as we waited for the coach to pull into the porte cochere. The morning was misty and damp, but the rain had let up.

"A very pretty shire," I said. "They've kept a lot of their forests in trees rather than trying to put every acre into crops. Excellent shooting out that way."

"You don't hunt game, guv."

Something about that diffident observation caught my ear. "You'd like to learn how to handle a firearm?" Boys not much older than Atticus had taken the king's shilling. Such lads had often ended up as flag-bearers, a hellishly dangerous job when capturing the enemy's colors was proof positive of victory.

"Someday," Atticus said, mimicking firing a pistol with his thumb and index finger. "Every 'prentice and drover who went to war knows how to shoot now. Guns aren't just for squires and gents anymore."

A troubling and true observation. "When you can read and write

French and English fluently, I will instruct you on the fine art of marksmanship."

Atticus's gaze became speculative when I'd expected resentment. "You mean that? When I can do the *parly-voo* and *bon-swar*, you'll show me how to shoot?"

"Read and write, my boy, both languages, and my French is fluent, so a few handy phrases won't impress me. I was raised to speak both languages with equal facility. Why do you want to learn to handle a gun?"

He began hopping up and down the steps that led from the terrace to the carriageway. "I just do."

The mysteries were piling up like linen on laundry day. "We will not encounter any highwaymen, Atticus, and if we do, John Coachman and I are both armed."

The coach jingled up from the stable, precluding any more discussion of Atticus's newfound fascination with firearms. He was welcome to ride inside with me, but preferred John Coachman's company up on the box. Better stories to be had from that perch, and scenery unfettered by window shades.

Atticus loved the outdoors, while my eyes appreciated the gifts of a cloudy day and a closed coach.

"Julian!" Osgood Banter trotted forth from the house. "Glad I caught you." He was freshly shaved, immaculately attired, and exuding the aura of a man whose slumbers had been enviably satisfying, the blighter. "A moment of your time, and then I'll see you off."

What now? "We're not in any particular rush."

"But you are in a general rush because you are investigating." Banter gestured at me to walk off a little way with him. Atticus switched to hopping up and down the steps on one foot, though I knew the lad could eavesdrop as well on one foot as on two.

"His Grace mentioned that Healy West has turned up difficult," Banter said.

"Disapproving, at any rate—of me. West insisted that he needed his sister back in Town to serve as his hostess, and now that she's heeded his summons, he doesn't appear to be entertaining."

"West does not enjoy the steadiest temperament." From Osgood Banter, who avoided speaking ill of anybody, that approached a scathing condemnation.

"Lady Ophelia mentioned a duel with Gaylord Montefort, who I believe is the oldest scion of the Montefort house."

Banter's gaze was on the windows at the corner of the house one floor up. The ducal suite, which had a lovely view of the drive, the park, and the home wood.

"Your godmother scares me, Julian, but then, West isn't always as discreet as he should be, and Montefort's seconds included his younger brother. Bellerophon Montefort claims no great stores of discretion or sense."

One did not forget that name. "Bell Montefort served in uniform for less than a year before selling up. I seem to recall the threat of a court-martial hanging over him, but the details elude me."

"I'd heard a general's daughter was involved," Banter said, "but one cannot trust club gossip. Montefort's other second was a Scot, Murdoch, another former soldier who had a reputation for battlefield rages."

I vaguely recalled mention of such a man. He supposedly killed with his bare hands, a demon in plaid, Ney's personal nightmare. The whispers had been half ghoulish and half in awe.

"If one is to have murderous rages," I observed, "the battlefield is the place to indulge them."

Banter left off making sheep's eyes at his true love's windows. "I suppose a soldier would see it like that. Murdoch seemed perfectly sensible to me. Lady Ophelia is right—there was a duel. A spat over cards—nobody is sure who started it—but West was the challenger. Montefort offered the usual apology—an excess of drink, a paucity of manners, meant no insult, et cetera and so forth—but West wouldn't have it."

"In my experience, the men who did not go to war are more likely to indulge in lethal stupidity than the men who did." Though officers could and did duel, despite Wellington's stated disapproval—Wellington, who had also defended his honor at twenty paces, of course.

"It gets worse." Banter's usually genial features were a mask of distaste. "Gaylord Montefort fired into the air, West wasn't half so gallant. Montefort was winged. Bell started yelling about murder, and dishonor, and the seconds must duel, but Murdoch and I put a stop to that damned nonsense."

"Who was Healy's other second?"

"He had only me. Nobody else wanted to dignify the lunacy by supporting him. I am accounted a fool for having done so."

"You probably saved his life." And for Hyperia's sake, that was a good thing. "Does Hyperia know any of this?"

"I doubt it, unless Lady Ophelia has told her. I agree with the general sentiment that the less said about any duel, the better. The law is increasingly intolerant of citizens indulging in premeditated murder in the name of honor."

"Not citizens, Banter. Almost invariably *men*. Grown men." Women dueled, though the occasions were vanishingly rare—at least with pistols and swords.

"Well, nobody has seen Gaylord Montefort since. Wounds fester, and if Healy is behaving badly, it might well be that he fears charges of murder."

"He'd be an idiot not to, and yet, there he is in the London residence, when he could instead bide quietly at the family seat until spring. He is also pulling his sister into a closer orbit. If scandal looms, he ought to be distancing himself from family and friends."

That had been my course a scant year ago.

"To lie low and play least in sight," Banter replied, "is the honorable, *sensible* course. I had hoped the whole business would blow over, but this happened in the spring, and my guess is Bell Montefort won't let it drop."

I knew the younger Montefort slightly, but he'd have no reason to listen to my pleas to exercise restraint. "I will apprise Hyperia of the storm brewing over her brother's head and offer what aid I can to Healy."

"Offer him one-way passage to the Antipodes. Better to leave of his own free will with his silks and linens stowed in the hold than on a convict transport ship."

Banter, for all his facile charm, was pragmatic at heart. "I might suggest that." Though how would Hyperia fare if her brother left England one step ahead of the law? "Please let Arthur and her ladyship know I might detour into Town on the way home. This news is best conveyed to Hyperia in person."

"Be careful, Julian. Healy West and Bell Montefort are a pair of hotheaded idiots. I'm sorry I involved myself in the whole affair, and your reputation will suffer if you get dragged into it too."

His words inspired a smile. "Banter, my honor is dear to me. My reputation in the clubs, among the churchyard gossips, and with the Mayfair scandalmongers matters less and less."

Banter smacked me hard on the shoulder. "Then have a care for Miss West's reputation, and my own, as well as your continued existence, my dear. If anything happens to you, Arthur will be inconsolable."

"If anything happens to Arthur, I will be... You must look after him, Banter. I will haunt you from the ninth circle of hell if you allow anything untoward to happen to my brother."

Banter patted the shoulder he'd just pummeled. "We understand one another. Safe journey, my lord, and good hunting."

⁓

Because Arthur kept teams along all the major routes to London, we made excellent time and were in Berkshire by midafternoon. Atticus had joined me for part of the journey—the drizzling part—and was bouncing with energy by the time we pulled up at The Lambs' Knoll.

Lady Ophelia had been unable to give me the name of a particular manor or its direction, but she recalled the village from which Sir Tristan Peele hailed. I thus needed local intelligence to find Lady Peele, née Barbara Hasborough.

"Pretty," Atticus said, scanning a village green ringed with shops. "Hills are bigger hereabouts, but not as long as ours."

"Not like the Downs, but not like mountains, you're right. Proper hills. Proper woods." Harvest was nearly complete in these surrounds, and many of the trees had lost most of their leaves. The autumnal air felt different from Sussex too. Sharper, with more of a damp tang.

"You could doubtless do with some tucker," I said, "and John Coachman and the groom will leave me at the nearest crossroads if we don't make time for at least a pint."

"I'll kick you out of the coach meself," Atticus said. "I'm that famished."

He was always famished, which I took as a sign of a boy catching up on his growth. Since joining my employ a few months earlier, Atticus had gained both height and swagger, and his diction was coming along. He'd also, thanks to Hyperia and Lady Ophelia, made a start on his letters.

"Help with the horses as best you can," I said. "I'll arrange for your comestibles."

I trooped into the inn's common, the fire in the enormous hearth a welcome respite from the damp and chill. With its whitewashed walls, blackened beams, high-backed settles and battered tables, The Lambs' Knoll could have been any one of a thousand inns in the home counties. The smell was pleasant—peat smoke and roasting meat—and the hygiene impressive.

"Sir, good day." A balding fellow with an apron about his belly welcomed me with a smile. "Thaddeus Howell, proprietor of this fine establishment." He was the quintessential English innkeeper, and I hoped he had the encyclopedic knowledge of his surrounds that usually attended that office.

"If you'd like a meal," he went on, "then take any seat in the common. If it's rooms you're after, we have four vacant at the moment."

He likely had two rooms and a pair of garrets under the eaves. The premises were clean, but exceedingly quaint.

"A meal would be much appreciated. My groom, coachman, and tiger will be hungry as well—and thirsty. The boy in particular is prodigiously fond of his food."

"A change in the weather puts an appetite on us, me missus says. On your way out from Town, sir?"

He was the chatty type, thank providence. "On my way into Town, as it happens, but I promised my godmother I'd detour from the King's highway to look in on an acquaintance of hers, a Lady Peele, married to Sir Tristan Peele."

"You haven't far to go, then. Peele Manor be less than a mile from the green as the crow flies. Sir Tristan will be in residence. Another month, and he'll be out on his hunter from dawn to dusk. Goes into a positive decline every spring, I vow."

"We have that type in Sussex too. Can't see it myself. Might I have the inglenook?"

"A good choice today. Frost is right around the corner, or my name's not Thaddeus Howell."

I settled onto the worn bench next to the fireplace and let my mind wander. I'd had hours in the coach to plan my interview with Lady Peele, but thoughts of Hyperia and Healy West had intruded. If Healy had to leave the country, how was Hyperia to go on? Healy was not her guardian, but he doubtless dealt with the solicitors on her behalf, played the role of head of her family, and kept the gossips from accusing her of being without male protection.

She was not quite old enough to be a convincing spinster and not young enough to be anybody's ward. *Feme sole*, as the law put it, rather than that legal non-entity, *feme covert*. Would she view marriage in a different—and more favorable—light if Healy exiled himself?

Meaning marriage to me... I hoped.

A plump, smiling tavern maid approached my table. "Good day, sir. Howell says we're to feed you and your fellows. We have beef stew with lentils and the best beer this side of Bristol." She was pretty, and I'd put her age at about twenty.

"Might you add some cheese toast to that order and something in the way of a pudding?" I was truly hungry and knew the folly of neglecting my belly when on campaign.

"Aye, and for your fellows too. We'll start you off with a pint."

"A small pint, please. I'm paying a call locally when I leave here, and I expect more libation will be offered then."

"Up to see Sir Tristan and his lady. They don't get many callers, other than neighbors, of course." The young lady was making me an offer—give up some information about myself and my business, and she'd hand over the local opinion of Sir Tristan and his lady.

Many excellent intelligence officers had never worn a uniform.

"I'm something of a neighbor to Lady Peele's oldest sister down in Sussex, and I've made the acquaintance of the youngest sister as well. We have mutual acquaintances in Town." Lina Hanscomb was a mutual acquaintance of a sort. "My godmother, who knows everybody, suggested a brief call would be an appreciated courtesy."

"They're lovely people," the tavern maid said, taking the towel draped over her shoulder and applying it to the spotless table. "Sir Tris is hunt mad—so's half the shire—but he's not too high in the instep. Doesn't begrudge a neighbor the time of day, pays his tithes, and sponsors the Christmas pageant. His gamekeeper is always bringing around a hare or some grouse to the widows, too, dontcha know. Lady Peele does the loveliest boxes at Yuletide, organizes the village fete, and makes sure we have a kindly vicar, which is more important than most grand folk realize. She's finding us a new schoolmaster—the old one was a dear, but has moved closer to family, which is understandable, of course, when he had a tyke to raise and no missus. Lady Peele also put together the lending library. She heads up the lady's charitable committee, too, and always turns out to cheer her husband on race day, though Sir Tris is never in it to win. Puts on a good spread afterward for the whole lot of us."

"That is a glowing report." More significantly, it appeared to be an honest report.

"Aye, sir." The maid finished polishing the table. "Her ladyship was country-born, and Sir Tris's people have owned the manor since the Flood. He served in the Low Countries and came back a baronet, and we're that proud of him."

As well they should be. "Anybody who survived that debacle deserves the unending respect of his country."

I had said the right thing, with the right sincerity, and my meal was abundant. By the time I was waiting for the coach and a fresh team outside the inn, Howell was inviting me back *anytime* to hoist a pint in honor of His Grace of Wellington, *may God keep that dear fellow into a great and lauded old age.*

All in all, a delightful encounter—deceptively delightful, as it turned out.

CHAPTER THIRTEEN

"Lord Julian Caldicott." Lady Peele read my card, then inspected me as if questioning whether I conformed to the universally approved specifications for a courtesy lord.

"Late of Caldicott Hall in Sussex," I said. "I am acquainted with two of your sisters and in search of the third."

Lady Peele was an amalgamation of her siblings, with chestnut hair and blue eyes. Not as robust as Margery Semple, not as fashionable as Ardath Deloitte, not as mannish as Evelyn Tait. The result was pleasant, sturdy, and—I hazarded—nobody's fool. When I'd been ushered into her presence, her ladyship was conferring with her head gardener regarding the organization of the conservatory for the coming winter.

Ferns and citrus sat about in pots, like second-form scholars waiting to be assigned a desk. Empty shelving lined three sides of the glass-enclosed space. The air was humid and redolent of earth, and the gardener's boots muddy. I abruptly missed Caldicott Hall.

"I'm afraid his lordship's business will call me away for a bit, Mr. Castle." She pocketed the card and sent the footman scampering off with a glance at the door. "You will excuse me, and please do not move the camellias in my absence and think I won't notice."

"Wouldn't dream of it, yer ladyship."

"Lord Julian, come along. I will have a word with the butler about where and how titled guests are to be received. No offense was intended, I assure you."

"None taken. It's a busy time of year."

She led me through a house that put me in mind of Tait's abode, but with a lady's conscientious touch. Cleaner, brighter, graced with cheery flourishes—a dried bouquet here; a sketch of a sleek, saddled hunter there; a stained-glass depiction of doves in the transom window over the conservatory door.

No preachy proverbs or boring samplers.

"The fire isn't lit in the formal parlor," her ladyship said, setting a brisk pace down the corridor. The Hasborough ladies all seemed inclined to traverse life in quick-march time. "I daresay you will be more comfortable in the family parlor. We haven't an informal parlor. Sir Tristan says callers are either high sticklers, or they are friends. My husband is blessedly pragmatic."

"I am not a high stickler."

She stopped outside a carved oak door and gave me another inspection, though I sensed no malice in her gaze.

"Margery wrote to me," she said. "Margery takes her correspondence and her status as senior sister seriously. John Tait set you to searching for Evelyn, didn't he?"

"He did." Margery had written to Lady Peele, but Margery had not mentioned that I should confer with Lady Peele. What did Lady Peele know that Margery sought to keep from me?

Her ladyship preceded me into a cozy, unpretentious chamber that avoided the cluttered quality of Margery Semple's sitting room. More sketches here, of Sir Tristan with a hunter in hand and hounds gamboling at his booted feet. He was a lean, genial sort, who probably changed for supper only on Sundays. Various smiling children occupied rectangular frames. A sleeping cat curled in a perfect oval merited an oval frame.

I looked more closely at an older couple posed on the steps of a church. They radiated gracious warmth, and I was reminded of the tavern maid's comment about the importance of a kindly vicar.

"Your local man of God?"

"And his wife. Vicar is getting on, but he has such a gentle way with village squabbles, and his missus knows every herb and flower planted on this earth."

Real affection colored that description, just as the artist's benevolent regard for the couple came through in the drawing.

"You created this?"

"I did. Old people make good subjects. They can hold still. My children, on the other hand..."

"How many?"

"Five so far. Sir Tristan says more would put Margery's nose out of joint, and it's always better if the daughters outnumber the sons. A chicken coop with too many roosters is a loud, unhappy place."

"An unusual perspective." Fatherly, rustic, and unconcerned with the cost of doweries. I moved on to another sketch, of a soberly attired young man, hair queued back, with a small child sitting on his lap. The adult gazed over the child's head with an odd seriousness for somebody cuddling a toddler.

The child, by contrast, was bundled against her companion—the frilly cap suggested the feminine gender—only a quarter profile visible. The portrait depicted shyness in the girl and the loving refuge offered by a reliable parent.

"Who have we here?"

"Our previous schoolmaster and his offspring. They were frequent visitors at our table, the child being the same age as one of mine. Mr. Keough was well-liked, but raising a daughter without benefit of a wife poses challenges. A few of the local ladies would have been receptive to a proposal, but a schoolmaster's wages do not easily support a family."

The next frame held a page from a child's copybook. The same quote had been written twice, once in a tidy, elegant adult hand and, directly below that, a more wandering, rounded, wobbling version: *He that hath wife and children hath given hostages to fortune; for they are impediments to great enterprises, either of virtue or mischief.*

"Francis Bacon?" I asked. The same fellow who'd likened money to manure—of very little use unless spread around.

"Sir Tristan named our youngest boy Francis in memory of the right honorable viscount. Mr. Keough chose the copybook quotes with that inspiration in mind."

A far cry from the proverbs favored by Mrs. Semple. I moved to the next frame. "And you have immortalized Thaddeus Howell." Standing on the steps of his inn, apron about his middle, a towel over his arm, lord of all he surveyed. The frame to the right depicted a burly fellow with a mallet in his hand, dark hair tied back, a horse nuzzling the man's pocket. "The blacksmith?"

"Blacksmith, horse doctor, and the finest bass singing voice you've ever heard. His wife barely comes up to his shoulder, but she can also work the forge when needs must."

"You love these people."

Lady Peele looked, if anything, amused. "*Love thy neighbor.* The greater curiosity would be if I did not love them, given that they *are* my neighbors, and good, dear, decent people."

Did Arthur, who had to be the most enthusiastically ruralizing duke in the realm, *love* his neighbors, or was his bond to them one of duty? The coming year might provide me an opportunity to see the question from Arthur's perspective.

"And you love your sisters, too, I take it?"

"Of course, though love and liking are far from synonymous. Shall we be seated?"

We took a pair of wing chairs worn to comfortableness. A hassock suggested the baronet passed many an evening, feet up, paper in hand, while his wife occupied her matching throne and enjoyed a book or a gardening pamphlet.

"How is John managing?" Lady Peele asked.

Interesting place to start. "Not as well as he wants the world to think he is." And I knew precisely how that felt. "He told himself Evelyn would come home of her own free will when she pleased to. Then he told himself that Evelyn must have gone to her reward, for surely she wouldn't leave him like that, no final communication, no terms of separation, nothing but questions."

"I know it has been difficult for him."

"Your sisters take a different perspective."

"That John is the worst of husbands and Evelyn never should have married him?"

The same footman who'd escorted me to the conservatory appeared in the doorway with a tray.

"Come in, Harold. A mug of hot cider on such a dreary day will be just the thing. You may close the door behind you when you leave."

Harold bowed and withdrew, though he got another good look at me first. Reconnaissance officers everywhere in this shire. I liked the sense that folk were looking out for one another and that strangers were kept under surveillance.

"John Tait," I said, "based on what the man himself has told me, was delighted to marry Evelyn. He thought her the perfect wife for a country squire and counted himself lucky to win her hand."

Her ladyship set a pair of biscuits on a saucer, added a mug of steaming, spicy cider, and passed it over. "Tea is all well and good, but one wants some variety, too, and this year's cider is ambrosial. As a younger man, Sir Tristan broke his fast with steak and mulled cider every morning. He claims years of that diet is what kept him healthy when half of his regiment was down with fever and worse."

"I was fortunate that my service was on the Peninsula rather than in the Low Countries."

"An odd sort of fortune. Is John thinking of remarrying?"

Her question was curious rather than accusatory. "He might be, but I doubt anybody is considering becoming his wife. He approaches the age of thirty, and that has brought to his mind financial matters and also the sheer passage of time."

"Evvie is to finally have her own farm at eight-and-twenty." Lady Peele rose and made a circuit of the room, touching a frame here, then tossing a square of peat onto the fire and poking it down into the coals. "She has earned it too. Don't get up, my lord. We aren't in Mayfair, and God be thanked for that."

"Where is this farm?"

"Kent, near Chiddingstone. Some ancestor forgot to entail the property, and some more recent ancestor realized that was a good idea, and thus it was available to be bequeathed to the child of Papa's choice."

Why were there no sketches of Ardath, Margery, or Evelyn in this family parlor? "Evelyn was the logical party?"

Lady Peele stood and stared at the fire. "Yes, and not just because Evvie is a first-rate farmer. She rides like a demon, never on anything less than seventeen hands. She is a dead shot, she can wrangle ledgers better than any clerk, and she is always reading at least two books. But Margery and Ardath have always spoken of Evelyn as if she deserves pity rather than respect."

"Pity?"

"Pity. 'Our Evvie is plain, but she has a good heart.'" Lady Peele had adopted Mrs. Semple's air of humorous condescension. "'You mustn't worry about having such large feet, Evelyn. Every solid structure needs a firm foundation.' 'No matter how stout you grow, Evelyn dearest, you will always have a good figure.' 'Not another book, Evelyn! You'll develop a squint.' 'Evelyn should have the family pearls. It's the least we can do for her.'"

"Damning with faint praise?"

"Damning with sororal lies. Evelyn's feet are no larger than Margery's. Evelyn was never fat—she was just *big*—until after she married, when she did put on weight. She can quote philosophers and Scripture and plays by chapter and verse. Evelyn is the best of us, and Margery and Ardath will never admit that."

Lady Peele did not speak ill of John Tait, and she showed no inclination to blame Evelyn for anything. She was comfortably situated, and her husband apparently enjoyed her warm regard.

I chose trust over suspicion. "I suspect Evelyn is in danger, my lady, if she's extant."

"She is extant, my lord. Evelyn is resourceful, practical, and has every reason to live. She and John are just too much alike. Not arrogant so much as proud, and both very assured in their opinions. Evelyn put up with our sisters carping and condescending, but she wasn't about to accept disrespectful behavior from a husband."

A confident pronouncement, but then, Lady Peele had been nothing but confident since greeting me.

"If Evelyn is extant, she is about to inherit a valuable property. If she is dead, or declared dead, then the proceeds of that property, as well as Evelyn's considerable dower funds, will be divided between Tait and Evelyn's surviving sisters. If Evelyn had had children, the outcome would have been different."

"John Tait would not scheme to kill my sister."

"Why do you say that?"

Lady Peele returned to her seat. "Because he wouldn't. Husbands can be stupid. Wives can be idiots. We are human, and we try one another's nerves, but John was raised largely in a household of women. Ladies, to him, are for protecting and respecting, or for diversion or flirtation, but to imply that John would take a woman's life, especially the woman he has vowed to cherish and protect... Such an act for John Tait would be not just ungentlemanly but *unmanly*. Beneath him."

Her words had the ring of something Hyperia might say and were similarly insightful. Tait might despise his wife, but he'd despise himself more should he ever raise a hand to her. He'd been too immature or spoiled to realize that infidelity would deal an equally bitter blow to a woman who lacked confidence in her appeal.

"Would Ardath or Margery scheme to kill Evelyn?" I asked.

Lady Peele picked up her mug, sipped, then sipped again. She had largish hands, competent rather than graceful. "I don't think so."

She *knew* John Tait was incapable of uxoricide, and yet, regarding sororicide, she hesitated. "Can you elaborate?"

"Both Ardath and Margery are in financial difficulties. Sir Tristan has forbidden me to lend them any more money, because I asked him to do so. Margery has taken to wheedling on behalf of my nieces. Ardath alludes to bearing all the expenses of putting me up in Town on my frequent visits."

"You don't visit frequently?"

"Not for a year, and when next we do travel to London, we will stay with Sir Tristan's sister."

"I'm sorry. Siblings can be the very devil." A year ago, I'd doubted my welcome at the Hall, but even then, I'd known that if I'd nowhere else to go, I'd have been given accommodations. I knew Arthur better now and knew that keeping my distance had tried him sorely.

"Families are complicated," Lady Peele said. "I don't want to think Ardath or Margery would wish harm on Evelyn, but they might refuse her aid or otherwise scheme to get a portion of her money. I hope you do find Evelyn. John is right that years can pass while we're planning what to do with our morning, and Evelyn deserves to be happy. I honestly don't know where she is, my lord, and I do worry about her."

I believed her—for the most part. "If Evelyn sends word to you of her whereabouts, please let her know that Tait is offering an annulment, if that's what she wants. He bears her no ill will and understands that he is obligated to support her if they remain married, even if that's under the terms of a separation."

I rose, and Lady Peele got to her feet without any assistance from me. Whatever else was true, the Hasborough women were vigorous.

"If I hear from Evelyn, I will pass along your message. It sounds as if John has done some growing up."

"Maybe a lot of growing up. Thank you for your time, Lady Peele, and with respect to the conservatory, we find at Caldicott Hall that regularly rotating which plants are closest to the windows keeps more of them healthy."

"I like that idea. Gives the gardeners something to do in the colder months. Interesting."

We parted cordially, and yet, Lady Peele had left me with her own brand of unease. She'd spoken highly of Evelyn and seemed to be a lady of surpassing common sense. Her every reference to Evelyn had been in the present tense—*Evelyn is a dead shot, Evelyn is the best of us, Evelyn is always reading at least two books...* Despite Barbara being the sibling most removed from the whole drama.

Not even Tait thought or spoke about his wife as if she were an immediate presence in his life, though he claimed to be haunted by her.

As I climbed into the coach and woke Atticus from his slumbers on the forward bench, it occurred to me that Evelyn Tait, possessed of common sense and some means, would have turned to Lady Peele for aid before calling on either Margery or Ardath.

I thumped the coach roof with my fist, and the horses started forward. The journey to London would take hours, but I needed that time to think. Lady Peele had been honest with me, but she also knew more than she was saying.

What was she concealing, and why conceal it from me?

᠎ ⁓

I risked breakfast at the Orion Club, a favored London haunt of former junior officers. My appearance merited raised eyebrows, and I would doubtless be a subject of talk by noon.

"Ignore them, my lord," the balding majordomo murmured. "The worst of the lot reason that if the Corsican can no longer oblige them with a big war, then they must start all manner of little wars out of boredom."

Cranbrook was a veteran of the American campaigns, and his father had been a viscount's younger son. He had a foot in several worlds, and I'd always liked him. I hadn't had any idea that he might return my regard.

"My hair catches them off-stride." I'd been born with chestnut hair. I was now blondish, having passed through a period of having an old man's stark white locks, courtesy of captivity and its aftermath.

"Your *survival* caught them off-stride, if I may say so, my lord, and well done of you. A table by the window?"

Cranbook offered me an opportunity to show off my presence at the club, windows in St. James's male bastions being more than architectural devices for admitting light. Who earned seats at a club window, what judgments they passed from their perches, and what hours they chose for viewing and being viewed were all fodder for gossip. Brummel had been king of White's bow window until recently. Now that the Beau had left for the Continent, creditors nipping at his heels, Lord Alvanley reigned in Brummel's place.

"Near the fire would suit me better, thank you, Cranbook."

"A sensible choice on such a chilly morning, my lord."

We wended our way through the dining room, past the odd stare or puzzled frown. Cranbook showed me to a table for two in a corner near the hearth, but not too near. A pair of folded newspapers were included in the place settings such that I could hide if I pleased to, and I could sit with my back to the room or facing the other guests.

I faced them, of course. I was not ashamed to have lived through horrors most of these fellows could conjure only in their nightmares.

By the time my ham, toast, eggs, and tea had arrived, I'd been the recipient of two cautious nods and one cut direct. The cut direct had been from some fellow I did not recognize, one who doubtless held me responsible for the loss of a brother or cousin. For a time, I'd served as the military's scapegoat at large, accused in the court of parade ground opinion of giving up all manner of secrets and hoarding riches in France gained by treasonous perfidy.

Harry's resting place was somewhere in France. Otherwise, the entire country held nothing and no one I valued.

I was nearly finished with my tucker and resigning myself to defeat when a likely prospect strolled into the dining room. He, too, took a table to himself and sat facing the room—and, most particularly, facing the door. His presence was something of a surprise—he'd been a volunteer rather than a commissioned officer—but the man had earned a few privileges with all the lives he'd saved.

I waited until his food had arrived before approaching his table. "St. Sevier, good day."

He could have nodded, picked up his paper, and indicated to me and to the whole room that my company at his table was unwelcome, but Hugh St. Sevier had been a French physician serving with Wellington's army.

He well knew what it meant to forge his own path in hostile territory. When facing the generals, he'd been fearless, loud, and occasionally profane in several languages regarding the welfare of the soldiers in his care.

"My lord." He rose slightly and gestured to the seat opposite. "A pleasure indeed. You look well, and one makes this happy observation with more than a physician's clinical eye."

He was a handsome devil, lanky with russet locks worn a tad longer than English fashion preferred. Military lore said he'd been born in France, raised near London, and educated in Scotland, where distinctions between physicians and surgeons were no longer made.

A doctor was a doctor, and we'd been pathetically grateful to count St. Sevier as our doctor. Every soldier who left the battlefield on a stretcher had croaked the same plea. *For the love of God, take me to St. Sevier. Don't let the surgeons get me.*

More than once, I'd seen St. Sevier propped standing against a tree or a tent pole, only to realize the man was asleep on his feet.

"I've eaten," I said, taking the proffered seat.

"Eat more," St. Sevier said. "You are too skinny, and the only meal the English do better than anybody else is breakfast." He moved a rack of toast to my side of the table, followed by jam and a dish of butter.

He made no effort to hide a slight accent, just as he wore a touch more lace than the typical Bond Street exquisite. His table manners were elegant, though I shuddered to think of the other skills his hands possessed.

"You are more rested than when I've seen you in the past," I replied.

He sipped his coffee. "You heard the guns. I heard the screams and moans. We both needed time to reacquire the art of restful sleep, but now we are on the mend, *non?*"

I realized why I'd been so impressed with St. Sevier on the Peninsula. He took on each case with the air of an investigator. What were the patient's symptoms? When had they begun? What of diet, upsets, exertions? Of all the courses of treatment available, how did they compare for ease of application? Unintended effects? Cost? Duration?

He had an analytical mind, and yet, he took on the air of a collaborator with his patients. *Now what shall we do about this foot of yours that tried so courageously to stop the wicked cannonball? One must deal sternly with such a wayward appendage. I am open to suggestions, provided they are made quickly.*

"You come here to keep an eye on your former patients, don't you?" I asked.

"Cranbrook keeps an eye on us all, but yes. The war is over. The suffering is not. I have no Harley Street consulting room, and these men would not come to me in such a location anyway." He spoke as if I had never inquired of him regarding my dysfunctional manly humors—we'd met by chance on a Hyde Park bridle path—and that, too, was part of his appeal. He respected his patients' privacy and dignity, and for that, St. Sevier deserved to be canonized.

"You should be practicing medicine properly," I said, biting into toast slathered with butter and jam. "You are too skilled to go to waste playing the charming French bachelor."

He smiled a little sadly at his coffee. "But I *am* a charming French bachelor. I have this on the authority of the Mayfair hostesses, and their judgment is infallible."

How lonely he must be, a Frenchman in postwar London, without professional colleagues, likely reviled at home for serving in the British army, and without family to speak of. Heaven be thanked for Cranbrook, who'd likely asked St. Sevier to drop by the club from time to time.

"Be careful of those hostesses, St. Sevier. One heard you are some sort of comte, and all manner of former French aristos are regaining their titles these days."

"Their titles and sometimes even a ruined chateau, but never their lands or wealth, *mon ami*. The hostesses know this, and I remind them of it often. What brings you to Town when you have a lovely family estate where you should be riding the countryside by the hour and making all the local maidens swoon?"

"I am biding mostly at the Hall these days, though I can't say swooning maidens come into it. I'm in Town to make a few inquiries. What do you recall of a Lieutenant Bellerophon Montefort?"

St. Sevier, while pouring himself more coffee, took a casual inventory of the room's dozen other occupants. We were early. The fellows sleeping off a sore head or determined on a morning hack despite the drizzle would trickle in at a later hour.

"Bell Montefort was a hothead, as you English say, and, by his own account, capable of vanquishing the Corsican one-handed and blindfolded. A pity we did not allow him the opportunity."

St. Sevier was rarely judgmental, but he'd taken this particular hotheaded young officer into dislike. Into contempt, in fact.

"I heard he attempted liberties with a general's daughter and was offered the choice of selling his commission or facing a court-martial."

St. Sevier, for the first time, met my gaze directly. "Your hearing is excellent, my lord. The young lady was ill-used, but she foiled his worst intentions. General Harcourt would have seen Montefort before a firing squad otherwise. As it is, Mrs. Harcourt insisted that the legendary English discretion must prevail. The whole matter was hushed up, and then we had another battle to fight."

Thus did a scoundrel return to London, safe and sound, to brag of his military prowess. "He suffered no punishment?"

"Montefort was hustled out of camp so quickly you'd have thought he had the plague. No chance for a thorough beating by passing Spanish brigands behind the officers' mess, alas."

"He might yet get that beating," I said, finishing my toast. "You've been very helpful, St. Sevier."

"One appreciates the opportunity to be helpful. I have properties, you know, here in England, but they acquired the habit of running themselves, and now... One can only read so many plays and waltz with so many incomparables before a restlessness takes over."

I could hardly believe what I was hearing. "You are God's gift to medical science, St. Sevier. London is teeming with illness, with military widows perishing quietly of melancholy. We have aging curates who can barely walk because nobody has taught them about willow bark tea and those other nostrums you prepared for us on the march. If you don't care to endure schoolgirl French by the hour, then get back on the horse, man. By virtue of divine providence and your own native wit, you can save lives and relieve suffering. You are languishing for want of a good case of gout, a lung fever, or a colicky baby. Go forth and make medicine."

He finished his coffee and regarded the small, empty cup. "You are much improved, my lord. Vastly improved. If you should relapse a bit, don't be concerned, because the worst is firmly behind you."

While St. Sevier, who had aided and saved so many, was floundering.

"If I am vastly improved, then it's because I have accepted that some of what I learned on the Continent still serves me, St. Sevier. I am a reconnaissance officer in my bones and probably always will be. I use that aptitude now to take on inquiries society has no other means of solving, and I like the work."

Not quite true. I liked the results, but I'd yet to face a failed investigation—until now?

"One hears this about you. You defend old ladies who lack champions and pull striplings from the River Tick. Last week, I heard something about a hound."

"Next week, I want to hear that St. Sevier has once again put his shoulder to the medical plow. The émigrés need you if Polite Society won't take their troubles to you."

I left him looking thoughtful while an excellent meal grew cold on the plate before him. I made a mental note to keep in touch with him, lest he become another casualty of peacetime, as I so nearly had.

CHAPTER FOURTEEN

I approached the West family town house well before noon, telling myself that I was being discreet, though I also wanted to return to the Hall and offer Tait my disappointing report. I was haunted by the sense that I'd missed relevant details, that a pattern had eluded my notice—an important pattern that might reveal to me just what had become of Mrs. Evelyn Tait.

I longed to discuss the whole mess with Hyperia, though I'd forbidden myself that boon.

"Good day, my lord," Deering said as I came in from the misty drizzle. "One hadn't heard you were back in Town."

"I'm once again on my way to the Hall, though I'd thought I'd..." Raised voices caught my ear, coming from the direction of the music room.

"Perhaps my lord would like a cup of tea in the formal parlor?" Which lay at the opposite end of the corridor from the music room.

Healy West's voice was loud enough that every word came to us clearly. "You lark about with a disgraced traitor, flout my authority as the head of your family, and refuse to conduct yourself in a seemly manner. I won't have it, Hyperia. The time has come for you to marry and marry properly."

I stalked down the corridor, Deering trailing behind me. He made a grab for my arm as I marched through the music room door, but declined to follow me into the lion's den.

Hyperia sat at the piano bench, facing her brother rather than the keyboard. A Beethoven sonata, black notes filling the page, lay open on the music rack. My dear Perry was paler than I'd ever seen her, while Healy was on his feet, attired for riding and looking choleric.

"You," I said, advancing on him, "will apologize to your sister this instant."

"What the hell are you doing here, Caldicott, and how dare you tell me how to act under my own roof?"

"Somebody had best sort you out, because Hyperia has better things to do than humor a fool and a bully in the person of her own brother."

Hyperia rose, hand on the piano. "Julian, good day." Her voice shook, and that nearly inspired me to throttle her idiot sibling.

I closed the door, though Deering, to his credit, had fled the scene. "I mean it, West. You apologize to the lady now. If Bell Montefort is blackmailing you, you won't solve that by offering him your sister's unwilling hand in matrimony."

Hyperia bent over as if she'd taken a blow to the middle, and I caught her about the waist and led her to the sofa.

"Julian, what can you be..." She subsided onto the cushions. "Healy, *what is Julian talking about?*"

I stayed by Hyperia's side rather than risk allowing myself within pugilism range of Healy. "I haven't heard an apology yet."

"How can you possibly know about Montefort?" West said, some of the ire leaking out of him. "I've been discreet. Bell promised he'd keep his mouth shut if..."

Puzzle pieces snapped together in my mind. "He'd keep his mouth shut, if you bankrupted yourself meeting his blackmail demands. Now that he's bled you dry, he wants Hyperia's settlements. You, having a modicum of fraternal decency—a dust mote's worth—realized that Hyperia ought to at least have the security of marriage if her portion was to be stolen from her, lest she be forced to enjoy penury at your worthless side."

West took up a heroic pose by the great harp, resting his forehead against the elaborate carving of the crown, his hand on the pillar as if for support.

"I killed Gaylord Montefort. I am at Bell's mercy. If I have spoken harshly, Hyperia, it's because I am a man in extremis."

Oh, for the love of bunglers in breeches. "You are a clodpate who owes his sister better than that." How I longed to leave a muddy boot print on those tight chamois breeches and on his stupid, selfish soul.

"Very well." He pushed away from the harp and stood straight. "Hyperia, I am sorry for words spoken in anger. I should not have addressed you thus, and it won't happen again." He was trying for sincerity, proof of some sort of self-preservation instinct.

"I would not marry Bell Montefort," Hyperia said in a low, ashy voice, "if he were on bended knee, possessed of a fortune, sober, and begging me. I would leave the country first, and so you should have left the country if what you say is true. This was a duel, I take it?"

Healy stared straight ahead at nothing. "A matter of honor. Fate did not favor my opponent. No more need be said."

"A great deal more needs to be said," I snapped. "Hyperia, might I be seated?"

She patted the place beside her, and some of my anxiety receded. My lady was regaining her balance, though I still wanted to kick Healy and aim a fist at his gut too.

Before Healy could launch a lament about his cruel fate and Montefort's rapaciousness and other farragoes of self-serving fantasy and stray facts, I posed the pertinent question.

"Who is managing the Montefort family affairs these days?"

Healy looked at me as if I'd asked who had taken the throne after Good King Aethelbald. "I beg your pardon?"

"Who manages the Montefort family affairs? Who meets with their solicitors? Upon whom are the bankers calling?"

"Bell has the reins," Hyperia said. "I've heard his mother complaining that he's not as generous with pin money as Gaylord was."

"What has that to do with anything?" Healy asked.

"Where is Gaylord buried?" I asked.

Healy looked truly baffled. "In the family crypt, I presume. The Monteforts bide in Kent, not far from Canterbury."

"So you've made discreet inquiries of their vicar? Had a look at the parish registry of births and deaths? Asked the sexton if you could quietly pay your respects?"

Healy scrubbed a hand over his face. "You're saying Gaylord isn't dead? He went off to the Continent after the... after the incident. He might have expired on the packet or in Calais or Paris. I have no idea where he was when he went to his reward."

Hyperia stated the obvious, that exercise apparently being necessary for her brother's benefit. "You made no effort to disprove Bell's claim—none whatsoever—before you emptied the family coffers into his lap. When Gaylord eventually came skipping home from France, I would still be married to his criminal of a brother, penniless, and likely *with child* to that... that walking disgrace. Healy, I understand pride, but you have been unforgivably rash and stupid."

"Gaylord has gone to his reward," Healy said, chin jutting. "I am a dead shot, and I saw the blood."

"The blood on his arm?" I asked pleasantly. "Where you might have grazed him while he was busy deloping, because that was his only honorable course after you refused his apology and took drunken mumblings for a dire insult?"

"You are not a dead shot, Brother," Hyperia said tiredly. "You are a profound disappointment."

Healy pushed away from the harp. "I was thinking of you, Hyperia. Devising a way for you to hold your head up, to have a roof over that head. I met Gaylord Montefort on the field of honor and behaved according to the applicable rules. He left the country and then expired, to the best of my knowledge. I am dealing with the consequences of my actions as best I can."

Hyperia stood as well, and I took the place at her side. "Then you should be committed to a facility that looks after the legally incompetent, Healy. You could have written to Cousin Penelope in Paris and asked if Gaylord Montefort had been seen socializing. You could have kept your damned hands off my settlements. *You could have told me what was afoot.* At every turn, you behaved with the myopic self-interest of a spoiled brat. If Julian hadn't come along today, you would have forged my signature on settlements that parted me from my freedom and my inheritance. If you ever think to act on my behalf again, Healy, I will disown you and let all of Mayfair know why. Get out of my sight."

"You don't mean that," Healy said, taking a step toward his sister.

"Julian, please make him go away."

Gladly. I caught Healy's right wrist, spun him by the shoulder, and jerked his hand up to the middle of his back. He was stumbling into the corridor before he could get off a single curse. I closed the door behind him and regarded a very upset, very dear lady whose worst fears had nearly come true.

∽

"Is Gaylord Montefort alive?" Hyperia asked, subsiding onto the sofa. "Healy is a fool, but I hope not a murderous fool."

She wasn't patting the place beside her, so I remained on my feet. "Healy reacted badly to remarks made over a hand of cards. I suspect the hour was late and the libation excessive. He then refused Gaylord Montefort's apology. Montefort deloped, and Healy shot to kill. I have this from an eyewitness whom I would trust with my life. Foolishness of that magnitude has resulted in many a death."

And not a few public hangings. Battle nerves were setting in, or after-battle nerves. If I'd left Town without looking in on Hyperia, if I'd let Healy's rudeness to me interfere with my attachment to her...

"Please do sit," Hyperia said. "I'd ring for tea, except I'm likely to smash the whole service to bits in my present mood."

I resumed the place at her side and took her hand. "Would he truly have forged your signature?"

"Yes. He said as much yesterday, and today when I told him I had some shopping to do, he denied me the use of the coach and said I wasn't to leave the premises until I'd *seen reason*. The footmen were apparently ordered not to let me out of the house and have been giving me worried looks all morning. I think even Healy knew not to involve Deering in such measures."

I should have rung Healy's bell so hard he didn't wake up for a week. "You had a plan?"

"I would have left by the kitchen steps in the dead of night, made my way to Caldicott House, and sent a pigeon to the Hall. A special license takes a few days to obtain, and I would have relied upon you to stop the foolishness."

Not a bad plan, assuming the dead of night on a London street hadn't ended in disaster, assuming the pigeon fulfilled its birdy office, assuming Healy didn't already have that special license.

"Marry me," I said, wondering where in the hell such a pathetic excuse for a proposal had come from. "Please, marry me. I nearly did not stop by this morning, Perry. I told myself the roads out to Sussex will be mucky, and I shouldn't be dithering about in Town. I told myself not to annoy your idiot brother, who is still deeply in debt and less trustworthy than a London pickpocket."

I went on, feeling more than a little unnerved. "Then I told myself that I had given you my word not to leave Town without paying a call, though that was last time, but I did not know when I might see you again, and I missed you, so perhaps I might consider that my promise was given to you in the general case, and then I was knocking on your door and overhearing a shocking breach of fraternal duty."

Hyperia did not laugh at my offer—at my babbling. I took courage from that.

"Marry you." She considered our joined hands. "If I were to marry anybody, it would be you, but, Jules... We are upset, we are angry, we are..."

"We are the best of friends, we are attracted to each other, we are of age, and I love you." And yet, Perry was right too: The circumstances did not lend themselves to clear thinking, and I was in a blithering panic at what Healy had nearly inflicted on the sister he was honor-bound to protect.

"Marriage cannot be undone," Hyperia said slowly. "You know how I feel about children, and I know you long for them."

"Do I? Or do I long to be the disgraced brother who saved the ducal title by virtue of imposing progeny on my wife? I'm not sure myself, Perry, but if Healy had forced you to the altar with that vile buffoon, I would not answer for the consequences."

"I might have done something drastic to foil that plan. I would not have spoken those vows."

I put the rest of the battle plan into her possession, not that she wouldn't figure it out herself soon enough.

"To save Healy's life, even to save his good name, you would have spoken those vows and been a dutiful wife. You would have put up with whatever indignities and dangers Montefort imposed on you."

A gust of rain pelted the windows while Hyperia leaned into me. "Hold me, Jules. Please, just..."

I wrapped my arms around her, and she held me too.

"After a battle," I said, some moment later, "camp was eerily silent, save for the infirmary, where all was moaning and shouting and rushing about. Men would sit and stare, or they'd polish a spotless weapon over and over. The enlisted men would get quietly drunk simply to find some oblivion. The aftermath is harder than the fight in some ways, because you can never erase the stain of that battle from your soul."

The killing, the wounding, the fury, the fear... Boxing all that up in a neat little mental square where it couldn't touch any other memories or present realities took time and effort. Repeated effort, for me at least.

"Healy is *my brother*, Jules. He put me in harm's way, lied to me, tried to steal from me..."

"This explains why he would not show his face at the Makepeace house party," I said, resting my cheek against Hyperia's hair. "He was afraid to move about in society lest he stir up talk about the duel, afraid to twist Bell's tail by leaving Town for even a fortnight."

"And I thought Healy was considering a run for the House of Commons."

Even the lower house didn't deserve a bumbler of Healy's rare distinction. "I suggest you meet with the solicitors yourself, Perry. I will happily accompany you, or I'm sure Lady Ophelia will serve as your rear guard. Find out first hand where the family finances stand. If you haven't done so already, move whatever funds you personally command to Wentworth's bank. Wentworth will guard your money as ferociously as Cerberus guards the gates of hell."

Hyperia was quiet in my embrace, and holding her helped soothe my nerves. She'd had a plan for foiling her brother's lunacy, and the law forbade a woman to be married against her will. Still, she'd been ambushed and betrayed, and I would not be easy in my mind until I knew she was safe.

"Is Gaylord dead?" she asked, sitting back and keeping hold of my hand.

"I very much doubt it. Your solicitors can inquire of the Montefort solicitors. It's possible that Gaylord has gone to his reward, but in that event, his will likely made direct provisions for his mothers and sisters. They would doubtless have had funds of their own, though perhaps held in trust, with Bell as one of the trustees. Bell would also have come into a considerable sum and have no need to blackmail Healy. Blackmail is a hanging felony, after all. Even Bell Montefort wouldn't undertake it lightly."

I'd personally remind Montefort of the standard punishment for convicted blackmailers.

"Healy never learned to think along such logical lines," Hyperia murmured. "If Mrs. Montefort is complaining about limited pin money, then Gaylord is likely alive. If Bell is roaringly flush, then Gaylord is likely dead. Logical conclusions, but just as Healy made no effort to prove Gaylord dead, my brilliant brother could not parse out the logic in the details. If only he'd told me... but no, of course not. He expects me to accompany him to a musicale tonight, Julian, and I cannot imagine how I will bear to share a coach with him."

"The mother of all megrims has befallen you, perhaps, or you might consider returning to Caldicott Hall with me."

She sat forward and regarded me over her shoulder. "You escorted me up to Town. I don't see how escorting me back to the Hall would cause any greater scandal."

It would cause no scandal at all if we were engaged. I knew better than to press that argument.

"I will send a note to the Montefort solicitors," I said, "asking if Bell enjoys the authority to act as his brother's power of attorney. I will imply that I am in anticipation of some business dealings with the Montefort junior scion, and that as the Duke of Waltham's prospective representative, I am exercising caution in all business matters."

"What does a power of attorney have to do with anything?"

This much at least had come clear to me on last night's journey from Berkshire. "If Bell holds Gaylord's power of attorney, the document is worthless unless Gaylord yet lives. The delegation of authority lapses irrevocably upon the principal's death." Hence, every officer serving under Wellington had been required to make a valid, witnessed will, not simply leave a power of attorney with a brother or uncle. "If Bell has no power of attorney..."

"Then Gaylord is dead of a certainty," Hyperia said slowly, "because the solicitors would not permit family funds to be expended without some proper authority in Bell's hands, by will, trust, bequest, or something of the sort. Send that note, Julian, by all means."

"You'll get packing?"

"I shall, and,"—she wrapped my hand in both of hers—"thank you, Julian. Matters were growing dire, and I was so shocked, so bewildered... I will never scoff at another Gothic novel. Healy has been keeping this imbroglio to himself for months, and if he'd only confided in me, I might have prevented much foolishness."

"How?"

She rose and regarded me. "Firstly, by confiding *in you*, of course." She let that salvo reverberate in my conscience for a moment, then headed for the door. "I'll meet you in the mews in thirty minutes. Feel free to use the library if you want to pen your epistle to the solicitors before we leave Town." She halted with her hand on the latch. "I love you too, Julian. Very much."

Not a complete rout, then, and she hadn't turned down my proposal out of hand either.

∽

I blew a kiss to the door Hyperia had left half open and took myself to the library, where I made use of paper, pen, sealing wax, and my signet ring. I put the requisite communication into Deering's keeping and found Healy at the escritoire in the family parlor, also attempting some correspondence.

"Hyperia will return to Caldicott Hall with me," I said, "and I have asked for her hand in marriage."

He sanded his epistle. "Did she accept?"

"She is considering my offer, which—might I remind you—comes from a ducal heir who is quite solvent and who was also mentioned favorably in Wellington's dispatches." I closed the door and took the decanter sitting at Healy's elbow back to the sideboard.

"I'll give you leave to court her, if that's what you're after."

I'd just removed a figurative noose from about Healy West's

finances, if not his neck *and* his good name, and he yet maintained pretensions to a position of authority over his sister.

"Your approval," I said evenly, "your opinion, your smallest passing comment on any undertaking of your sister's is of no moment whatsoever, nor will it ever be. If Bell Monforte would blackmail you into betraying your sister, what sort of husband do you think he'd have made?"

Healy finished his drink and rose. "Half of polite society finds themselves in unhappy unions. Hyperia's the resilient sort. She'd have managed. She always does." He ambled over to the sideboard as if intent on a refill.

Foolish of him to come that close to me.

I applied my fist to his jaw, not hard enough to dislocate anything serious, save for Healy's pride. He had the sense not to attempt a retaliation.

"I deserved that," he said, rubbing his chin. "I've been an idiot."

"We are all idiots at some point or other," I said. "I followed my brother into the night, broke a standing order to do it, and possibly got him killed in the process. The issue for you, West, is how to make amends. Your sister doesn't feel safe under your roof, and she is an eminently sensible woman."

He moved his jaw from side to side. "I never meant... I suppose that's all water under the bridge. Will you permit me to attend the nuptials? People will talk otherwise, and I'm so bloody tired of worrying about talk."

I sympathized, very reluctantly and only a little. "Here is what you need to do. Right now, immediately, send a note to the solicitors explaining that an accurate accounting of the family's finances is to be made available to Hyperia, who will likely share it with me. You will inform her when the solicitors have confirmed their understanding of your direction."

"She's good with numbers. Does all the household books. I'm not drowning, but another month of Bell's demands, and I would have had to mortgage something."

If Healy had avoided mortgages thus far, the situation was salvageable. "You will remind Bell Montefort that his scurrilous behavior with General Harcourt's daughter could soon become common knowledge in the better clubs. Nobody was sad to see Montefort all but drummed out of the regiment, and every former officer will amplify the tale if it gets loose in Mayfair."

Healy sank back into the seat behind the desk. "Blackmail the blackmailer?"

"It's not blackmail if you ask for nothing in return for your silence. You will merely be making Montefort aware that you have been put in possession of certain facts."

"I want my money back."

How could this bleating dolt be any relation to my dear Perry? "I want many things I will never have, West. Montefort doubtless put nothing to you in writing and invariably insisted that you pay him in cash or fungibles—a blooded colt, jewels, a Caravaggio landscape. Proving that he's a felon will be nearly impossible."

Though Montefort was a successful felon, suggesting Healy was not his first victim.

"For God's sake, Caldicott. Why can't I destroy the bounder's reputation? He's the one who suggested marriage to Hyperia."

I marshaled my patience and acquired some sympathy for the drill sergeants responsible for turning an infamous army into an effective fighting force.

"You cannot engage in a battle of insults and accusations, West, because you have a sister to consider. Montefort could involve you in another duel, for starts, and even winging his brother qualifies as assault with intent to maim, if not attempted murder. Cut your losses, make an orderly retreat, and hope that, someday, Hyperia forgives you."

I wasn't sure I ever would. As I waited in the mews for Hyperia, I reflected that Healy's folly, immense as it had been, had also given me an opportunity to act as Hyperia's champion, rather than as her lover or friend. A husband had uses, in other words, even to a lady determined to safeguard her freedom and her health.

I assisted Hyperia into the coach, took the place beside her on the forward-facing bench, and considered whether I ought to obtain a special license, strictly in an abundance of caution.

But... no. Not without consulting Perry first. From her perspective, Healy's worst transgression had been a failure to confide in her, and I was—to the limited extent of the Tait investigation—guilty of the same behavior.

As we rattled over the cobbles and headed for the first turnpike, the rain started coming down in earnest. This was fortunate, because the racket made conversation difficult, and Hyperia did not appear to be in the mood for more talk.

CHAPTER FIFTEEN

"Babs was the peacemaker," John Tait said. "The sister who never made a fuss and often poured oil on troubled waters. She flattered her elders, cosseted Ardath, was the prop and stay of her mama. Then she quietly stole a march on the lot of them, marrying an actual baronet."

We met on neutral ground at the Bamford coaching inn, the same establishment where Evelyn had begun her flight from her marital difficulties.

"Lady Peele asked after you," I replied as a serving maid brought us two tankards of ale. The day was cool and breezy, but I was glad for the wind if it dried out the roads more quickly.

"Babs is a decent sort," Tait said, blowing foam onto the floorboards before sipping his drink. "She sends me a note at the end of the year. Just a few lines to let me know of births, illnesses, and how Sir Tristan fares. He's a capital fellow. Could have been a considerable soldier-statesman, but does the jolly squire instead. They have two sons and three daughters."

A wistful observation. "Would Evelyn have sought refuge with Lady Peele?"

We occupied the snug, which sat at the far end of a polished oak bar at a slight distance from the rest of the common. The bartender was wiping glasses at the other end, and the midmorning hour found the room otherwise deserted.

"Babs might have taken in Evvie for a time, of course. She is nonetheless the most distant of the siblings and in some ways the most socially visible. Sir Tristan is well-liked, very much *the* squire. He and Babs do the village fete, the hunt meets, the Sunday suppers, and so forth. I can't see Babs stuffing Evelyn into a broom closet for five years."

I couldn't see Evelyn Tait contenting herself with a clandestine existence, based on what I'd read in her diaries.

"Lady Peele is also worried for her sister," I said, letting my ale settle rather than disrespect the flooring. "I explained the situation to her as best I knew it. Evelyn made a first stop in London to liquidate jewels, then a departure from Town to no fixed address. Her coin is running out, and Margery and Ardath have attempted to befuddle me. Lady Peele considered my recitation credible."

I was still haunted by the sense of having missed something, something that in hindsight would mock me for its obviousness. I was sure that were I conferring regularly with Hyperia, a woman of surpassing acumen, the puzzle would be solved.

She'd been quiet the whole way down from London, and by the time we'd reached the Hall last evening, she'd been sleeping at my side. She'd not come down to breakfast, so I'd explained the debacle in London to Arthur and Lady Ophelia and made arrangements to meet Tait.

I wanted to quit the investigation, my first failure on home territory—not my first failure on a mission, by any means. The knowledge that Evelyn Tait, a woman alone, might be facing penury and all the hazards attendant thereto prevented me from deserting the regiment.

"Does her ladyship share your concerns regarding Margery and Ardath?" Tait asked, downing more of his ale.

"Yes, though she wasn't quite willing to accuse her sisters of murder. She implied they might have blackmailed Evelyn, demanding coin in exchange for silence regarding Evelyn's whereabouts."

"Now you think they've lost her too?"

"As best I can puzzle it out, Evelyn had no choice but to run. If she could no longer pay Margery and Ardath hush money, and she didn't want to reunite with you, then she was bound to leave whatever safe haven she'd found."

"Where is that doting sea captain when my wife needs a refuge?" Tait muttered. "Where am I? I never thought Evvie hated me. I thought all couples quarreled, and I wasn't the worst husband, and she wasn't a perfect wife, and we'd sort it out... Why not communicate with me somehow? Get the business dealt with and move on?"

"Perhaps Evelyn fears you will do her a mischief if she returns?" A plausible theory because it explained her continued absence. Many an itinerant shearing crew walked from York to London or London to Cornwall over the course of a season. From Sussex to Berkshire, if that's where Evelyn had bided, would have been a few hard days on foot for a fit woman, less than a day by public coach.

Why hadn't Evelyn returned to Tait's household, the one place where she was legally entitled to room, board, and at least a grudging welcome? That question struck me as one I should have considered earlier and at length.

"We are back to the possibility that Evelyn cannot come home," Tait said. "At some point since selling the last of the pearls, she met with foul play or misfortune and left no means by which anybody would know to notify me."

"Or notify her sisters or her dear friend Lina Hanscomb."

We sipped our ale in silence as a London stage clattered into the yard, disgorged one passenger, changed teams, and trotted off again.

Tait shifted a curtain partly blocking the window. "That's not... no. For a moment, I thought Mrs. Ingersoll just got off that stage. I'm not sleeping well. The mind plays tricks."

"Are you and the widow no longer cordial?"

He finished his drink and did not call for another. "I was a bit unforthcoming with her originally, but she wasn't precisely forthcoming with me. I thought surely a widow with a small child would be receptive to a gentleman's sincere interest, and she appeared to be, up to a point. When I did explain my situation to her, she wanted no part of a man who lied about his marital status by omission."

That turn of events had apparently flummoxed Tait, so much so that he imposed the rest of his confession on me as well.

"I would have told her about Evvie," he said, "before matters progressed much further. She informed me that matters would never progress at all as long as honesty figured so poorly in my dealings with women. Damned if she wasn't as good with a scold as Evvie was, and even that... My lord, I am a sad case these days."

"You should have confided in her." Hyperia's protracted silence mocked me bitterly for that hypocrisy.

"Yes, I should have, but I didn't. This sadder and wiser business hasn't much to recommend it, you know. I like Mrs. Ingersoll, my lord, purely like her as I haven't liked a woman since I courted Evvie. She doesn't suffer fools, and she'd give her life for that little girl."

I offered the only advice I could. "Apologize. Don't pretty it up. Don't make excuses. Apologize and tell her it won't happen again, and then *don't lie to her again.*"

"She's not about to walk home from services with me when I'm married to another."

A sad case indeed. "Tait, you are not apologizing to advance your chances of getting under the lady's skirts. You apologize because you have wronged her, and honor demands you acknowledge the harm you've done."

"Apologize." He tasted the word and found it off, apparently. "Evvie and I were awful at apologizing. We'd fume for days, sleeping on opposite edges of the same bed, waking up all tangled together, and then recalling we were at war... It should have been amusing. Then she demanded her own apartment."

Amusing, were it not so sad. So lonely and stupid and

preventable. "I want to confer with my godmother regarding a few possibilities, Tait, but I am otherwise at *point non plus*. I am sorry to have disappointed you."

I was sorrier to have failed Evelyn Tait. She deserved at least the security of a separation agreement or the freedom of an annulment.

"You're giving up?"

"What else would you have me do?"

He rose, and I got to my feet as well. "Reread Evelyn's diaries, for one thing. I'm too... too involved to read them as anything other than the memoirs of my embittered wife, but you might see something you missed the first time. You've met the sisters, talked to Lina and the jewelers. Evelyn was smart enough to put things in code, you know. She made all manner of funny marks on the calendar in the library, and I had no idea what she was keeping track of. Candles, possibly, half days, poor-box donations, all of the above."

"And you didn't ask her?"

"She ran the household, my lord, and ran it well. I ran the estate, and she left me to it, for the most part. We'd chat about whether to switch half days for the footmen or leave a field in clover for another year, but our responsibilities were in different spheres."

And children, even one child, would have been a common sphere. "Send the diaries over, and I'll give them a closer reading. I would also like to discuss the whole business with Hyperia West, who is once again a guest at the Hall."

Tait winced. "You promised you wouldn't air my linen with Miss West."

I moved my half-finished pint across the table, out of dashing-in-Tait's-face range. "I am asking to be released from that promise. Pride cost you your wife once, and now, the same pride might cost you a chance to regain that wife if I cannot confer openly with Miss West. She knows the worst about me, Tait. She knows which of the rumors about my actions in uniform are true, which are baseless slander, which fall somewhere in between. She will not judge you or Evelyn for being human, and Miss West might claim the perspective that solves the riddle of Evelyn's whereabouts."

Hyperia was a true friend, in other words, and whether she and I ever married, I wanted no more of this weight that my obligations to Tait—and to my pride—had placed on that precious friendship.

"Tell her the worst, then," Tait said. "Show her the diaries if you must. Soon, there won't be a woman in Sussex willing to speak to me. I do believe you've made matters worse rather than better, my lord."

He put an ironic emphasis on the honorific, though he was entitled to his pique. I *had* made matters worse for him. He was held in contempt by Margery and Ardath, pitied by Lady Peele, and thanks to my inquiries, he'd landed in Mrs. Ingersoll's bad books as well. All of that might come under the heading of Tait's just deserts.

My real concern was that I had made life worse for Evelyn, whose situation was undoubtedly more precarious. Perhaps it was a mercy that no children were involved.

"If I have made matters worse," I said, "I apologize for that. You have the consolation now, though, of having searched thoroughly for your wife. That can only aid any petition you eventually make to the courts."

Tait put on his top hat and produced riding gloves from a pocket. "The only real comfort I have these days is looking after my patch of ground. I do that well. Even Evvie would concede that I am a conscientious and competent farmer. To my acres, I shall return, the same acres I should probably never have left."

"Apologize to Mrs. Ingersoll," I called as Tait stalked away, "and send me those diaries."

He waved a hand without turning. I resumed my seat, and while I finished my ale—the summer ale would soon be done for the year—I composed an apology to Hyperia. No prettying up the truth, no making excuses, and it was a damned uncomfortable exercise.

Only as I was back in the saddle and cantering in the direction of the Hall, harvest in progress all around me, did I realize there was one more place to look for Evelyn Tait, a place that should have been obvious to me from the start of the whole inquiry.

∼

"If you can spare me the better part of a day," I said, "I'd like your company on an excursion over to Chiddingstone." I'd found Hyperia in the ladies' parlor, which had been the solar of the medieval keep predating modern incarnations of the Hall.

Afternoon sun flooded the room, hence I wore my blue spectacles. Atticus, perched at Hyperia's side, regarded me with open resentment.

"Whyn't you go to Kent on your own, guv? It's not that far."

"You've been studying maps, my boy?"

His expression turned guarded. "Aye. Leander has a map in the schoolroom with all the counties on it, and London and the ports. France is down in the corner, across the Channel. Scotland sits up top. Wales is over there." He gestured to the left, which also happened to be the west.

"Where is Africa?"

He looked confused, then grinned. "Thataway." He pointed out the window, which was south.

"Correct. No reconnaissance officer lasted a fortnight in Spain without a good sense of direction, and you have one. Now be off with you and let John Coachman know that if the weather is fair tomorrow, I'd like to nose about Chiddingstone."

Atticus bounced to his feet and charged toward the door, then stopped halfway across the room. "Miss Hyperia, may I be excused?"

She bestowed on him a smile of such warmth and approval, I was jealous of my tiger. "You may, and we will resume our studies on your next idle afternoon. Take Aesop with you, and you can ask me the hard words later."

He took the book and assayed a bow. "I don't find as many hard words as I used to, do I?"

"Barely any," Hyperia said, beaming at him. "You'll be reading Shakespeare next."

"Hear that, guv? I'm learning me letters."

"Then we'll soon have to start you on French. *Vite, vite, à l'écurie avec toi!*"

"Quick, quick," Hyperia translated, "to the stable with you!"

"Miss Hyperia knows everything." Atticus whipped open the door. "I'm off, *vite, vite!*"

I took the place beside Hyperia that Atticus had vacated. "That child does everything *vite, vite*. Where does he get his energy?"

"From Cook's abundant victuals, from a night spent safely in a warm bed, from the affection and regard of those around him. Leander thinks Atticus is the pinnacle of boyish achievement."

"Leander is my next stop, but I wanted to talk to you first." I was in fact dreading our discussion and sought to have it behind me. "How are you?"

She eyed the door, which Atticus had left open. "Too relieved for words. This drafty old Hall feels more like home than the town house where I was born. When did my brother become a fool?"

"I have been a fool, too, Hyperia, so I can't judge Healy too harshly, but I am wroth with him for involving you in his difficulties."

She rose, closed the door, and returned to my side. "Jules, you cannot endlessly flagellate yourself over Harry's death. He chose to leave camp without explaining himself to you, and he had to know you'd be concerned. You went on reconnaissance, just as he would have in your shoes."

"Possibly not—Harry tried not to hover over his little brother—but my conduct on that occasion is not what bothers me now." A silver lining, that. I was finding more and better things to fret over, finally.

"You never took drunken offense to a passing remark," Hyperia said, "then refused an honorable apology and shot to kill. I know you didn't."

I wanted to take her hand, to say my piece while we were

wrapped in each other's arms, my face pressed to her shoulder. Instead, I stood.

"I have wronged you, Hyperia West, and I am here to apologize for the hurt I've done you. John Tait's privacy is not more important to me than your counsel and friendship. To imply that conferring with you would in any way compromise Tait's dignity or my honor was ridiculous."

She rose and faced the windows, which looked out over the gardens. The flower beds were growing bedraggled, with a few chrysanthemums trying to keep up appearances, despite some borders having already been trimmed back to winter height and others gone weedy. Yellow leaves spattered the walkways and floated in the pools of the tiered fountain.

"When men talk about honor," Hyperia said, "they usually mean pride. True honor goes about its business without making speeches or taking umbrage over a hand of whist."

Hyperia was lumping me in with her brother, and she wasn't wrong.

I moved to her side. "I was jealous of Tait. You and he were on the best of terms, and you pled his case for him. He has a place in your heart, clearly." More than that, I would not say.

Hyperia crossed her arms. "If you turn up dunderheaded over every male who has a place in my heart, then you should be jealous of Atticus, Banter, Leander, Arthur, and Atlas, for starts."

"I am, a little."

"Jules, be serious."

I hadn't been teasing. "I am seriously sorry that I promised Tait you would have no part in this investigation. Not only was that an insult to you, it was a disservice to Tait himself. He has released me from that promise, hence my request that you join me on tomorrow's outing."

"What's in Chiddingstone?"

"Evelyn's farm."

"Do you expect to find her there?"

The subject had changed, for which I was grateful. My apology had not, however, been accepted.

"No, or not really, but it will soon belong to her. If she can make her money last until her twenty-eighth birthday, then she becomes a landowner, likely through trusts and remainders and other legal machinations. The income from the farm is hers, and I can't see Tait interfering with that." He would have a right to that money, too, of course, a reminder of just how absolute a husband's dominion over his wife could be.

"Evelyn has needed a safe haven, and you suspect the farm might be it?"

"I have no idea what to expect, Perry, but I haven't seen the farm, and I am at dead ends in all directions. If you don't want to come with me, I understand. Having shoved you out of this inquiry, I admit you are entitled to leave me to it. Please tell me that my apology has nonetheless been accepted."

"You are apologizing for keeping the investigation to yourself?"

Though Hyperia sounded merely curious, I knew myself to be on boggy ground. She'd come with me to the Hall of necessity. That I could be a friend to her when she faced daunting exigencies sat on one side of our ledger book, rendered in black ink. I had still given offense by excluding her from Tait's situation, which sat on the other side in bold red ink.

"I am apologizing," I said, "for allowing anything—Tait's privacy, my own pride, notions of gentlemanly discretion, *anything*—to come between us. That business about, 'I could not love thee, dear, so much/Loved I not honor more,' is fine for doomed poets and hotheaded soldiers, but I have faced doom, Hyperia, on the battlefield and off. I would rather have been solely responsible for the defeat at Waterloo than lose your respect and trust."

I hadn't planned those words, but I meant them.

"What's that from?" she asked, "that bit about 'loved I not honor more'?"

"Richard Lovelace, 'To Lucasta, Going to the Wars.' I fancy his

'To Althea, from Prison' more, though his loyalty to Charles I ruined him in the eyes of others." Lovelace's poetry had consoled me deeply when I'd been locked in a French dungeon. Ruin in the eyes of others had never dissuaded that old fellow from the loyalties he'd held dear. He'd written his truth in those verses. He hadn't merely penned a Cavalier's gallant tripe.

"What's the one you prefer? 'To Althea'?"

"Lovelace was jailed for loyalty to his sovereign, and it was not his first incarceration. He used the time as a sort of monastic retreat, and he wraps up with this verse:

Stone Walls do not a Prison make,
    Nor Iron bars a Cage;
    Minds innocent and quiet take
    That for an Hermitage.
    If I have freedom in my Love,
    And in my soul am free,
    Angels alone that soar above,
    Enjoy such Liberty.

"Oh, Jules." Hyperia sank onto her bench. "You know all about stone walls and iron bars. I hate that."

"I hated it, too, at the time." I sat beside her, not sure where the discussion had taken us. "I hated myself for landing in such a place, against orders, with nothing to show for my folly save a guilty conscience and a wrecked mind." And a dead brother—mustn't leave that off the list. "I sometimes think that if I could just see Harry's grave, I could put the whole business to rest with him, except he was likely buried in the French equivalent of a potter's field, if not heaved over the parapets for the crows."

"Don't think like that. Harry is soaring with the angels, and they are buxom and friendly angels too."

We sat quietly for a time. I was vaguely bothered by a need to get to the nursery, but more aware that I'd not mended my fences very well with Hyperia. What had prison poetry to do with anything? What good was an apology without better behavior going forward?

"In future, my dear Perry, should more investigations come my way, I will refuse the task if consultation with you is not an assumed part of my services." That felt right. A castle of certainty I could defend zealously.

She curled her arm through mine. "What does that mean, Jules?"

"I delight in solving these puzzles—once they are solved. I haven't found Evelyn Tait yet, but I mean to continue trying. When I came across that wretched missing hound, when I discovered the particulars of Leander's situation... I felt useful and challenged and alive. But when I have wronged you, I am unbearably ashamed. Going forward, I choose you over any other inducement. If I hadn't kept you at a distance, you might have refused Healy's summons, and that whole donnybrook in London could have been avoided."

"Put off perhaps, not avoided. Bell Montefort had found a pigeon he could pluck endlessly. Sooner or later, Healy would have helped himself to my settlements."

Well, yes. "Am I forgiven, Perry?"

She sighed and leaned against my arm. "It hurt, Jules, to think you'd keep me out of an inquiry I could possibly help with. It hurt more than it should have. When a woman has a household to run, she justifies her existence. I have no household, no children—by my own choice, let it be said—and I have enjoyed whatever minor role I've had in your investigations. I hadn't realized how much."

"Your role is far from trivial. You might not spend as much time in the saddle as I do, but you are with me every mile. You are the commanding officer who expects my safe return, the authority for whom I draft mental dispatches that make sense of what I find in the field."

"You will be asked to undertake more investigations, Jules,

whether or not you find Evvie Tait. You are gaining a quiet reputation for managing the impossible."

"Have I managed an adequate apology, Perry?"

She sat up. "Yes. Yes, you have, and I have an apology of my own."

"Whatever for?"

"I never thanked you for your proposal."

She'd never *seriously considered* my proposal. "The offer remains open and has nothing to do with your idiot brother or your settlements. I want you to have the protection of my name, such as it is, and in all my inadequacy and shortcomings, I love you madly."

"Your sentiments are returned, Julian—in all *my* inadequacy and shortcomings—but there's a bit more to a marital pact than an enduring friendship, isn't there?"

What was she wittering on about? "An enduring friendship is no small boon, Hyperia."

"It's not, of course, but in your case, there's the title and the entailed properties, and... Jules, I love teaching Atticus to read. He's so eager and funny and serious about it. So dear. Leander is stealing my heart one bowl of porridge at a time. He likes cinnamon on his. I missed them both when I was in Town."

Did you miss me? "I am responsible for both boys, Perry. Nobody will snatch them away from you." Though Millicent could, in theory, snatch Leander away if she pleased to.

Hyperia leaned against me as if weary. "What I'm saying is that there's more to motherhood than giving birth."

Oh. *Oh.* "Much more, one hopes, and all of it less painful than the actual parturition. Some of it positively joyful."

"I thank you for your proposal, Jules, and for your apology."

"Are they both accepted?" I managed to sound fairly calm when I put that question to her.

"Of course not. No woman wants to accept a proposal offered strictly to avoid disaster. That's not a sound basis for a marriage. As for that other, apology accepted. Off to the nursery with you, Julian, or Leander will sack Paris in your absence."

My commanding officer had dismissed me with further orders. I kissed her cheek, bowed, and withdrew, my heart curiously light. I wasn't foolish enough to think that all was well, the status quo ante restored, no harm done. I had hurt my beloved's feelings and made only a start on repairing the damage.

She had refused my proposal of marriage for good reasons—the moment had been all wrong. There would be other, better moments, though. Much better moments. I would make *sure* of it.

Leander and I sacked Paris loudly, then we besieged Amiens and blockaded Marseille. The boy had a positive genius for military strategy, a talent he'd no doubt inherited from his father. By the time we returned to a hero's welcome in London, nurse was eyeing the clock.

"Uncle Julian, will you teach me how to write my name?"

A delaying tactic, of course. I had been a boy once. I knew exactly what the proper response was.

"If tomorrow morning, Nurse tells me your evening went well and that you scampered off to sleep with nary a peep of protest, then after you've broken your fast, I will show you how to write your name."

Leander saluted with his left hand. "Nary a peeper of protest, Uncle Julian. My name starts with L, like linnet and lace."

"Good to know. Until tomorrow, General Leander."

I left the nursery in good spirits, though tired. I returned to my rooms to change for supper and found Evelyn Tait's diaries sitting on my vanity. When the dressing bell rang, I was once again engrossed in young love's early raptures, and this time, Evelyn's panegyrics to her devoted spouse struck me as sweet and sad rather than silly.

CHAPTER SIXTEEN

Teaching a boy to make a signature was not the simple undertaking I'd envisioned. Leander could draw his letters in fine straight lines, but for his name, he'd wanted the cursive versions. He and I were still debating the best style for a majuscule L when Hyperia joined us.

"One can get all flourish-y," she said, pulling a third stool up to the schoolroom table. "But legibility is more important than putting on airs. Oh, I like that one." She pointed to a rather staid rendition of the letter in question. "Has dignity, and I can tell it's an L."

Leander had been enjoying wild loops and curlicues, though he wrote with a pencil rather than a quill pen. A world of artistry was possible with a pencil that became so much smudging when attempted in ink.

"Uncle Julian, is plain better?"

"Legible is better, meaning words and letters that can be easily read. Perhaps Miss West would favor us with a demonstration of her signature."

Hyperia obliged. I knew her hand intimately, and yet, watching her form the letters of her name was a pleasure. Her penmanship was steady, graceful, forthright... like the lady herself.

"There," she said, pushing the paper over to Leander, who sat between us. "My H can only be an H. My W can only be a W. Lord Julian, your turn."

I dutifully applied my moniker to the page and returned it to Leander. "My J is a J. My C is a C."

"A monogram is something different from a signature," Hyperia said. "A monogram is made up of only your initials and can be quite fancy. You can allude to the family crest, add symbolic flowers, choose your favorite colors."

Leander traced a finger along the letters of my last name. "I wish I were a Caldicott. Mama says I am, but Uncle Arthur hasn't made it official. My papa was Lord Harold Caldicott. He was a soldier who died fighting against the Corsican monster for Good King George."

Hyperia hugged the lad briefly. "We were all very proud of your father, and now we are proud of you. Not every boy is as conscientious about learning his letters."

"I was terrible at it," I said when it looked as if Leander's little chin might start quivering. "My governess despaired of me. I thought letters were boring, but I did rather enjoy numbers."

"I like numbers," Leander said. "They have to come out right."

Leander's mother walked through the doorway. "You get that from me. I'm a fiend for my ledger books. Good morning, Miss West, Lord Julian." She curtseyed, and Hyperia and I reciprocated with gestures that seemed too formal between family in the nursery.

How long had Millicent been lurking in the corridor, and how much had she overheard?

"We're debating the style of Leander's signature," I said. "Leander has a flair for embellishment." I passed her the paper, and she smiled.

"My son is a calligrapher. My lord, if you can spare me a moment, I'd like a word."

"Go," Hyperia said. "Leander and I will attack the vowels."

Millicent accompanied me into the corridor and kept walking until we were at a window overlooking the garden.

"That's a fetching frock," I said. "The color becomes you." A raspberry hue between red and purple.

"Your mother has yards and yards of it, and I do like the shade. You are very kind to spend time with Leander, my lord."

More than Millicent's wardrobe had improved. She'd lost some of her perpetually fretful air, and she was fashioning her hair into a coronet rather than a governess's severe bun.

"He is my nephew and a delight. I am fond of him and hope he's learning to enjoy his Uncle Julian's company." A pony should soon be added to his life. Caldicotts loved to spend time in the saddle, and whatever the boy's name might be, he was a Caldicott.

"He's learning to adore his uncles," Millicent replied. "He's a bit cautious with the duke—afraid that His Grace might meet Napoleon in France, that sort of thing—but you are his idol."

"I am not the stuff idols are made of."

"You are a good man," Millicent said, with a degree of earnestness that made me uncomfortable. "His Grace has settled a sum on me. Not in trust, not an annuity. A sum I can do with what I please. A substantial sum."

Well done, Arthur. "You have earned the right to some security, Millicent, and Arthur and I both know Harry meant to marry you."

She grimaced. "Can you see me as a duchess?"

Where was this discussion going? "If the old Duke of Chandos could find his second duchess at a wife sale, then yes, I can see you as Her Grace of Waltham. You'd be surprised at what some duchesses have got up to, Millicent. I myself I am not a Caldicott by blood."

"Of course you are."

"Afraid not."

"But you look exactly like the old duke. He must have half a dozen portraits scattered about this house. You have his nose, his chin, his eyebrows. They sort of swoop, so you look haughty until you smile."

As a child, I'd overheard my parents discussing the irregularity of my provenance. Papa hadn't minded, Mama hadn't seemed very repentant, and I'd only made sense of the conversation some years later.

"You did not haul me to the end of the corridor to discuss ancient history, Millicent."

"In a sense, I did. I'd like to go home."

You are home. Except she wasn't. For all that she was making free with the fabric stores and had been given some independent means, Millicent was still taking supper in the nursery and avoiding public occasions.

"You are the sole authority over Leander," I said, though the words cost me. "If you want to establish your own household in your home shire, Arthur and I will assist you to do that." Though Arthur had already taken ship in spirit and would soon be traveling in fact.

"Leander is happy here," Millicent said, some of her old diffidence leaching confidence from her words. "He's settling in. I haven't been home for years, my lord. Haven't seen my brother, have never met his children. I thought I'd make a visit, without Leander. They don't know about him, you see, and it might be easier—be kinder—if he remained here when I reestablish family ties."

I detested this plan. Millicent had tried to slip quietly from her son's life once before, and without having seen the splendor of the Hall or having had the benefit of independent means.

"He can't lose you," I said, wanting to physically restrain her from going anywhere. "You are all that boy has, the center of his universe."

"He won't lose me. I intend to visit over in Surrey, my lord, nothing more. A few days, a fortnight. I'm welcome there, and I miss it. My parents are buried there, as is my sister. I need to pay my respects."

As I longed to pay my respects to Harry's resting place, even if it was somewhere in bloody, bedamned France.

"I cannot stop you from going, and I will take the best care of my nephew in your absence. You will take the traveling coach, crests turned. An indulgence from your last employer, whose late wife remembered you kindly in her will."

Simple, useful falsehoods, not that far from the truth. How easily the old skills of an officer in enemy territory leaped back into service.

"I was planning on something like that, but the traveling coach won't be necessary."

"Yes, it will. The mother of my nephew shall not be subjected to the indignity of the public stage." Then too, I wanted John Coachman's report regarding precisely where Millicent had gone, whether the place was thriving, and how she'd been received.

"You aren't angry?" she asked as laughter drifted down the corridor from the schoolroom.

"I understand the pull of home, Millicent. Thoughts of home, of the lime alley in particular, saved a portion of my sanity once upon a time. I am nonetheless terrified that you will gather up Leander and take French leave."

I paced off a little way and considered her silhouetted against the window. She was a lovely woman, but life had been unkind to her. She was entitled to do whatever she saw fit for Leander, and yet, I had to state my piece.

"He just got here," I said, "and while I know the Hall isn't exactly cozy, I had a lovely childhood on this property, and I hope Harry did too. You are traveling to Surrey on reconnaissance, but I fear you will send for Leander two weeks hence." And I would lose my brother and nephew all in the same week. "Promise me you will give us more time with him than that."

"Who is 'us,' my lord? His Grace leaves for extended travel shortly."

She had been a housekeeper for the middling orders. Decent homes, all, until she'd crossed paths with my philandering brother on winter leave. She had little appreciation for how a large estate functioned as its own village and extended family.

"'Us' is the entire household. Lady Ophelia, Miss West, myself.

Everybody from the butler to the boot-boy is pleased to have Leander here. Mrs. Ingersoll has assured me she will accept the next invitation to have her daughter call on Leander, and I know many other local children who'd enjoy making Leander's acquaintance."

Don't take him away when we've just found him. He's all we have of Harry, and ducal connections bring many benefits. I kept that powder dry, suspecting I'd need it for a subsequent skirmish.

"I will leave on Monday, if you can spare the traveling coach," Millicent said. "My purpose is to reconnect with family, to revisit good memories, to renew some old acquaintances. You and His Grace have made that possible, and I thank you for it."

Hyperia emerged from the schoolroom. "I've been banished," she said. "Putting together seven letters in the right order requires practice and concentration. I hadn't the heart to tell the boy how many more letters will soon demand his attention."

"I will admire our scholar's efforts thus far," Millicent said, dipping slightly at the knees. "Enjoy your outing to Chiddingstone, my lord, Miss West."

She repaired to the nursery, her new skirts swishing gently.

"Not here," Hyperia said quietly. "Children have the ability to hear thoughts." She escorted me down to the waiting coach, and we began our eastward journey.

As the vehicle turned through the gate posts, I explained that Millicent was intent on visiting her old village, but that Leander would remain at the Hall for now.

"You're concerned she'll take him home with her?"

"She might, once she has scouted the terrain. Arthur would say that could be for the best."

"What do you say, Jules?"

I considered my answer as the horses picked up speed. "I say that Millicent is Leander's mother and has legal authority over him. Were he legitimate, other considerations would pertain, but he's a bastard, and thus her claim to custody is valid. If she does take him to dwell in some hamlet in Surrey, I will be the most doting, meddlesome, visitatious uncle in the history of uncles."

"Visitatious isn't a word."

"Neither was vexatious until somebody deserved the epithet. I've brought Evelyn's diaries. Would you like some reading material?" I was changing the subject, lest I descend into ranting.

"I would. Let me start at the beginning, when all was rose petals and birdsong, at least for a time."

I handed Hyperia the first volume and resumed reading where I'd left off the night before, with the second volume. Paradise had become purgatory. Evelyn's entries were less and less frequent and more and more bitter.

Hell hath no fury... I was so troubled by the notion that Millicent would take Leander away that I could barely focus on Evelyn's angry chronicle. I called upon a soldier's discipline, and by the time we'd reached Chiddingstone, I'd finished the second volume and made a good start on the third.

～

"I ask myself, what did Evelyn want?" Hyperia posed the question as we strolled the length of Chiddingstone's Tudor high street. The town—a village, really—showed to good advantage under the autumn sun. The lone inn was a red-brick edifice of substantial proportions, and the conical chimneys of an oast house suggested a local crop of hops.

The predominant building style along the street itself was whitewashed half-timbered architecture, mullioned windows, and window boxes overflowing with pansies and herbs.

The place charmed me at first sight, and I suspected Evelyn Tait had fallen under its spell just as quickly.

"Evelyn," I said, "wanted to get away from a husband who flirted with everything in skirts."

"John has always had charm. She liked that about him at first. He offers his arm as willingly to me as to the local beauties or their grandmamas."

That Hyperia did not include herself among the local beauties... "You describe a gentleman rather than a flirt. Tait broke his vows, though, and that is not gentlemanly in the least."

I could make that observation to Tait's devoted friend because Evelyn's diaries had made it for me first.

"Evelyn wanted children," Hyperia said. "Truly wanted them, and leaving John was a certain step away from that objective."

The aroma of baking bread wafted on the breeze, and my belly reminded me that the day was advancing.

"Evelyn wanted children, you're right, but she also wanted a husband she could trust. This must be the famous Chiding Stone."

Nobody knew where Chiddingstone got its name—perhaps from the corruption of an old Norse name—Cidda's town—or perhaps from some Saxon reference lost to antiquity. The place was named in the Domesday book, after all. Another theory suggested that we beheld the location where villagers gathered to remonstrate with scolding wives, habitual inebriates, or mischievous children. The list of possible etymologies also included Druid worship, though the Druids must have been a busy lot if they used every stone oddity in southern England as a place of worship.

The stone itself looked like a large lump of sandstone dough—six feet high, perhaps ten feet across—set on a ledge of stone that gave it another ten feet or so of height at the front.

"Only in England," Hyperia muttered. "It looks like a rock outcropping to me. A place for children to play that their mothers forbade them to climb upon. Evelyn truly did want a child."

"Children, plural," I said as we resumed walking. "She envisioned a loud, happy supper table and filling the Tait pew at the local church. She must have been very angry with John to cut herself off from that dream."

"Leaving certainly punished John, if that was her aim." Hyperia clearly did not approve, which was just too bad. She'd wanted to join me in this inquiry, and we'd reached the *for better or for worse* part of the proceedings. Darling John had behaved like an ass, and dear Evvie had retaliated in similar form. That was the plain truth as far as I knew it.

"She's sold her every worldly good," I pointed out. "She has vexed and worried her sisters and courted scandal to stay away. Why do that unless she hates, truly hates, the idea of rejoining Tait's household?"

"Marry in haste..." Hyperia murmured. "Shall we try the local ale?"

We more or less needed to if we were to learn the exact whereabouts of Evelyn's farm. I had not mentioned this excursion to Tait, because I hadn't wanted him galloping hell-bent for Chiddingstone and confronting Evelyn without witnesses—or referees.

Then too, I might be wrong about Evelyn's location, in which case Tait's hopes would have been raised for nothing.

The innkeeper was a jovial fellow of substantial proportions. He girded his middle with what looked like a red-checked tablecloth made over into a half apron, an interesting variation on turning a worn sheet.

"A farm owned by a lady over in Sussex?" he asked, wiping his hands on his apron. "You mean the Hasborough place? Good land, lovely situation, fine little manor house. The acres are prospering under Henry Mainwaring's hand. You couldn't ask for a better tenant. Henry and his sons know the land, and Maudie keeps the dairy and the garden in good trim. We get some of our winter butter from them because they always have a few fall heifers."

Before mine host could name the heifers and describe their markings, I asked for the private dining parlor, where Hyperia and I enjoyed ham sandwiches and excellent ale.

The innkeeper had explained how to reach the farm—Hasborough Cottage—which lay about half a mile from the village itself. We chose to walk, having spent much of the morning in the coach, and I was glad for a chance to move about.

"Do you still need those tinted spectacles?" Hyperia asked, striding along at my side, "or are they more of a habit now?"

I took them off, regretted it, and put them back on. "Still need them. Autumn sunshine is supposed to be mellow, but as we lose the leaves, I find the sunbeams brighter than in summer. Bright sun on snow is a recipe for a megrim."

"You dread winter?"

I had missed her so in the few days she'd been in London. These conversations that meandered into random corners of my soul were good for me, and I hoped Hyperia enjoyed them too.

"I dread the Hall without Arthur as the unfailing prop and stay of the household and the estate. Now Millicent is making noises about leaving, though she never promised us we'd have Leander for long. Even Banter is a frequent visitor, and he's good company." I was dodging the hard part, of course, and that would not do. "If Lady Ophelia goes to Paris, you cannot bide with me, Perry. I know that. I will miss you dreadfully."

If we were married, we'd never need to be parted, though I couldn't see Hyperia tolerating a husband who lived in her pocket.

"I am quite at sixes and sevens," she said as we started up a hill. "Dwelling with Healy is unthinkable, but at the family seat I'll be by myself, as you will soon be, and that will cause a bit of speculation. Not quite a scandal."

"Can you recruit an auntie or companion?"

"Old women have companions. I hadn't thought in that direction."

I knew for a certainty that, despite my infirmity and inadequacy, I wanted to marry Hyperia. I knew with equal certainty that this was not an opportune moment to renew my suit.

"Lady Ophelia will certainly know of willing and appropriate parties who can serve as your companion. We'll ask her."

We topped the rise, and Hasborough Cottage lay in the dell

below us. The neighborhood was much given to oaks, and several grand specimens provided the backdrop for a two-story manor in the local red brick with a crown of chimneys and a wealth of mullioned windows.

"Tidy," Hyperia said.

"Prosperous," I replied. "Not a weed on the walkways, not a shutter dares sag." Evelyn, by her own account, found weedy paths untenable. "The door is painted red." Tait Manor had a red door of the exact same hue.

"You think she's biding here?" Hyperia asked as we started down the lane that led to the little manor.

"If what she wanted was independence, this was the most direct path for her to that goal. She could wait here until she inherited control of the land and the leasehold, then deal with John from a position of strength. Unless he wants to look a perfect fool, he'll not gainsay her decision to live apart from him."

"He already looks a perfect fool, to hear some tell it. The property is lovely. Merry Olde at its bucolic finest."

The people inside were lovely too. We'd caught Henry Mainwaring lingering over a midday meal, two of his grown sons with him, Mrs. Mainwaring at the foot of the table, and a nearly grown daughter present as well.

No Evelyn Tait, but then, she'd likely keep to herself when in the area.

"Knew your old steward, my lord," Mr. Mainwaring said when Hyperia and I had been inveigled into joining the family for a delectable serving of apple tart. Cinnamon and nutmeg underscored the Mainwarings' relative wealth, and the whipped cream slathered over our sweets was a paean to fall heifers.

"I learned a lot from Sean Gorman," Mainwaring went on. "Was a great one for reading every pamphlet, and he does love those Welsh herding dogs."

"As does his son," I replied, though the connection surprised me when it should not have. Villages were no longer worlds unto themselves, and enterprising fellows in these modern days often left the home shire in search of opportunity.

Hyperia was smiling at her tart, and I could have spent a lovely quarter hour simply watching her consume it.

"What brings your lordship to our humble abode?" Mrs. Mainwaring asked, sending a pitcher of cider around.

"We're looking for Mrs. John Tait," I said. "The Taits bide not far from Caldicott Hall, and I am under the impression that Evelyn Tait has come this way." Vague, and husband and wife sensed I was treading lightly, based on the glance they shared.

"Fanny, boys, away you go," she said. "You can finish your tarts in the kitchen."

The boys were twenty if they were a day, their sister perhaps sixteen, and away they did go, desserts in hand, after taking a proper leave of Hyperia and me.

"If you want to buy the property," Mr. Mainwaring said, closing the door after his offspring had decamped, "you're too late, my lord. I've signed a contract of sale with Mrs. Tait, right and proper, duly witnessed, and I'm to hand over the coin in a fortnight or so. I don't blame you for wanting this farm—it's excellent land, and Mrs. Tait has been a wonderful landlord—but you'll not have it from me at any price. My children were born here. My boys will work this land when I'm gone. Mrs. Mainwaring has said it shall be so, and thus I am bound."

I poured more cider for Hyperia, though Mainwaring's revelation left me mentally reeling. "I am not in the market for more acres, Mainwaring, and I can see that you are taking excellent care of this farm. Might I be so rude as to inquire what you're paying for the property?"

Husband and wife exchanged another look, this one unreadable to me. Mrs. Mainwaring named a sum that would allow Evelyn Tait to leave for continental parts unknown and spend the rest of her days there, living in safety and comfort, if not outright luxury.

Damn and blast. Outmaneuvered again.

"You weren't completely wrong," Hyperia said as the coach rattled away from Chiddingstone. "Evelyn is apparently set on independence, and she did see the farm as her haven of last resort."

"But she conducted the transaction entirely by post, Perry. *Where in perdition is she?*"

"Could her sisters be selling the property out from under her?"

Hyperia's question gave me a bad turn—for a moment. "You've read Evelyn's diaries, seen pages and pages of her handwriting, and you might have noticed her name in the front of each volume. The signature on the contract looked to me to be Evelyn's signature. The penmanship on that letter Mainwaring showed us looked like hers to me. What did you think?"

"Hers," Hyperia said after a moment's reflection. "She makes a little production out of the initial T in Tait and crosses the final T with a markedly upward slash. A vigorous signature, much as I picture Evelyn."

She hadn't set foot on the farm itself for more than five years, but she'd corresponded regularly, congratulated the Mainwarings on good harvests, and condoled them on wet springs. She'd convinced them to try the Russian wheat that was planted in fall and came up in spring, and she'd approved a dam on the stream to facilitate irrigation for dry years.

A good landlord indeed. Involved. Conscientious.

"Do you recognize the address she used in Town?" Hyperia asked.

"Doubtless a poste restante of some sort, maybe the first of several she set up in a series to make tracing her whereabouts more difficult." And Tait had never thought to inquire of his wife at the farm, very likely because the quarterly rents had come in regularly.

"Julian, do you have the sense that Evelyn isn't simply hiding from Tait, she's hiding from her sisters too?"

"You put your finger on a notion that has been plaguing me since my first discussion with Margery Semple. Who is the villain of this piece? I want it to be Evelyn or John—apologies for that, my dear, but his wife left him for reasons—but that's too simple."

"Promise me something, Julian. If ever we are married, and even if we're not, we won't quarrel for five straight years, until neither one of us recalls exactly what justified our pique in the first place. Evelyn's behavior strikes me as that of a runaway horse. Once the beast panics, its own panic fuels more headlong flight."

I had ridden runaways, and Hyperia was right. Once fear got a grip on the beast, any attempt to assert reason over the situation provoked worse and more dangerous hysterics.

"And John became passive," I replied, "waiting for Evelyn to come home or demand a legal separation by correspondence, anything to put matters in order. He'd still be waiting, but you got him off his backside, so to speak. I can't imagine holding a grudge that long, Perry, or that hard."

"You bear a grudge against France."

She had me there. I did have a grudge against France, and as long as my brother lay moldering in French soil, I would hold that grudge hard. The rest of the wartime dead were lamentable casualties and even tragedies, but Harry's death was a personal grief. I could not avenge him. I could not reconcile myself to his passing. A grudge was all I had.

"Let's get comfortable," Hyperia said when we'd made the only change of horses the journey necessitated.

"I am comfortable."

"*Comfortable*," she said, leaning forward and opening the opposite bench so it folded out flat.

"An excellent suggestion." Excellent and bold. The Caldicott traveling coach was a luxury conveyance, and thus its interior could be fashioned into a rolling bedroom. We shed boots, and I removed my coat, and Hyperia was soon resting against my side on our makeshift mattress, her head on my shoulder.

"Will you be insulted if I fall asleep, Jules?"

"I will be honored to serve as milady's pillow. You didn't find much rest in Town, did you?"

She stirred about, sighed, and tucked an arm across my middle. "I grew fretful. Healy's behavior made no sense. I feared for his sanity, and from there, all manner of mental flights took hold of me. If Healy was legally incompetent, what would become of his properties and income? Who could become his trustee? Who would marry him if he continued to behave erratically? He needs a wife."

So do I, by God. One particular wife. "Why do you say that?"

"I tell you things, Jules. That I was terrified in London, that your investigations give me a purpose I hadn't realized I needed. You *listen* to me. Healy needs somebody to listen to him, to tell him his fears are reasonable but he's equal to the challenges he faces. He needs somebody who reposes her most personal confidences in him."

I traced the curve of Hyperia's shoulder and drifted my fingers across her nape. "The listening is mutual, Perry. You sort me out." And she cuddled so sweetly too.

I inventoried my bodily state and found no real stirring of desire, but instead, a sense of... wellbeing. Of comfort and comfortableness.

"I'm falling asleep," she murmured. "Sorry."

I commended my beloved to the arms of Morpheus and soon joined her in his embrace, but something in Perry's observations, about a spouse being the one who listens, plucked at my heartstrings. When Evelyn locked her door to her husband, she'd turned a deaf ear to him in more than the basic conjugal sense.

He had become deaf to her wifely concerns too. Their disregard for each other had made a bitter mockery of the vows. I thought of Mainwaring and his wife, their gazes speaking volumes without a word. They likely indulged in carnal pleasures rarely, and yet, they were clearly, devotedly, married.

"They aren't *my* investigations," I said to my sleeping beauty, "they are *our* investigations." Hyperia would not see it as I did, but she'd known that for me to exclude her had been wrong.

I drifted off, bemused by the notion of John Tait having nobody to talk to, and when I awoke, I realized that I had yet another party to interview in the ongoing search for Evelyn Tait.

CHAPTER SEVENTEEN

Mrs. Emelia Probinger was in her garden, where she and I had conversed on occasions related to previous investigations. She was a thirtyish military widow who had followed the drum, and we shared a natural sympathy based on that common experience. She was practical, attractive, self-assured, and given to going her own way, deeming that a widow's right.

"Have you and Miss West been introduced?" I asked.

"We have," Mrs. Probinger said, smiling at Hyperia. "We've admired each other's bonnets in the churchyard. Miss West, a pleasure to see you. Will you have lemonade, cider, or tea? Meadow tea for you, my lord, if I recall correctly."

"I will join you ladies in your drink of choice."

"Cider," Hyperia said. "His lordship and I have spent considerable time in the traveling coach today, and I have a thirst for a cool glass of cider."

Much of that time had been in a pleasant, dozing cuddle, and when I'd asked Hyperia if she had the stamina for one more call, she'd answered in the affirmative.

Mrs. Probinger set her secateurs in her trug, pulled off her gloves, and led us to a wrought-iron grouping on her back terrace. When last I'd been here, the trellised roses had been in vigorous form. Now, the best display was from a potted morning glory climbing to the second story on a lattice of twine. Given the late afternoon hour, some of the blooms were closing, but the display was still a lovely riot of blue-violet flowers.

"We'd like to talk to you about John Tait," I said when the drinks were before us. "We're searching for his errant wife at his request."

"Good," Mrs. Probinger said, pale green eyes narrowing. "That man has been lovesick for years, and time is not improving his situation." She was a petite woman with strawberry-blond hair and piquant, angular features. One would not expect such a dainty creature to indulge in blunt speech and hearty laughter, but Mrs. Probinger did. She was a particular kind of military widow—tougher and more pragmatic than many of the civilian variety, hard to shock, and willing to enjoy life's fleeting pleasures where she found them.

Her company was bracing, her cider excellent.

"Lovesick for Evelyn?" Hyperia asked.

"Of course for Evelyn. He maundered on at tiresome length about how he'd fallen from her favor, he did not understand his wife, he had no idea what troubled her and knew not how to woo her back. This was all years ago, but never was a widow less entertained by a gentleman's company. I recall the interlude clearly. I suspect he thought we were both bereaved in a sense, and I'd be sympathetic to his situation. I am sympathetic. A sullen wife is a problem. A broken heart is a problem, but those were Tait's problems, not mine."

Her pity for Tait came through in her words, as did a certain bewilderment. Mrs. Probinger's union, I had reason to know, had been no bed of rose petals. She'd mourned for her husband properly, and that was that. A husband in perpetual mourning for an extant wife would have made no sense to her.

"What exactly were John's intentions toward you?" Hyperia asked.

"To bore me silly?"

"To make Evelyn jealous?" I suggested.

Mrs. Probinger's gaze ranged over her garden, gone overgrown with the advanced season. "Possibly."

"How exactly," Hyperia asked, "did you and John tryst?"

"Tryst?" Mrs. Probinger laughed. "Heaven defend poor Evelyn if that is her husband's idea of a tryst. He fell in step beside me a few times on my way home from church. Evelyn preferred to take the coach when wearing her Sunday finest. He offered me his arm, and I took it, though I am quite capable of walking unassisted. Mr. Tait struck me as considering himself something of a gallant, the squire with some Town bronze generously bestowing his handsome company on the rural widow."

"He's charming," Hyperia said.

"Charming?" Miss Probinger pushed the pitcher of cider across the table. "Wellington is charming, Miss West. He likes women and treats them as friends. I'm fairly certain His Grace considers his best friends to be women, in fact. Lord Julian is charming. I suspect his sisters put the manners on him, and being the youngest brother, he was smart enough to acquire a few airs and graces too. John Tait is... tedious."

What a delightful woman, and yet, I was honor-bound to pursue the truth wherever it led. "Was Tait tedious on purpose?" I asked.

Hyperia poured me more cider while Mrs. Probinger stared at me hard.

"Yes," she said at length, "I think he was, now that you put it like that. He knew my reputation would stand up to a bit of flirtation, or the appearance of a bit of flirtation, but he had no more interest in me than I have in once again trudging across Spain in high summer. I tried to kiss him, if you must know.

"He acted surprised," she went on, "and gave me a pretty speech about neighborly friendliness, and 'aren't friends life's greatest blessing?' He didn't happen upon me on the way home from church again after that, and I counted myself relieved." She took a biscuit from the plate in the center of the table. "Men are so odd. The shy ones can be full of hidden fire, the accomplished flirts are usually capable of little else, and the exquisites turn up exquisitely selfish when consideration would most be appreciated. Don't you find it so, Miss West?"

Hyperia's smile was the embodiment of mischief. "Precisely, but watch the quiet ones, and your vigilance is often rewarded."

Whatever did she mean by that? The ladies were in perfect accord on some matter that escaped the understanding of a mere adult male. I stuffed a biscuit into my mouth and took refuge in lordly silence.

"He loved Evelyn," Mrs. Probinger said. "His sentiments struck me as a combination of calf-love and genuine bewilderment at a spouse turned cold. Not a pretty sight. I hope he finds his wife and can arrange a resolution with her. John Tait is not a bad man, and no marriage is perfect."

She spoke with the voice of experience.

"I don't think Evelyn had access to such wise counsel as you offer." I was coming to suspect just the opposite.

"If you were hiding from your husband," Hyperia asked, "where would you go?"

"Interesting question. I often hid parts of myself from Dewey, and he returned the courtesy. But the whole of me? London, I suppose, but London is expensive, and I would eventually be recognized by some old acquaintance from the regiment. Where would you hide, Miss West?"

"If I were Evelyn," Hyperia said, "I'd masquerade as another man's wife. Nobody would give me a second look then."

"Miss West, you have an interesting grasp of the protections of matrimony. Many a rogue will only poach on another man's preserves in hopes that the resulting cuckoos are born into some other fellow's well-feathered nest. Such men prefer experienced partners, and wifehood confers at least that dubious blessing. I have shocked myself with these observations. I have doubtless shocked you. I do apologize."

She did seem a bit chagrined, while I was glad to see the assumption that wifehood equated to invisibility questioned. How many negative associations could Hyperia have with one conventionally venerated institution?

Even as that question occurred to me, I also realized that John Tait had known where he could credibly appear to stray. Petty of me, but that was not the tactic of a paragon. That was the tactic of a fool in love, but a fool all the same.

We made our farewells and, having sent the coach back to the Hall, walked the final distance across the fields.

"Where could Evelyn be, Jules? I asked you to undertake this inquiry because I thought John needed to move on, but now... I hope she's alive."

"Only a living woman could arrange to sell that farm, Hyperia, but if we don't find her in the next few days, she will have all the means she needs to live in comfort on the Continent, assuming her sisters won't steal the proceeds from her. In either case, Tait will be left to wander in a purgatory of Evelyn's making forever." Not entirely of Evelyn's making, but Evelyn was certainly the party perpetuating the separation.

"We won't allow that."

Hyperia's faith was reassuring, but not until we reached the Hall, and I was leafing through the day's correspondence, did I acquire a smidgeon of hope that we might find Evelyn in time.

~

True to her word, Mrs. Ingersoll had accepted a second invitation to bring Merri to the Hall to meet Leander. The occasion was set for the afternoon following the excursion to Chiddingstone, and thus I had an evening to ponder my battle plan. I acquainted nobody with my suspicions, but sent a note to Tait asking him to attend me at the Hall at two of the clock.

And if my note was a bit mysterious, well, I'd earned the right to some minor theatrics. More were to follow, I hoped, if all went well.

"You look as if you're home on leave again," Arthur said at the noon meal. "Watchful and distracted while you exchange pleasantries in all directions."

We dined on the terrace, though the day had that heavy, humid feel of a gathering storm. The sky was a cottony expanse of white batting and the air unusually still.

"Leander is expecting a guest this afternoon," I said. "A young lady. He was full of questions about whether girls can have ponies and speak French."

"Yes to both," Lady Ophelia said, selecting a profiterole from the epergne in the middle of the table. "We can also shoot, swear, and tell naughty jokes. If you fail to inform that lad of the foregoing, I will provide him demonstrations when he's a bit closer to his majority."

Something about the odd weather, or perhaps my acquaintance with Evelyn's bickering, backbiting sisters, produced a wave of affection for her ladyship. She made it possible for Hyperia and me to be together, she was a font of knowledge useful to my investigations, and she kept an eye on the nursery and on Arthur while I went gadding about.

All the while pretending that fresh country air was her reason for biding at the Hall.

"Thank goodness," I said, "that somebody's on hand to show the boy how to go on. I wonder if he has an extant godmother."

Hyperia patted my hand. "He does now." She popped a petit four into her mouth.

Had Leander been baptized? A question for Millicent, who was preparing to leave the Hall and still unwilling to join even family meals.

"Anything interesting in the post, Julian?" Arthur asked, taking the last raspberry tart from the epergne.

"You should have turned the post over to me as soon as I mustered out. I needed rest above all else at that juncture, and the mail is a reliable soporific. Three reports on the progress of harvests on the properties in Surrey and Kent. A half-dozen invitations you will not be on hand to accept, as polite society well knows. Some invoices from Bond Street. You will be the best-dressed traveler on the Continent."

The post had also included some good wishes for Arthur's safe travel from his cronies in the Lords, and I was reminded that His Grace had a large and demanding life. Holding the reins for him would be a challenge for any brother, especially one prone to lapses of memory and regarded poorly by much of Society.

"Banter is more fashionable than I am," Arthur said. "The dignity of my office and all that." He smiled self-consciously, a happy man contemplating a dream come true. Perhaps it was a day for sentiment, but as much as I'd miss Arthur, I was also—for the first time—fiercely glad he and Banter were going abroad.

Their dream was simple—a shared life, with all the ups, downs, delights, and doldrums attendant thereto—and for a time they could have that dream.

"Be outrageously fashionable on the Continent," I said. "Cast Banter into the shade. Paris will fall at your feet. Miss West, might you join me for a postprandial stroll about the garden?"

"I'd best, as much as I've eaten. Mrs. Gwinnett is a treasure."

Our cook was indeed a treasure, and she made the most scrumptious meadow tea too.

Hyperia and I wandered down into the garden and were soon by the three-tiered fountain at the center of the formal parterres.

"Keep me moving, Jules, or I will find a convenient bench and commence basking in the sun like an old tabby cat. How do you find taking on the ducal responsibilities?"

"I'm not taking them on, really. I'll be more of a house steward. The parliamentary rigamarole, the occasions of state, the commission of the peace—all that will simply muddle on without His Grace. It's a testament to Arthur's integrity that he makes the time to ensure the Hall prospers as well as it does."

"But he attends to the Hall in part because it's the family legacy, and the only fellow who can inherit it is you."

"And I have no intention of inheriting anything for a good long while. The very idea gives me the collywobbles. Will you do me a favor this afternoon, Hyperia?"

"Of course." The herbaceous borders had been chopped back, the potted citrus moved into the conservatory. The garden had the feel of a lady stripped down to chemise and petticoats. Not conventionally attractive when shorn of her finery.

"I've invited John Tait over for a briefing, which will occur in the library. I'd like you to keep Mrs. Ingersoll company on the mezzanine while Tait and I converse."

"You want me to eavesdrop with a guest? A guest whose presence will cause John some embarrassment?"

"She can't cause him any more embarrassment than he has already caused himself, and she—like Mrs. Probinger—is in a position to hold Tait accountable in ways you and I cannot."

"What aren't you telling me?"

That was my Perry. Able to leap where angels feared to tread and to land precisely on the truth. "I have a theory," I said, "and at first it struck me as outlandish, but my theory fits all the facts. Hear me out."

I explained, and when I expected Hyperia to laugh, she looked pensive. "I'll do it, Jules, but you'd better be right. John has been through enough."

I quite agreed, and thus when my caller arrived, I had him shown to the library. Tait did not notice the quiet click of the door latch when company joined us on the mezzanine, but I did. The allies and opposing forces had arrived, and so, I hoped, had the end of Tait's purgatory.

Whether his next destination was heaven, hell, or the prosaic joys of married life would be to some extent up to him.

CHAPTER EIGHTEEN

"I brought the calendars." Tait strode across the library, a satchel in hand. "I have no idea why you'd want to see them after all these years, but a farmer keeps records almost as religiously as a clerk tends his ledgers." He extracted a stack of documents and passed them to me.

He looked hale, windblown, and worried. He'd galloped cross-country, in other words, rather than sedately hacking about on the lanes or impressing the grazing livestock with his majestic coach.

"The calendars are appreciated," I said, putting them on the reading table, "and Evelyn's diaries are on the sideboard. Care for a drink?"

"Lemonade would do. I'm not in the mood for spirits."

I poured him some of Mrs. Gwinnett's meadow tea. "Try this. I adore it. Has a touch of sweetness, very refreshing. The honey blends well with the mint and the whisper of black tea. Mrs. Gwinnett says reused tea leaves are the secret."

He sampled his drink. "A fine libation. My compliments to your kitchen, but, my lord, what the hell am I doing here? Have you news that cannot be entrusted to a messenger?"

"You are hearing a report I would not set down in writing because letters can be intercepted or misinterpreted. I visited Hasborough Cottage yesterday, though it might soon be renamed Mainwaring Manor."

Tait wandered to the French doors with his drink. "Evvie's farm. A lovely place. Every few months, I ride over that way and have a gander at it. They pay their rents to the penny, and the land prospers. I wish I could tell Evvie that."

I poured myself half a glass and took a seat at the reading table. "You don't drop in on the tenants?" I searched through the calendars until I found the year Evelyn had gone missing.

"The Mainwarings are not my tenants," Tait said. "They are Evvie's tenants, and she was very protective of that place. It was hers, or soon will be."

"And she, or somebody impersonating her, has arranged to sell it to Mainwaring for a very tidy sum. With that money in hand, she'll be able to live comfortably in Paris for all the rest of her days."

"Paris?" Tait pushed away from the doorjamb. "You think she's in Paris? My French is awful, but harvest is going well, and the packets from Dover run nigh daily anymore."

"Tait, I do not know what Evelyn plans to do with the proceeds of the sale. I do know you've been lying to me."

"About what?" He was annoyed, a man who'd been at the end of his tether too long, and for our audience to hear just how far he'd been pushed was a good thing.

"You were faithful to your wife. Those widows and jaded women and bed-hopping countesses were actresses in a drama you put on for Evelyn's benefit. I've spoken with Mrs. Probinger, and she said when she tried to so much as kiss your cheek, you all but climbed the nearest oak tree to get away from her."

"Bold little thing." He was affronted that one of his fellow performers had had a script of her own. "I couldn't very well plant her a facer for taking liberties. A little gallantry to another woman was all it took to get Evvie fuming, but I never meant... There are more lonely women on this earth than one rural bachelor can fathom, my lord. In any case, my tactic failed. Evvie stopped noticing with whom I exchanged flatteries, and then she just got quiet.

"I hated that," he went on. "When she grew indifferent. That's the worst. We talked about everything at first, and then we couldn't talk about anything. As if I could ever be with another woman after speaking my vows to Evvie. She spoiled me for all others, and then she wouldn't have me. She got it into her head that I was straying, and I got it into my head that she needed to see that others would have me even if she wouldn't. The quintessential marital impasse, and I still don't understand how it happened."

With any luck, that was about to change. "If you could speak to your wife now, what would you say to her?"

Tait sighed, closed his eyes, and tilted his head back. "That's easy. I've had five years to consider what I *will* say if providence should reunite us. I would tell her that I love her, that I'm sorry. I am just so perishing sorry, and I miss her until I ache with it, and please come home. If she won't come home, I simply need to know that she's well and happy. If she wants an annulment, a separation, to live in Town or Paris or Cathay... I cannot dwell in uncertainty without her anymore."

From the mezzanine above, I heard a stirring, but Tait, so far gone in his lamentations, apparently hadn't.

"What about that business with Mrs. Ingersoll?" I asked. "You were dishonest with her, and you appeared genuinely interested, according to the lady."

Tait opened his eyes and sent me a quizzical look. "Damnedest thing, that. She reminds me of Evvie, in a way. She's not as grand as my Evvie, not as fashionable, not quite as sharp-tongued, but she gives as good as she gets, and she's devoted to that child. Evvie longed for children, and I sometimes think..." He resumed his tragic post at the French doors. "All that's neither here nor there. I suppose I'd best pack for Paris."

A substantial tread set the metal frame on the spiral staircase shaking. Mrs. Ingersoll, looking like the Avenging Angel of Wronged Womanhood, descended the steps and stalked across the room to the French doors.

"A fine speech, John Tait, but you did not know your own wife when you attempted to kiss her."

Tait's mouth opened. He raised a hand a few inches from his side, dropped it, shut his mouth.

Hyperia came down the steps more quietly as I rose from the table, and Tait studied the lady before him.

"Evvie's hair was curly. People's hair doesn't change."

"Damn you, John Tait. I used the rubbishing curling tongs nigh daily to look pretty for you." A world of despair lay in that admission and queendoms of hurt and anger. "I know I've lost a good deal of weight. Between worry and penury, a body forgets to eat. But I am still your wife even if you can't recognize me, and I want an annulment. *I will have an annulment.*"

"Evelyn." Tait was smiling at her as if he beheld salvation itself rather than a woman at her wits' end. "You are well. You are *alive*, and you are well."

"An annulment," Hyperia said quietly, "means Merri becomes illegitimate."

"That can't be true," Evelyn spat, though Hyperia had voiced a simple, legal fact.

I collected the calendars from the reading table. "It shouldn't be true, but that's how an annulment works. Might I offer you some libation, Mrs. Tait?"

"I don't want any wretched libation, and I don't want to be married to this... this rural rogue. I'm selling my farm to get away from him once and for all."

"Evvie," Tait began, "please don't be so angry. If you love another, you can tell me. Something went awry between us, and I don't like it—I hate the very notion, in fact—but if Merri's father is your choice, then I will reconcile myself to that reality."

I'd never heard Tait speak so plainly, so quietly. "Look at the calendar from five years ago, Tait. You'll find an X marked about every twenty-eighth day for the whole year until September. No X in September. Merri is your daughter."

Tait blinked, and then the farmer in him handed the sense of my statement to the husband. "Evvie? Is his lordship correct?"

"You won't believe me if I say yes." Evelyn was no longer fuming. Instead, she'd taken on some of Tait's martyred resignation. "I know you won't believe me, but yes, she's your daughter. No other candidates in the running. Plain, overly tall women running to fat don't get those sorts of offers."

"You're not plain," Tait said. "You were never plain. You were never fat or overly tall. You were grand and robust, and now you are positively striking. Curse me all you like, Evelyn, but don't say a single word in self-denigration."

She sank into a chair at the reading table. "Spare me your gallantries. You will need them for every other woman in your ambit. I heard all that blather about keeping your vows, John. You kept your pants on, possibly, but you betrayed me just the same, and you will never change."

I understood in that moment why a sensible village would have a designated spot for remonstrating with scolds, inebriates, and reprobates. We had no Chiding Stone at Caldicott Hall, but we didn't need one.

We had Lord Julian Caldicott, who now, apparently, included the resolution of marital discord among his varied talents.

"It seems to me," I said, joining Evelyn at the table, "that *you*, madam, are the party who is overdue to mend her ways. You need to stop listening to that pair of harpies you call your sisters and uphold the vows you took on your wedding day."

A younger Evelyn might well have slapped me for that bit of pomposity. This one regarded me with glittering, hurt-filled eyes.

"I did not imagine John's behavior," she said with considerable dignity. "He's the consoler, flirt, and cajoler at large."

"He's friendly," I retorted, "not too high in the instep, and you used to love that about him. But allow me to speculate. Mrs. Margery Semple kindly passed along to you some incident she claimed to have observed, where John had his hand on a lady's person, or was whispering in some belle's ear behind the livery. In a fit of pique, you took to locking your bedroom door."

Evelyn's ire drained into puzzlement. "How could you know that?"

And thus was my theory of the case confirmed. "Just as you were talking yourself into forgiving John," I went on, "for a slight that was, I suspect, entirely imaginary, Margery would come up with a gentle warning about John bantering with some sweet young thing. Ardath would pass along an on-dit from some source she never named, though John was always painted as the villain. This spite was reluctantly poured into your ear with the best of sororal intentions, of course, or so they claimed. You could have told them both to shut their mouths and leave you in peace, but instead, you locked your bedroom door."

"I unlocked it," Evelyn retorted, "any number of times. I told myself I had to try again, to be patient, to look for the good. Then Margery said John had nearly compromised Ardie, and unlocking my door became harder and harder."

"*Me?* Compromise *Ardath?*" Tait sank into a chair opposite Evelyn's. "That is rank... Ardath threw herself at me, Evvie. She was your little sister, like my own sister, or so I thought of her. I didn't realize she had designs on my person until I was all but peeling her off of me. I told Margery that Ardath needed a husband before the blasted chit attempted the same behavior on a less gentlemanly victim."

"And now," Hyperia murmured, taking a seat at the foot of the table, "Ardath blames John for precipitating a less-than-satisfying union."

Evelyn tidied up the stack of calendars until they were perfectly aligned. "Ardath said John all but ravished her. That was my first clue that my sisters were not exactly impartial where John was concerned. John wasn't that fond of Ardath. He spoke of her as a pest, giddy, foolish... He might have bussed her cheek or put an arm around her shoulders, but near ravishment was an exaggeration at best. Even I knew that, or I eventually figured it out."

I was at the head of the table, not by design. "Ardath overplayed her hand. Did anything else in your sisters' behavior give you pause?"

Evelyn twisted the ring on her fourth finger, a simple gold band like a thousand others, much plainer than the hoard she had sold.

"When I left," she said, "I was furious. John had forgotten our anniversary. Margery warned me that husbands do that, but I thought John would be different. He'd always remembered before... but Margery was right, and I was exhausted and out of sorts. Breeding, though I didn't know it at the time. I have a temper. It's a failing. But I could not take another excuse, another apology. I presented myself on Ardath's doorstep, and she was so welcoming..."

Evelyn removed the ring and peered at the inside. "Love conquers all. That's what's inscribed here. In Latin, because John knew I love my letters. *Amor omnia vincit.*" She put the ring back on. "Ardath said she didn't know how I'd lasted as long as I had under John Tait's roof, and in the mood I was in—then—that sounded like sympathy and understanding. I craved sympathy and understanding."

"That wasn't all she offered," Hyperia muttered. "Her sympathy came at a cost, didn't it?"

"Of course. Not much at first. Ardath claimed having me in her household meant she had to increase her staff, spend more at market, do more laundry... She hated to ask me, but I did have 'all those pearls,' and 'money doesn't grow on trees.' I never liked Grandmama's pearls. Pity pearls, I called them. We should have split them up and given them to our granddaughters, but no. I was to parade around in the lot of them."

Why hadn't Dante fashioned a circle of hell for jealous, conniving siblings? "Then you realized that you were with child," I suggested, "and the situation became more complicated."

Tait, who had been silent for some time, regarded his wife with utter seriousness. "Merri is our daughter? Your word on that?"

Evelyn's gaze roved from the shelves marching along the inside wall, to the spiral staircase, to me, to the calendars.

"I have already given you my word, John. Ardie and Margery insisted you would not believe Merri is yours. I refuse to spend the rest of my life begging you to accept that truth. Do you believe she is our daughter?"

The fate of the marriage hung on that one quiet question, as did the potential happiness of one small, innocent child.

"Your sisters told you that you were plain," Tait said gently. "They were wrong about that, Evelyn. They were wrong about a lot of things."

Evelyn sat up very tall. "But?"

"But nothing," Tait replied. "If you say Merri is my daughter, then she's my daughter, and there's an end to it. You need to know I will not consent to have my offspring made illegitimate just so you can be free of me. Living apart will be scandalous for such as us, though the nobs consider it fashionable, but if that's what you want, then we'll dwell separately."

Evelyn stared at her hands, mannish in their breadth and strength and trembling slightly. "And Merri? Will you take her from me? Ardath and Margery insisted you would, that it's your right, and they aren't wrong about the law."

The sheer meanness of Margery and Ardath's scheming would have shamed Old Scratch himself.

"That pair of hissing vipers," Tait muttered. "God pity their husbands and children."

"Merri is your daughter in fact and by law," Evelyn said, voice low. "*Will you take her from me?*"

We had finally reached the part of the investigation that answered the *why* questions. Why not come home, negotiate a truce, and resume life? Why not write to the estranged husband and demand terms? Why not pursue the annulment? Why such desperate measures for so long? The explanation was simple.

After years of longing for a child, Evelyn Tait had one daughter. Her worst fear would be losing that child to an angry, vindictive husband. A husband who grew more entitled to his bitterness with each passing season. She'd spent too much time in the company of siblings intent on exploiting that fear as only siblings could. Then too, her conscience had whispered that her precipitous flight had been a mistake, compounded by the further mistake of trusting her sisters.

Evelyn was guilty and afraid but, above all, determined.

"Why can't Merri have you both?" I asked. "If an annulment is off the table, and separation means the child remains a stranger to her father, why not consider the remaining, sensible option?"

Tait looked at me as if I'd burst forth with a Basque drinking song. "And that would be?"

Hyperia stated the obvious. "You can reconcile. No annulment, Merri has two parents, and Margery and Ardath have nothing to say to anything, *ever again*."

The silence that sprang up was complicated. Then Evelyn began to cry. Tait came around the table, took the seat beside her, and passed her his handkerchief.

"We'd like some privacy," he said, patting Evelyn's shoulder. "Please, we'd like some privacy *now*."

Hyperia nearly raced me to the door, slowing only so I could open it for her. I'd barely set foot in the corridor before she was in my arms, sniffling against my shoulder and holding on to me for dear life.

CHAPTER NINETEEN

"I still have questions," Hyperia said, accepting my handkerchief and dabbing at her eyes. "Many questions, but I'm honestly a little consoled too, Jules."

I escorted her into the family parlor, which sat across the corridor from the library. I left the door open, the better to hear any shouting from the Taits' direction.

"Consoled," Hyperia went on, "because Healy was stupid and arrogant and ridiculous, but he'd never undertake the sort of siege Margery and Ardath laid on Evelyn's happiness."

"And on her worldly means." I sank into a wing chair, unaccountably tired, despite the midafternoon hour. "I hope Evelyn and John can come to some sort of reproachment."

Hyperia took the seat behind the escritoire. "Because you adore a happily ever after?"

I did not trust or believe in happily ever afters. "Because those two have suffered enough, life is short, and all it takes is a horse shying at a rabbit and a loved one has met an untimely end. Merri needs all the loving family she can find. She'll very likely be an heiress of some sort, and her aunties will prey on her if John and Evelyn should be prematurely gathered to their celestial rewards."

Hyperia brushed a white quill feather against her chin. "I dislike intensely that you can think like that. At the same time, I admire your shrewdness. Lady Peele should be Merri's godmother, Sir Tristan her guardian in the event of parental demise."

We were quiet for a moment, both thinking of siblings, no doubt, and children, and how complicated family matters could become.

"You aren't gloating," I observed. "You are entitled to."

Hyperia twirled the feather between her palms. "Gloat? You've apparently solved another puzzle, though I'm not sure how. Why should I gloat?"

"You said Tait was a good man. You were right."

Hyperia laid the feather in the pen tray. "He was a complete dolt too. Evelyn was a prize ass, and they wasted so much time, Jules. As much as sibling mischief has figured in this tale, I'd still hate to think Merri will be an only child because her parents spent five good, healthy years apart out of sheer foolishness."

An interesting sentiment coming from a woman who emphatically didn't want children, ever, on any terms.

"Evelyn is hardly ancient, and both of them are robustly healthy. I wonder how much that locked door had to do with their empty nursery."

Hyperia rose and came around the escritoire. I had just formed the thought, *She's about to sit in my lap, and how I delight in the very notion*, when Tait and Evelyn joined us from the library.

They weren't holding hands, but they appeared to be in a tentative sort of charity with each other. Progress. Napoleon hadn't been defeated in a day, or a year, or a decade.

I rose and gestured to the wing chairs. "Please do join us. Miss West was just remarking that we're still mystified as to a few of the situation's particulars. If you're up to the telling, Mrs. Tait, we'd like to hear the story from your perspective."

"Do call me Evelyn, please, my lord. John says you've worked a miracle." Tait assisted her into a chair while I settled with Hyperia on the sofa.

"Hardly that," I said. "You simply forgot to change your handwriting. Mrs. Ingersoll wrote her notes to us here at the Hall in precisely the same hand as the woman who filled those three journals on the sideboard. She also writes—I commend you, madam—in the hand of the schoolmaster employed by Lady Peele."

He that hath wife and children hath given hostages to fortune; for they are impediments to great enterprises, either of virtue or mischief. Young Francis's copybook had stayed with me, both for the odd quote and for the penmanship.

"Then too," I said, "you nearly quoted Francis Bacon when I conversed with you on the village green. Your turn a phrase was something about it being impossible to be in love and sensible, but the precise quote is that 'It is impossible to love and to be wise.' Young Francis Peele's schoolmaster gave him a longer quote from Bacon to copy. You do enjoy your philosophers, don't you?"

"She was always quoting somebody," Tait murmured. "She read his *Novum Organum*. Actually read it in the original Latin."

"You remained devoted to Bacon," I went on, "and you forgot to change your walk. Ardath Deloitte striding across her garden reminded me of somebody, and that somebody was you—Mrs. Ingersoll—marching about the back gardens with me here at the Hall. You claimed to be a Londoner born and bred, but London ladies never learn how to *hike*. Evvie Tait, by contrast, never learned how to stroll, mince, or meander. Even Lady Peele moves with a sense of purpose that echoes your stride."

Hyperia was smiling slightly, while Tait was staring at his wife and trying not to be too obvious about it.

I kept talking, mostly to fill a vast, complicated silence. "Then too, you told Merri that you'd explain the situation to her when you and she were home, and Tait had told me that Evelyn was clever enough to devise codes. You and Merri had a little code, probably a lot of little codes, and 'I'll explain when we're home' was only one of them. I was slow to put the pieces together, but your handwriting doesn't lie."

The mantel clock ticked softly three times while Evelyn regarded me. "Your lordship is observant."

Hyperia looked pleased, while Tait was clearly concerned. "You were a *schoolmaster*, Evelyn?"

"I was," she said, smiling slightly, "and a good one, and I enjoyed it more than you can imagine. I had to get away from Ardath and Margery. Ardath kept demanding money for this and that, and I soon realized it was hush money. The sister who'd claimed I should have left John years earlier than I did was periodically consumed with guilt for putting asunder those whom God had joined. Ardie should have been a thespian."

"Or a confidence trickster," Tait muttered. "You went to Lady Peele?"

"I told Ardath I wanted to get Merri out of the foul London air, and I did. Babs was a true refuge, and when I proposed giving me the schoolmaster's post, she agreed. I cut off half my hair, borrowed some of Sir Tristan's old clothes, and carried a battered satchel with me everywhere. The job came with a small stipend and a cottage, and for a few years, we managed."

"All the while," Hyperia put in, "you were being bled dry by Margery and Ardath."

"Ardath's demands ceased, but Margery dropped hints that my nieces would appreciate a holiday token from me, that had anybody known I was to inherit Hasborough Cottage, 'all those fabulous jewels' would never have come to me. They were good pearls, but the best of my jewels were given to me by my husband. Parting with those hurt."

Tait, to his credit, responded on cue. "I can buy you more, Evelyn. The jewels don't matter."

Evelyn shook her head. "I don't want jewels. I always felt like mutton dressed up as lamb in them. I haven't missed the curling tongs either. I did miss you."

To be listed along with curling tongs and cameos was hardly a profession of undying devotion, but Tait looked bashful. "Is that why you came here when you left Berkshire?" he asked. "Because you missed me?"

"I'm curious as well," I said. "Did you think Tait wouldn't recognize you? Was it a final test?"

"A test which I failed," Tait said, looking not too upset with his bad marks.

"I knew I would soon come into possession of Hasborough Cottage and that Ardath and Margery were already planning that I should sell it and dower their daughters with the proceeds. I, who was living by my wits, was to dower young ladies who have perfectly doting papas to see to the matter. That bothered me, I can tell you. What of Merri? Who would dower her, for pity's sake? She was growing old enough to be puzzled by a mama who played dress-up every time she left the house, and the whole deception was becoming insupportable. I realized that Margery and Ardath would never stop unless I could manage to disappear. I didn't even tell Babs where I was going."

"And the one place you would never be expected to go," Hyperia said, "was your home shire."

"Two villages over," Evelyn said, "but yes. Not quite under John's nose, but close enough that Merri might catch a glimpse of him. I thought someday she might need a memory of his appearance, if anything happened to me. Or that's what I told myself. The years have been kind to you, John Tait. I nearly hated you for that."

"The years have been lonely, Evelyn. Never doubt it." Tait patted her hand, and for the love of all things ridiculous, Evelyn blushed.

She soldiered on with her narrative before the color was receding from her cheeks. "Lord Julian told me—told Mrs. Ingersoll—that you wouldn't allow anything in my rooms to be changed, that you'd read my diaries. I thought you might, and the notion was a comfort when it should have annoyed me."

"You left them behind," Tait said slowly, "because you thought you were coming back, didn't you?"

Evelyn peeped at him from beneath lowered lashes. "I hoped I would, eventually. At first. The whole situation grew so muddled, and I didn't carry Merri well, and Margery made certain that I was apprised of your every peccadillo and amour. Miss West is one of your particular favorites. To hear Margery tell it, the two of you cooed audibly throughout the village fete and nearly sat in each other's laps at the quarterly assemblies."

"Oh dear." Hyperia smirked at Tait. "And here I am, all unaware of your tendresse, John, and utterly uninterested in same."

"I will cope with the rejection," Tait said, "believe me."

And I would have a word with Lady Ophelia, who'd apparently heard gossip instigated by none other than Evelyn's own sisters.

"I had another reason for returning to home territory before I sold the farm," Evelyn said, gaze on her husband's countenance. "I wanted to see for myself what I was giving up. I wanted to make the decision to move on based on current evidence, not on Margery's bile or Ardath's spite. I wanted to say farewell in my mind to what might have been, not to the tarnished tale my sisters concocted. And then John turned up charming, and I wanted to bash him over the head with my parasol."

"You used to do that," Tait said wistfully. "Showed me no mercy, and we always ended up laughing."

"You have a hard head, and I pulled my punches."

Tait took her hand. "You also kept your worries to yourself, Evelyn, and I can't blame you for that." His expression was as serious as I'd seen it. He focused on Evelyn's plain gold wedding band. Not all wives, and certainly not all widows, wore such rings, but Evelyn had not only kept hers, she displayed it.

"We should have confided *in each other*," Tait said slowly. "I had no one older or wiser to urge that behavior on me. Margery and Ardath were bent on destroying our trust in each other. They were jealous of us. I can see that now. We should have confided as husbands and wives are exhorted to do. Cleaving only to each other..."

Not a sentiment Margery Semple would ever immortalize in a sampler, and that realization gave me a passing sense of pity for her. Her life would be the envy of many, as would Ardath Deloitte's, and yet, those women seethed with discontent.

"I wanted somebody to confide in," Tait went on, "and that somebody was my own wife. Her door was locked to me, repeatedly, and I did not know what to do. I am sorry, but I promise you now, before these witnesses, that if you will honor our vows, then when I am next unsure what to do, jealous, or confused, I will entrust my worries to you before taking any other action."

Hyperia was staring at Evelyn as if she'd will Tait's wife to rise to the honor she'd just been paid.

"I hated the curling tongs," Evelyn said. "I couldn't even tell you that. The fripperies and lace looked ridiculous on me, and I felt ridiculous and so lonely, John. I'd go up to the nursery and cry because I knew you wouldn't look for me there. I didn't want to disappoint you, and I have, and I am so, so sorry."

I eyed the door, which was open, for pity's sake.

"I was awful," Tait said. "Flirting like an idiot, ignoring my wife when I should have simply asked you what was amiss."

Evelyn stroked his knuckles. "You were awful. I was awful-er. I wouldn't have told you why I wept. I knew marriage to you was too good to be true, and Margery said all honeymoons end. I wanted to strangle her. I wanted to strangle you. I often wanted to strangle myself."

"Oh, my love." Tait perched on the arm of her chair, and to the extent a man could in that awkward posture, he took his lady in his arms.

Hyperia and I once again withdrew, before anybody's weeping became audible. We closed the door behind us and sought refuge in the library.

Hyperia and I had dawdled among the biographies for a good quarter hour before she looked up from *Chesterfield's Letters to His Son* and snapped the book closed.

"John Tait is a good man," she said. "I was right about that."

I put down a musty tome by Mr. Gibbon, wherein he'd been maundering on about my imperial pagan namesake, Julian the Philosopher. "Agreed. Tait is a fine fellow." *Let the gloating begin.*

"He was also a dolt, and Evelyn was flighty and gullible, but they will muddle on, thanks to you. All that is behind them."

I maintained a diplomatic silence. In my experience, all of life was a matter of muddling on, and the past never truly left us in peace for long.

"John was right about the trust, Jules. When two people are committed to one another, they should be in each other's confidence."

Committed to one another? "The principle of mutual trust between halves of a couple does have a certain appeal."

Hyperia stepped closer and looked me right in the eye. "*I* should have confided in *you*. If my brother's behavior was scaring me—and it was—I should have told you. Instead, I sent you away and pretended I'd be just fine. I wasn't just fine. I was considering desperate, foolish measures, and if you hadn't come..."

"I came. I will always come." *What was my darling lady going on about?*

"Not if I keep sending you away. You should have told me that you suspected John and I had been lovers." She patted my cheek while she fired that Congreve rocket at my pride.

"Your past is your business, Hyperia. I have no right to any recounting, and I never will. Men of my age and station are expected to have a catalog of mistresses and liaisons. Were I to propose to you, you'd be expected to overlook the lot and hope for fidelity going forward. I cannot think it fair to have such latitude on my side of the ledger book, while your side is supposed to be filled with nothing more than chaste pecks on the cheek."

Hyperia linked her hands at my nape. "Jules, there's a difference between respecting my privacy and tormenting yourself with lurid imaginings. If there's a next time, and you want to know what exactly is on my side of the ledger book, please ask. You've told me so much about your years in uniform, your terms at Oxford. Don't let your honor be the reason you put distance between us. If I'd like to keep something private, I will explain that to you, and you will show me the same courtesy. Agreed?"

I wrapped my arms around her and spoke against her temple. "I will make this pact of mutual confidence with you, Hyperia West, provided we seal it with a kiss."

She consented—enthusiastically, to my relief. I kissed Perry out of a need for closeness rather than at the prompting of exuberant animal spirits, and my pleasure was no less for being based more in emotion than in physical yearning. We hadn't weathered five years of estrangement, but this investigation had parted us temporarily, and not only because of Healy's bungling.

I had missed Hyperia profoundly. I might have lost her. We were in accord that we must not allow such a risk to imperil our bond ever again. She and I were still agreeing apace on these conclusions when some idiot cleared his throat over by the door.

"Beg pardon," Tait said, standing hand in hand with his wife. "Was going to ask for the loan of a carriage. Evelyn and I would like to take Merri home with us, and the lady is not attired for riding."

"You can't stay for supper?" I asked, disentangling myself from the most luscious barnacle in all of England—in all the world. "His Grace will preside, and I'm sure Leander would appreciate a supper guest in the nursery."

"No, thank you," Evelyn said quite firmly. "John and I have much to catch up on, though we appreciate the invitation."

Not as much as they'd appreciate a fast team and a well-sprung vehicle apparently.

"The traveling coach," Hyperia said. "It's roomier, and Merri will be delighted to ride up on the box. John Coachman is an old hand with the infantry."

Tait readily agreed to that plan, Evelyn preened, and within a quarter hour, we were wishing our guests a cheerful farewell.

I was enduring Tait's heartfelt thanks—again—while the ladies stood off to the side, awaiting Merri's arrival from the nursery.

"You must be patient with his lordship," Evelyn said quietly, putting a hand on Hyperia's arm. "When I was a schoolmaster, I was befriended by the other young men in the village. You would be appalled at what a lusty lot they were, but fretful too."

I was not meant to hear this, but a reconnaissance officer developed the ability to nod agreeably and murmur appropriately while monitoring three different conversations in three different languages. Tait maundered on about the best harvest he'd had in years and some strain of sheep that never got foot rot.

"Men worry, you know," Evelyn went on. "About pleasing us. About making us happy, about earning our respect. They try to joke about, to make light of their fears, but I was quite surprised by what they will say and not say when private."

I'm sure you were. I silently prayed for the damned coach, Merri, a plague of locusts, anything to interrupt the tête-à-tête going on to my left.

"They worry about"—Evelyn leaned closer to Hyperia—"*satisfying* us. Plagues them without mercy, and then I went and locked my door to my own husband. I have amends to make. Indeed, I do, Miss West."

Tait was a lucky, doomed man. I wished him stamina and lots of chubby, happy babies, in that order.

"Mama!" Merri shot forth from the house, arms extended. "Mama, Leander and I beat Old Boney to flinders. Lee-Lee was Wellington, and I was Blücher. We smashed Old Boney to bits!"

"Did you now?" Evelyn took her daughter's hand. "I feel much safer knowing that we haven't Bonaparte to worry about. Do you see that coach, my dear?"

"Yes, Mama. It's big. I wish we had big horses like that. I want toy soldiers, too, so Lee-Lee can come and play with me."

"We are going for a ride in that coach to Mr. Tait's house. You may ride up top with John Coachman if you promise not to fall off."

Merri's eyes grew huge. She clapped her hands and spun around. When Tait tossed her up to the bench, she nearly snatched the reins from John Coachman's hands. As the carriage pulled away, Merri waved to us, to the nursery windows, to the stable, and to the very clouds, and then the vehicle disappeared in a plume of golden dust.

"And they lived happily ever after," Hyperia murmured. "Or happily much of the time ever after. Well done, Jules."

I felt another bargain-sealing moment coming on, but my aspirations were interrupted by a rider galloping up the drive. Because the Taits' dust had yet to settle, he emerged as if from a cloud of fairy sparkles, his horse lathered and laboring.

"Are you expecting an express?" Hyperia asked.

"I am not and neither, to my knowledge, is Arthur."

A groom jogged up from the stable yard and took the horse's reins when the rider slid to the ground. "Express from Lyme Regis for Lord Julian Caldicott," he panted. "I'm to put it into his lordship's hand and no other's."

"I am he." Though, at that moment, I was fairly certain admitting as much was a mistake. I came down the steps and was put in possession of a single folded missive sealed with my mother's signature lavender-scented purple wax.

"Your horse will be well cared for," I said. "Take yourself around to the kitchen and tell Mrs. Gwinnett you're to be stuffed to the gills and given a bed for the night, or for as long as you need to recover from your exertions."

"Thankee, milord. Hope it ain't bad news." He tugged a dusty cap, nodded to Hyperia, and trudged after the groom who'd taken his horse.

Hyperia came down the steps. "From Her Grace? Will she see Arthur and Banter off?"

I slit the seal and held the epistle so Hyperia and I could read it at the same time—no secrets and all that.

"We are invited to another house party," I said. "Her Grace has a problem with some missing letters."

"She's gallivanting about at house parties rather than bidding Arthur farewell? She's too busy playing whist to wish her firstborn son a safe journey?"

Said the lady who did not want children. "Her Grace would not ask—would especially not ask—*me* for help unless she needed it. Might I inveigle you into spending some time with me by the sea, Miss West?"

Hyperia gave me a long, searching look, and then a smile started in her eyes and poured like sunshine over a new and wonderful morning. "We've an investigation on our hands?"

"My dear, I believe we do."

"We'll take a proper leave of Arthur?"

"We shall." Possible only because Her Grace's present venue lay in the direction of Dover.

"Then yes, Jules. I will happily accompany you on this excursion, and we will find Her Grace's letters, and we will enjoy this investigation *together*."

As it happened, Her Grace needed assistance, heaps of luck, and a small miracle or two, though she was forced to make do with my humble self, abetted by Hyperia's good offices. The problem was larger than a few missing *billets-doux*, of course, and I became personally entangled in the whole far-from-enjoyable business, but that, as they say, is a tale for another time!

Made in United States
North Haven, CT
20 May 2025